FALSE LIGHT

*An Art History
Mystery*

by CLAUDIA RIESS

LEVEL
BEST BOOKS

First published by Level Best Books 2019

Copyright © 2019 by Claudia Riess

First edition

ISBN: 978-1-947915-20-6

Cover art by SRS

Praise for the Art History Mystery Series

for FALSE LIGHT...

"Riess has outdone herself. From the very first pages FALSE LIGHT explodes into motion. There's excitement, intrigue, and intricate painting of characters. It is fast-moving and mind-grabbing. The author's best yet."
—Alan Covey, M.D.

"What an enchanting read! The narrative pulls you along at a great pace. Not only is the love relationship of the two leading characters, Erika and Harrison, delightfully told, but the complexities and criminal activities of the art world are revealed dramatically. Mystery. Passion. Crime. All in one. What more could a book-lover want."
—Elizabeth Cooke, award-winning author of the Hotel Marcel Series

for STOLEN LIGHT...

"In this art-world thriller, Riess draws the characters with a broad brush, but they have all the capabilities, chemistry and give-and-take of a strong mystery-solving duo...complex and intriguing."
—*Kirkus Review*

"Riess uses words as an artist uses a paint brush; the pages come to life."
—Joseph Epstein, Ph.D

in memory of Bob

"Letters can destroy nations, raise up and cast down religions, and with what contemptuous ease alter our personal histories. But like all dangerous things there is something fascinating about them."

ERIC HEBBORN
DRAWN TO TROUBLE
CONFESSIONS OF A MASTER FORGER
RANDOM HOUSE 1993
ORIGINALLY PUBLISHED BY MAINSTREAM
PUBLISHING PROJECTS LTD.
EDINBURGH, 1991

Prologue

Owen Grant was ebullient—"ripped with joy," his beloved wife might have said. He smiled, remembering the flutter of her eyelids that accompanied her minted phrases. Now that she had died and his arthritis no longer permitted him to jog up a sweat, he satisfied his lust for life—which remained, five years after retirement, as vigorous as it had been in his teens—with voracious reading and clay sculpting. Today, however, he satisfied it with the *Art and Antiques* article that had set his heart racing when he'd come across it this morning while sifting through his mail.

He stole another glance at the newsletter on the kitchen table. In the article, a used and rare bookshop owner spoke about having acquired a copy of a memoir by Eric Hebborn, the infamous art forger. "It was in a carton I picked up at an estate sale," the owner had said. "The author's handwritten note on the title page literally blew my mind!"

Hebborn's note was displayed in a photograph. Owen had recognized the handwriting at once. Imagine, after decades of searching for this copy of the book—placing ads in all the art magazines, later in their online versions, finally giving up—proof of it had fallen into his life as he was about to venture another sip of his scalding morning coffee.

Now it was 8:30 p.m., and there was nothing more to prepare for. Owen had contacted the shop owner—how young and breathless she had sounded!—and they had made plans to meet. He had invited his longtime friend and colleague, Randall Gray, to collaborate with him. Randall, twenty years his junior and still in the game, was more current in his knowledge of the world of art crime and eager to have a look at the book as well.

Owen was on a skittering high, unable to concentrate on his usual avocations. Rather than wear a hole in the carpet pacing in circles, he opted for a walk in Central Park.

He headed for the nearest pedestrian entrance at Fifth Avenue and 72nd Street, two blocks from his luxury apartment building on 74th. There, he chose the rambling path leading to the Lake and Loeb Boathouse. It was a balmy night, on the warm side for mid-April. He might have stepped out in his shirtsleeves, but his conditioned urbanity, always at odds with his truer self, had held sway, and he had worn his suit jacket.

Aside from the couple strolling up ahead and the sound of laughter coming from somewhere south, Owen was alone. There had been an uptick of muggings lately, but his frisson of fear only piqued his excitement for the adventure shimmering on the horizon. As he walked, he silently chatted with his wife, Dotty, as he often did, so that their separation would not be absolute. He commented on the moonless night and looked up, for both of them, at the rarely visible canopy of stars. For a few seconds he was lost with her, until, without warning, he felt a hard object pressed against the back of his skull—the skull that held all memories, like Dotty's fluttering eyelids and the smell of new clay. He knew what the object was without ever having touched one.

He was a man of reason, not a fighter. He flung up his hands. "I have money. Let me get to it."

There was no response.

He reached into his pocket for his wallet—how warm the leather was against his thigh—and his keys jangled of homecomings, and the child in him whimpered please no, before the explosive pop of a champagne cork ended him and Dotty and all the rest of it.

Chapter 1

Erika Shawn-Wheatley sat at her desk in what had been her husband Harrison's late grandmother's dressing room, with their chocolate Lab, Jake, dog-purring at her feet. Her desk faced the window with its privileged view of Madison Avenue, but right now she was more absorbed in what was on her computer screen.

She was bent over her computer in tank top, draw-string sweatpants and flip-flops, her newly cropped hair in disarray. Her back was to Harrison as she heard him creep into the room. She guessed he was about to swoop down on her, and her hand went to cradle her belly, preparing its cargo for the oncoming jostle. Instead, he eased into her space.

"Morning, sweetheart," he said.

The words, heard without visual reference, sounded new, and she thought, startling herself almost: wasn't it in truth *all* new? They had met barely a year ago when she was an unattached editor at *Art News* magazine; he, a professor of art history at New York University's Institute of Fine Art. Erika's boss had hooked them up, deciding that her rookie could do with an academician's input on her art recovery assignment. Their attraction had been immediate, knocking them out of their comfort zones, where the word "love" had been ejected; hers by her father's abandonment, his by his ex-wife's infidelity. They had worked seamlessly together. Is *that*

3

how they had healed each other? Is *that* how the word "love" had crept back into their vocabulary? Erika took another moment to revel in the mystery before turning toward Harrison and smiling, giving him license to swoop. Wrapping her from behind, he burrowed his face in her neck.

"You smell good," he said. "It's barely six o'clock. How long have you been up? Did you already have breakfast?"

"Since five o'clock, and no. Grab a chair."

He let her go and pulled up the vanity chair that had been his grandmother's.

"What are you so engrossed in?" he asked, his voice brimming with contentment.

"I'm reading up on Eric Hebborn. I'm sure you know all about him." She raised a wicked brow. "Being a polymath and all."

"Hardly."

"In the art world at least."

He grinned. "Okay, I'll give you that. So. Hebborn was a brilliant forger who produced hundreds of works misattributed to such masters as Titian and Boucher. His fakes—"

"Not fakes," she countered. "According to Hebborn, they were works *in the manner* of whomever. Not copies."

"*Now* who's the expert? You're right, of course," he conceded.

She gave his thigh a motherly squeeze. Six weeks pregnant, and already her maternal instincts were spilling over into what had once been exclusively their love life. "My generous professor," she said, sliding her hand to his groin as he moved in for a kiss, which she warmly returned.

"Come look," she said, turning back to the screen before things went further. She directed the cursor to her most recent email, from a bookshop owner in Greenwich Village. "This came in after midnight, after we had gone to bed."

"How routinely you portray our sex life. I love that."

She flashed him a look. "Have I become a habit?"

"No, darling, an addiction."

"That's better. Now, look here." She opened the email.

Harrison read it. "Fascinating."

"You think we should take her up on it? Meet her at her shop this afternoon—three-thirty?"

"I don't know. You shouldn't take on too much." He stroked her belly.

"This is strictly an academic endeavor. Not like our first case."

"*First* case?"

She smiled. "Our Cuban caper," she said, alluding to the art recovery assignment that had brought them together and had turned out to be a perilous venture.

"I thought that was a one shot deal. What are we now, full-time sleuths?"

"The shop owner's a friend of Natalie Gilmore, a prime player in the Cuban affair. Natalie was pleased with our work, so she recommended us. As I said, it's strictly academic."

"That's what you said the first time around. Before you got knocked unconscious, that is."

She shrugged off the comment. "The woman is scheduled to meet this guy Owen Grant tomorrow to talk about this fascinating discovery of hers. She wants us to go instead of her. Why don't we drop by her shop later today and then decide. Fair?"

"She wants us to go *instead* of her? You'd think she'd be more excited about her find," he said. "But I suppose we can at least discuss it with her. I've got an Art History class at ten and a department meeting at the School of Fine Arts building at eleven-forty-five, so I can be back here by two. Or do you want me to meet you at *Art News*?"

"Home is good. Sara says it's fine I work at home this morning. I'm researching my article on the fashion-as-art debate."

"Your boss is flexible," Harrison said. "I'm counting on her giving you a lengthy maternity leave."

"Let's not push it. She just promoted me to senior editor. We've got plenty of time to think about my leave of absence. Our baby is the size of a pumpkin seed."

"Is that what your pregnancy bible says?" he asked, beaming with pride.

"Yes."

"When does it sprout ears?"

She laughed. "I'm not up to that chapter." She typed a quick response to the bookshop owner, confirming their get-together at 3:30. She shut down the computer and rose from her chair. "Let's have breakfast."

"I thought you'd never ask," Harrison said. He stood up, then tucked the vanity chair back into its niche from where it was rarely moved, like the museum piece it was. Beneath the desk, Jake stirred.

"Come on, boy," Erika beckoned, heading for the door.

The old Lab lumbered to her side, Harrison heeling along with him. Erika had moved in six months ago, following her and Harrison's windswept wedding on a beach in the Hamptons, and Harrison's faithful hound had taken an immediate preference to her. Harrison had expressed delight about this, as if Jake, in his unassailable judgment of character, had proven Harrison's own.

Even after all these months, Erika felt more comfortable walking through the halls of the Wheatley mansion as part of a triumvirate rather than on her own. Her makeshift study on the third floor of the home was strewn with her office-related papers and files and was the only space she could occupy without feeling like a visitor, albeit a welcome one. She was still awkward about being mistress of this grand abode, her egalitarianism challenged to its limit. Harrison, as un-*Downton Abbey* as she, and maybe even more militant about it, was nevertheless content with the commodious digs because they reminded him of his grandmother. His residency here fulfilled her dying wish, to boot.

The group trundled down the staircase to the living, dining, and kitchen area on the second floor, passing up a ride on the elevator both to give Jake the exercise and to spare Erika the experience of elevator claustrophobia, hardly diminished since move-in day.

Grace Jones, their spry, near-centurion live-in housekeeper and virtual member of the Wheatley family for over fifty years, had made fresh biscuits for them before leaving at the crack of dawn for her day off. For kick-boxing practice, Erika imagined.

"I want to hold you," Harrison said, as they were finishing their second cups of coffee. His voice was matter-of-fact, but his eyes were dewy with longing.

"You're irresistible," Erika said, close to tears at his raw vulnerability. "Will you be late for class?"

"I hope so."

"Harrison!"

"No, I won't be."

They cleared the dishes, and then hand in hand, like children in a fairy tale, they found their way to their bedroom on the third floor, Jake trailing after them. When they arrived at the door, Jake, presumably familiar with their pre-conjugal scent, knew to plop down in the hallway, resigned to being left out in the cold.

* * *

Erika slipped off her clothing. Harrison, dressed for class, stripped down to his briefs then kicked them off as Erika lay on her back over the rumpled bedclothes.

Harrison sat beside her. "You are beautiful," he said, as if he'd never seen her before.

"You're no slouch yourself," she said, her gaze roaming down his sculpted torso, defined by genetics rather than at the gym, the lucky bastard. Her lower abdomen ached with the wanting.

He ran his hand over her breasts, watching the nipples become taut, clearly marveling at the response to his touch, as if his prowess was bewildering him. "God, I love you."

"Even without them?"

"Without what?"

"Tits."

He grew solemn. "What a thing to say. Do you think I'm so shallow? Your tits are one way to move you." He softened. "Among others." He bent to kiss her mouth, stretching over her as their lips met.

He slipped into her. Raising his head to gaze into her eyes, he rose and fell, rose and fell, each time with greater urgency.

She panicked, suddenly afraid for her fetus.

He lay still. "You're holding back," he said, caressing her hip.

Hearing it vocalized solidified the thought: she imagined its evolving form mutated by their pleasure-seeking. "I'm afraid we'll disrupt something."

He withdrew, but he remained lying above her. "Not according to the doctor," he said, almost lightly.

"Science is imperfect." She squeezed her hand between their bodies to touch her belly. "This is bigger than both of us."

"That's what we say when he's seventeen," Harrison said.

There was no resentment in his tone, but she felt it in his essence, or maybe in the way he'd assigned a sex to their being-in-the-making without consulting her.

"I know it's off-the-wall, but I can't shake it," she said. "I want to make love so badly, but I feel I have to protect the baby, even from myself. Maybe as a man you can't understand." Her voice sounded cruel to her, as if she meant to drive a wedge between them. An image of her father percolated to consciousness—her father, incapable of resisting his primal urges and abandoning his wife and daughter to fulfill them. She thought she'd conquered her fear of being like him. Maybe not. "I'm sorry, I didn't mean that," she said.

"It's okay if you did." He rolled off her and for a moment lay still. Then, caressing between her thighs, he moved down along her body, his lips skimming along her flesh.

He was on his way, she knew, to satisfy her with the safer penetration of his tongue. "I shouldn't need to be serviced," she murmured.

"Another insult," he said, soothing. "I love the way you taste. I love to make you come. Your pleasure is mine, don't you know that?"

"I like how it sounds when you say those words, but what about you? You're still…"

"Tumescent?"

They laughed. "Yes," she said.

"Don't worry, we'll get to that. But first…" He spread her legs wider to part the dewy lips and pressed his own between them, burrowing his desire into hers.

Chapter 2

With its cobblestone streets and nineteenth-century townhouses, the West Village in Lower Manhattan looked more like a little European town than a district in a bustling metropolis. Yet for all its old-world charm, its sophistication and diversity rivaled any other area on the borough's grid. Erika always felt like she was coming home whenever she visited the West Village, although she had never lived anywhere near it.

Harrison's longtime driver, Bill, pulled his silver Lexus up to the curb at the corner of Bleecker Street, directly in front of The Book Den. Erika and Harrison slid out from the back seat.

Erika glanced at her watch: three-thirty on the nose. She poked her face up to the driver's window. "How do you do it?"

"How do you think? I'm a pro." Characteristically reserved, over the last year Bill had been gradually loosening up with Erika's relentless camaraderie. "Shall I wait for you guys?" he asked, focusing on each of them in turn.

"Sure. We might be as much as an hour," Erika said. "You have something to read? Eat? Want me to get you something?"

"I'm good, thanks. My wife fixed me a sandwich, and I've got a copy of *Time* magazine."

"What, not *Art News*?" she asked, with mock chagrin.

He smiled back. "Next time," he promised, disingenuously.

Erika and Harrison approached the entrance of the shop. The vibe was both chic and cozy, in the area's characteristic style: the gray slate façade and the black awning with white block lettering gave the exterior a sleek modern look, while the interior, visible through the large plate glass windows, hearkened back to a pre-search-engine time of leather-bound classics and atlases that contained worlds to get lost in. Examples of both were displayed on heavy oak tables and open to pages whose texts and geographies were just beyond vision's reach. A pair of maroon leather armchairs were tucked between two of the well-stocked bookcases against the far wall, inviting a cloistered browse.

Through the panes of the wood-frame door, the couple could see three women standing around the reception counter. None of their faces were visible. An engraved notice bidding visitors to "ring bell" was affixed above the door handle. Erika did so, and a buzz releasing the lock immediately followed.

As they entered, one of the women broke from the threesome. "Ms. Shawn?" she chanced, as she hurried toward them. A petite woman with a pixie cut and ears studded with tiny stones, she looked to be in her mid-thirties, with a smile as beguiling as a child's.

"Wheatley, actually," Erika replied, with a sidewise smile at Harrison. "I've kept my maiden name for professional use only. But please call me Erika." They shook hands.

"I'm Charlene Miller," the woman offered. "Soon to be changing *my* name," she added with a lilt.

"Congratulations," Erika said. "And this is my husband, Harrison, an art prof at NYU Fine Arts, and my—"

"Co-conspirator," Harrison finished. He smiled and shook Charlene's hand.

"You can't imagine how highly Natalie Gilmore spoke of you—both of you," Charlene said. "She was so pleased with what you did on behalf of her mother. And on behalf of herself," she added with a grin. "She and your artist friend, Rodney Smitts, are still an item, as they say. She's his patron saint, more like it. He's become quite the hit among collectors."

"Yes, we know," Erika said, exchanging a look of understanding with Harrison as she remembered the sometimes-trying maturation of Rodney's love life.

One of the women at the reception counter pocketed her credit card and left the shop with her purchased book. The second woman approached the awaiting group and smiled broadly. "Hi!" she said warmly, immediately endearing herself to Erika. Taller than Charlene, and with dark hair reaching mid-back, she seemed light as a feather and disarmingly open.

"Meet Andrea Stein, my partner," Charlene said.

"I didn't realize the shop was co-owned," Erika said, after their round of handshakes.

Charlene laughed. "Andrea is my manager—and life partner. The nomenclature will be easier when we're married in two weeks."

"God willing," Andrea appended, suddenly a shade off cheerful.

The doorbell rang and Andrea excused herself. As she strode to the counter to beep in the customers, she paused to look back. "I'll take care of things, and you'll answer the phone, Charlene?"

"Of course, Andy."

Andrea directed a hand-flutter at Erika and Harrison with a friendly "Later!" and walked off.

Charlene shook her head. "She's worried about her parents," she said, as much to herself as to her guests. "We've been together for eight years, and this has been our hardest week. Andy's parents are Orthodox Jews. They can't accept our relationship, and our wedding plans are making them more agitated. Andy will be an unhappy bride unless they come to terms with our decision. Forgive my venting."

"I thought Judaism had formally approved same-sex marriage," Erika said.

Charlene shrugged. "The American Branch of Conservative Judaism did so some years ago. Not so in Europe or Israel. As for Andy's parents, when it comes to this issue, they're as strict as it gets. God could appear on Fox News to say it's okay, and they'd scold Him for not standing His ground."

"So you'll just have to go for it on your own," Erika said. "Hope they'll come around eventually."

"Yes, of course, but we're going to give it one more try. We're meeting Andy's parents in their rabbi's chambers tomorrow. It took months for us to get them to agree to this negotiation, and we're not going to cancel."

"And that's why you need us," Harrison said, answering his question from earlier in the day.

"Exactly. We're counting on your brainstorming with Owen Grant tomorrow at his ex-business partner Randall Gray's office building in Midtown."

"The individuals you mentioned in your email to Erika," Harrison said.

"Yes." Charlene paused. "In fact, what with our preoccupation with our wedding plans and keeping the shop running, we'd really like you to act on our behalf for a while." She smiled. "As long as you keep us in the loop. It's such an intriguing mystery, we wouldn't want to miss out. I should say that although Mr. Grant did make it clear he wanted his ex-business partner, Randall Gray, to be in charge of the project, he was in fact delighted that we'd be part of it."

Harrison eyed Erika. "What do you think?" He looked hesitant.

"Let's hear Charlene out," Erika said. "See how much time would be involved. Right now we do have a lot on our plate."

"We'll do any kind of research you assign us," Charlene encouraged. "I'm primarily into geography and maps, but Andy's specialty is rare art books, and when it comes to researching, she's meticulous. I mean far beyond the reaches of Google, although what she can come up with going from link to link can be quite exhaustive—and exhausting."

The phone rang. Charlene scanned the room. Andrea was chatting with the new customers at the other end of the shop. Charlene started toward the reception counter, indicating with a nod that her guests follow. When they arrived, she gestured to the nearby nook that harbored the maroon leather armchairs before picking up the phone.

"Hello, yes, it's Charlene," she said, running the words together, as if there was no time to lose. "I'll tell her, Mrs. Stein. Looking forward to seeing you tomor—" She hung up after clearly being cut off. She threw up her hands, grabbed a book from a shelf below the cash register, and carried it and the stool from behind the counter to the browsing niche. She sighed before planting the stool between the leather chairs.

"That was Andy's mother," she explained, sitting down. "She calls every Friday afternoon to wish her daughter a Good Shabbos, then hangs up. She has thus fulfilled her duty while holding her ground."

"In essence snubbing her daughter," Erika suggested.

"Exactly." Charlene patted the book she had placed in her lap. "No more of my complaining. Let's get to it. Are you familiar with this book?"

She held it up so they could see the front cover. It pictured a spoofy self-portrait of the author, Eric Hebborn, as an angel plucked out of a Renaissance painting. His finely tapered fingers directed the viewer to the title: *Drawn to Trouble: Confessions of a Master Forger.*

"I've been boning up on Hebborn," Erika said, "but I haven't read the book. I have seen the cover on Amazon, though."

"The man had quite a penchant for devilish fun," Harrison said. "We're all clear on that, I take it."

Charlene nodded. "Which brings us to the crux of the matter." She turned to the frontispiece and handed the book to Erika. "Take a look at the handwritten inscription."

Erika read the neatly penned script:

Dear Reader,

You are in luck. With this book, but alas only in the company of another marked copy that resides at an undisclosed location, you can track down numerous works of mine that purport to be those of the masters. If you succeed, you will be rewarded for your efforts by grateful curators, insurance agencies, and collectors—the ethical ones, that is. Let me assure you, the individual in possession of the second book will be diligently searching for its mate. Keep a keen eye.

Drawn to mischief,

Eric

August 1992

Erika reached over to hand the book to Harrison. He grinned after reading what in effect was a dare.

"So, Charlene," he began, "how did you come across this book and make

14

contact with Owen Grant, the owner of the second book?"

"My copy was in a carton of books I picked up at an estate sale. I found it fascinating, so I contacted the editor of *Art and Antiques*, a newsletter I subscribe to. They offered to interview me. Quite serendipitously, Grant happened to read the interview. He'd been searching for the book in my possession for years and had just about given up on finding it."

"Not so serendipitously, then," Harrison said. "Since he was ever on the lookout."

"Of course you're right," Charlene said. "He was so excited when he spoke to me. His excitement was contagious. I said we could meet tomorrow, thinking I could get to the appointment with the rabbi later in the afternoon. But I'd be a wreck, worrying I wouldn't get there in time. Andy's parents would leave in a huff. I know they would."

"You could have postponed the meeting with Grant," Harrison offered delicately.

"I guess so, but he was so eager—and as I told you, Andy and I are really bogged down with—"

"We'll help you out," Erika cut in. "At least until after your wedding. I'm intrigued." She turned to Harrison. "Yes?"

"Who can say no to that look? Sure, I'm game."

Charlene's shoulders relaxed. "Thank you both."

Andrea had returned to the reception desk with her customers. Charlene caught her glance as she was wrapping up a sales transaction. She directed a confirmatory nod at Andrea, who signaled a thumbs-up.

Charlene smiled broadly at Erika and Harrison in turn. "We're happy you've agreed to come on board," she said. "If only to give us a jump start. Where do we begin?"

"Of course we'll have to wait to see the second book before we can come to any conclusions," Erika said, "but in the meantime, we can check this one for any superimposed signs of some sort. Have you looked for filled-in letters—the letter O, for instance?" She turned to a page of text. "It's a serif font. Any extended or added serifs? Any subtle markings which would indicate a code or spell out words? Have any lines been added to the illustrations?"

"Any *words* tucked into the illustrations?" Harrison chimed in. "The caricaturist Al Hirschfeld used to weave his daughter's name, Nina, into every one of his drawings. Maybe Hebborn employed a similar technique to provide clues."

"We'll have to look under an ultraviolet lamp to search for invisible ink markings," Erika added.

"Amazing," Charlene marveled. "You see why we wanted your help?"

Andrea, done with her customer, trotted over to the group. "You all look pleased with yourselves," she said. "Have you discovered something?"

"Only that Natalie was right about these two," Charlene said. "I'm so glad they've taken an interest."

Andrea stood by Charlene's chair and rested her hand on her shoulder. "Whose arm did you have to twist harder?"

"Neither," Harrison replied, jumping out of his chair. "We were easy marks. Here, sit down."

"No, no, I'm good." Charlene slid over on her chair, and Andrea planted herself on its edge.

Harrison sat back down and began to flip through the book. "Say, here's a pencil drawing, copied from a painting by Gericault." He held it up for Erika to see. "*Portrait of an Insane Man*. Not bad, right?"

"Right," Erika said, flashing back to their first night of passion, at the Russell Hotel in London, when she'd walked in on him as he was working on his book on Gericault. Her smile was irrepressible.

"What?" he asked, noticing.

"Thinking of the Russell," she said, with a cryptic smile.

"Speaking of *codes*," Charlene remarked to Andrea, a wink in her tone.

"We won't pry," Andrea reassured, playing along.

"Harrison has written a book on Gericault," Erika said evenly, though acknowledging their nuances with an upturned corner of her mouth. "In fact, he's scheduled for a college book tour in a couple of weeks. Would you like a copy of his book?"

"We'd love one," Charlene said. She suddenly turned to Andrea. "Your mother called to wish you Good Shabbos," she said.

"Nothing else?"

"No, hon. At least they didn't call off our meeting with the rabbi."

"Not yet, anyway," Andrea said, with a dip in buoyancy.

The doorbell sounded, and Andrea hopped up to the reception desk to buzz the customer in. It was a man Erika guessed was in his mid-forties. He had on a windbreaker, navy jeans, and dress shoes. He had a confident air about him, which made the conflicting styles look modish. He strode to the reception desk, where he removed something from his pants pocket and showed it to Andrea, who visibly flinched. He spoke to her in hushed tones and then followed her to the seated group.

Andrea's expression was blank. "This is Detective Keith Lenihan," she said flatly, as if she were reciting an inscrutable line from a play.

The man displayed the laminated ID card he had shown Andrea. Shoving his credentials back into his pocket, he said, "I'm from the Central Park precinct. Which one of you ladies is Charlene? I'd like to have a word with you in private."

"I'm Charlene, and these are my friends," Charlene said, sounding cool as a cucumber, though her cheeks had reddened.

"He said Owen Grant was murdered," Andrea said, her dazed expression unchanged.

Erika and Harrison sat up, as if a puppeteer had yanked at their strings. Charlene shot to her feet. "What? I just spoke to him yesterday! What on earth happened?"

"Your shop number was one of the last recorded on Mr. Grant's cell phone," Lenihan said, addressing Charlene. "What did he call about?"

Charlene summarized her conversation with Grant as Andrea stroked her shoulder. "As experts in the art field, Erika and Harrison have agreed to help us sort out the academic side of the project," she concluded.

"'Academic' being the operative word," Harrison added emphatically, hurling Erika an anxious look. "What exactly occurred, Detective?"

"I'll ask the questions," Lenihan replied. Turning to Charlene and Andrea: "May I ask where you were between the hours of five and ten last night?"

"At a dinner party with friends," Charlene answered. "Celebrating their fifth anniversary."

"Can this be corroborated?"

"Yes," Andrea said.

"Are there any facts you feel you are at liberty to impart, Detective Lenihan?" Erika asked, all tact.

"At this time the incident is regarded as a probable mugging," Lenihan said.

"So why are you questioning these women?" Harrison challenged, rising to his feet.

"I don't appreciate your confrontational behavior," Lenihan warned. "Tell me, where were *you* two during that same time span?"

"We were at home, sir," Erika said evenly, compensating for Harrison's stance. "Our live-in housekeeper can attest to that. I'll give you her cell phone number, or you can drop by for a visit."

"A call will suffice, at least for the time being," Lenihan said, mollified. He whipped out a pad and pen from the pocket of his Oxford shirt tucked beneath his windbreaker. He scanned his audience. "Let's have the names and numbers of those folks who will vouch for your whereabouts. It's all a matter of form, you understand." He regarded Harrison in particular. "Didn't mean to ruffle your feathers, buddy."

"No problem," Harrison muttered, jaw clenched.

* * *

After taking their information, the detective exited the shop as a young woman caught the door, almost on cue. She held it open as a group of her coevals brushed past her. All were burdened with heavy-looking backpacks. College students, Erika guessed.

Andrea looked at Charlene. "You good?"

"I'm fine," Charlene said. "You take care of the kids. We'll wrap up here." She rose from the stool as Andrea walked toward the newcomers. "Let me get Randall Gray's contact information. I've got it at the reception desk."

Harrison raised his hand. "I think we'll pass. We can't be taking chances. My wife is in a fragile state."

"Oh?" Charlene said, flashing Erika a look of concern.

"Not so fragile," Erika objected.

"I thought you'd...," Harrison began, but he stopped. He turned to Charlene, whose expression was turning to one of confusion. "Erika is pregnant. We want to be careful." He held out the Hebborn book for Charlene to take back, but Erika grabbed it before Charlene had a chance to lay her hands on it.

"No danger in perusing a book," she said. "May we keep it for a while?"

* * *

"Why so miffed?" Harrison asked as he and Erika climbed into the Lexus. "I thought surely you'd want to withdraw." He shut the divider between them and Bill.

"I thought we weren't going to say anything until the second trimester," she said.

"Sweetheart, I'm sorry. I wasn't thinking."

"You also made the unilateral decision to back out of the project *entirely!*"

He stroked her knee. "That's a corollary of my first fuckup. It shouldn't count as a second."

She shook her head. "You're incorrigible." She kissed his cheek. "I can understand why you were confused. One minute I'm neurotically protective of our unborn child, and the next it looks like I'm ready to involve it, however minimally, in a project associated with a murder."

"Make that two murders, my love. You do know Hebborn was himself murdered."

"His cause of death remains inconclusive. The incident took place in Rome over two decades ago, in 1996, and it's a well-known fact that he had belittled critics, gallery owners, art historians. There was a lot of animus swirling around him at the time."

"This coincidence of events is not at all disquieting to you?" he asked.

"No."

"What is it, then?"

"Ironic."

His laugh was close to explosive.

"I think of this project as a responsibility," she said. "Running away from it would be selfish. I suppose I'm afraid more of my self-indulgence causing damage to our baby than anything else. You know, set a bad example."

His laughter melted into a revelatory smile. "In case our baby is listening. Priceless."

She nudged him with the Hebborn book, which she had been clutching to her chest. "Doesn't playing even a bit part in unraveling the mystery of the forgeries excite you? It excites me just *thinking* about the possibility of righting a few wrongs in the art world."

He gave her a quizzical look.

"The crime," she said. "I know. It sounds heartless, but I think the juxtaposition of Owen Grant's murder and the surfacing of the second book is another tragic coincidence. From what little Detective Lenihan revealed, the incident in the park was in all likelihood a mugging that ended in a killing."

"In all likelihood," Harrison repeated. "That's a good one."

Erika patted his knee. Maternal again. She wondered if it was hormonal. "Our involvement will be peripheral and short-lived, okay?"

"How about we call our own personal detective, John Mitchell, for his stamp of approval on our involvement?" Harrison asked. "As long as you agree to abide by his decision."

"I do," she said. She opened the partition between them and their driver. "Sorry, Bill, we didn't want to distract you with our intimate conversation," she said, feeling obliged to provide an excuse for excluding him.

"Perfectly okay. I've got a spy cam back there, anyway," Bill returned, putting her at ease.

* * *

"I knew you'd come through for us," Erika told John Mitchell that evening when he responded to the message she'd left.

"I haven't told you anything yet," John laughed.

"No, but you will," Erika said.

"There's no surprising you, is there?"

"Don't bet on it," Harrison pitched in, joining their conversation on speakerphone. "Tell us what you know, John. We've agreed to act on your advice."

Erika and Harrison had a great deal of respect for Mitchell's intelligence as well as his level-headedness. He had investigated the homicide associated with their Cuban art recovery investigation, and since then they'd become fast friends. Five months ago, Mitchell had quit the force and turned private eye. The move, at age fifty-three, had been precipitated by the untimely death of his younger brother, the victim of a kite-surfing accident. The absurdity of the accident was as much a cause of Mitchell's decision as the loss itself. He had told the couple that he had dealt firsthand with the gory facts of homicide throughout his career, but that this was the first time death had grabbed him "by the balls," as he had put it. He had seen the end of his life as clearly as his morning cup of joe, and he was going to prioritize his time before it ran out, which included spending more of it with his wife and kids.

"I reached out to an officer I know who's been attached to the Central Park precinct for decades," Mitchell said. "He was very forthcoming, especially when I swore on my mother-in-law's life that your lips would be sealed."

"Your mother-in-law?" Erika said.

"Hell, you think I'm one hundred percent sure I can trust you?"

"You can," Harrison said firmly.

"I shouldn't be joking when the subject is homicide," Mitchell chided himself.

"That's okay, it takes the edge off," Erika said. "What did you find out?"

"It took a while to pin down the victim's ID. They traced it through a dry cleaner's receipt found in his jacket pocket. His pants pockets had been turned inside-out with only some loose change found at the scene. It looks like it was a straightforward robbery with the worst possible outcome: the man was shot in the back of the head, execution style. From the posture of his left hand, his finger was broken and abraded, presumably when a wedding ring was torn from it after he went down. The finger was deeply indented at the site where the ring would have been, a good indication that it hadn't been removed in a very long time."

"I hate to sound brutal," Harrison said, "but is your contact sure the crime was random?"

"As sure as he could be at this stage of the investigation," Mitchell said. "But of course all explanations must be ruled out."

"Blowing up a man's brains for a wedding ring and a couple of bucks seems to be overdoing it," Harrison said.

"Not everyone values life the way you do," Mitchell said.

Harrison shook his head. "The robbery may have been a tactic meant to mislead. I don't like it."

"We agreed to abide by John's decision," Erika declared. "John?"

"I don't appreciate being put in this position," Mitchell said. "How important is this project to you, anyway?"

"Very," Erika replied. "People have been deceived, and the deceit will be passed on to others. Perpetuating a hoax is intolerable, at least to me."

"These people," Mitchell said, "they've been hurt by the lies?"

"If you've bought a forgery of an Old Master, you've got an imposter hanging on your wall, only you don't know it."

"But it doesn't harm you."

"The truth matters. Art is truth."

Harrison's shoulders drooped.

"We'd be in it for the short term," Erika said. "And only academically," she added for good measure.

"Then I would go for it," Mitchell said, with audible restraint.

"Not the answer I was looking for," Harrison said.

"Just keep in mind, anytime you need me, I'm here for you," Mitchell said. "You want a personal bodyguard, you got one."

"Thanks, that's good to know," Harrison said, with the barest lift in his demeanor.

"Thank you," Erika said, wrapping Harrison in an embrace. On the desktop, she could see the impish self-portrait on the cover of Hebborn's book, egging her on.

Chapter 3

Randall Gray's work space was located in a swanky modern office building on 42nd Street, between 6th Avenue and Broadway. After checking in at the building's marble-topped security desk, Erika and Harrison were permitted to swing through one of the turnstiles leading to the multiple banks of elevators.

The double-doors of Randall's office faced them as they stepped off the elevator on the fifth floor. From the look of things, there were no other businesses occupying the floor. Tasteful script etched on the doors' milky glass panes read:

G&G Art Consultants

Authentications and Appraisals

The left-hand door opened as Erika reached for the buzzer.

"Security called to say you were on your way up," their greeter said, by way of disclaiming his clairvoyance. "I'm Randall Gray." He ushered them in.

Randall Gray looked to be in his mid-fifties. His rough-hewn good looks were framed by thick black hair, artfully shagged to effect unruliness. He wore a black dress shirt open at the collar, black jacket and trousers. Erika pictured him wielding a conductor's baton.

"We wanted to say in person how sorry we were," Erika began, after

Harrison had initiated a round of handshakes.

Randall stiffened. "No need. Must keep moving. Must go on."

"As we said on the phone last night, we would have been happy to postpone our meeting," Erika continued. "We can still do that, you know."

Randall shook his head, vehement. "What's the point? To give me a day or two more to obsess over the insanity of Owen's death? He wouldn't have tolerated it. He wouldn't have wanted me to waste a day. His voice is in my head, telling me to get on with it."

With an impatient hand gesture, he indicated that they should follow him. He led them past his receptionist's desk and down the hallway, stopping at the first open door. "Here's my office," he announced. "No staff here on Saturdays." He spun around, almost colliding with Harrison. "Wait. Let me show you the lab first so you can get a feel for what goes on here. Come with me." He strode past them, heading farther down the hallway, Erika and Harrison tagging after him.

Midway down the corridor, Randall halted at a steel door and punched in a security code on the panel above its latch handle. "This is my lab. It wouldn't exist without Owen." He led them inside, halting two feet from the doorway, facilitating a panoramic view. It was a huge space. On one side were metal tables arrayed with test tubes and trays of mysterious instruments; on the other, a gathering of large pieces of equipment with limb-like protuberances.

"Formidable," Harrison commented.

"Owen Grant was a pioneer in art forgery detection," Randall pronounced, as if he were inducting him into a hall of fame. "His specialty was infrared spectroscopy and techniques that can identify materials down to the molecular level. He was an expert in stylistic analysis. His instincts were impeccable. This lab is his legacy to the art world. My obligation is to sustain it."

"May we have a look around, Mr. Gray?" Erika broached.

"Randall—please," he said. "It would be better another day, when our lab assistants are on site."

"That's fine," Erika assured him. "And as I said, you don't have to trouble yourself with a meeting of any consequence today. I know it must be difficult for you, however anxious you are to get started."

Randall heaved a sigh. "Owen would expect it of me," he replied, with dirge-like solemnity.

"May I ask what *your* field of expertise is, Randall?" Harrison put in, deflecting from the gloom.

Randall shook his head, as if to clear it. "My own proficiency is in the historical end of things—establishing the provenance of a work of art and acquiring all the associated documentation. Its genealogy, so to speak. Sometimes an expert's authentication is overturned after a thorough examination of its history."

"Its upbringing, as it were," Harrison suggested.

Randall cracked his first smile. "Exactly." He gestured for his guests to exit the lab and followed them out, shutting the metal door behind them. The snap of the lock engaging had a distinctive note of finality.

Randall led them back to his private office, a large room furnished with an L-shaped desk and a floor-to-ceiling built-in bookcase where books, framed photographs, and objets d'art shared occupancy, as well as a round conference table with six broad-bottomed captain's chairs. He directed Erika and Harrison to the table, on which lay a copy of Hebborn's *Drawn to Trouble*. The book was encircled by three legal pads and three sharpened pencils.

"I thought pencils would be safer," Randall said. "We wouldn't want to chance making any indelible marks in our books. I assume you brought Charlene's copy?" He sat down on one of the captain's chairs, and the Wheatleys positioned themselves opposite him.

"Here it is," Erika said, removing the manila envelope that contained the book from her tote bag. She passed it to Randall. "Take a look at Hebborn's inscribed letter."

Harrison reached for Owen Grant's copy. "May I?" he asked, not quite waiting for a reply.

"Of course," Randall said, staring down at the letter Hebborn had penned to the unnamed reader. "Fascinating."

Harrison opened to the title page of Grant's copy and set the book on the

26

table so that he and Erika could read the note together. Erika kept the book open by delicately pinning the covers against the tabletop with the tips of her fingers.

Owen,

I am ambivalent. You praise my work, yet you unmask my Titian. I want to both thank you and torment you. How do I do this?

Aha:

With this copy of D to T, along with a second copy—gathering dust or encircling the earth—you will be able to track down a bunch of my paeans to the Masters, including a couple of splendid oils. I believe you are a Good Samaritan. So, here is your chance to save an untold number of future art patrons from vandalizing their retirement accounts; insurance companies from depleting their reserves.

You only need to find that book!

Break a leg.

Eric

August 1992

There was a moment of wordless taking-it-in.

"Randall, is Hebborn referring to a specific incident in regard to the Titian?" Erika finally asked.

"Yes, he is," their host replied. "In 1985 Owen discouraged a sale in progress of one of Hebborn's forged Titians, overturning the authentication on record. Owen contacted Hebborn about it and shook his finger at him, but he also complimented his talent. He agreed with Hebborn that his Titian imposter was a drawing that could stand on its own merits. The art community, by and large, did not harbor such kind thoughts."

"And so a friendly enmity was born," Harrison submitted.

"Well put," Randall said.

"I imagine Owen used all the equipment on hand to examine the contents of his book," Erika said.

"For a time he practically lived in the lab," Randall confirmed. He paused. "Which brings up the point that for efficiency's sake it would be best to keep the research in-house, where we're equipped with the necessary technology and experience. I should purchase Charlene Miller's copy of the book."

The Wheatleys were taken aback. Harrison spoke up. "According to Charlene, Mr. Grant made it clear that you were to be in charge of the project, but that he was happy to have her and her partner, Andrea, collaborate."

"I believe 'delighted' was the word he used," Erika said. "But of course if you want to offer to buy Charlene's book it's your call, Randall."

Randall shook his head. "No, no, the last thing I want to do is cause any misgivings. Let's get on with it." A sudden frown displayed consternation. "We should start with Owen's notes. They were copious. He kept them in the company's safe deposit box. He left them there for security purposes even after he retired. They're off premise, at a local bank. I didn't think to get them today. Stupid of me."

Erika raised a brow. "Under the circumstances? Hardly!"

"We can at least compare the two books now," Randall said, still agitated. Nostrils flaring, he reached for a pad, then pushed it away, causing it to fly off the table. "Leave it!" he cried, as Harrison bent to retrieve it.

"Randall, this is understandably a bad—*impossible*—day for you," Erika said.

"The police came to my apartment to interview me last night. Would you believe it? Not a word of sympathy. Frightened my wife half to death!"

"You're not alone," Erika said. "There was a detective in Charlene's shop yesterday. She and her partner were questioned, too. It was very disconcerting."

Randall seemed not to hear her.

"Actually, we all had to produce alibis," Harrison said, taking hold of his wife's hand and drawing it to his lap, where he cuddled it against his thigh.

"They said my number was in Owen's recent calls," Randall fumed, hardly in response to Harrison's remark. "I had to tell them where my wife and I had been during the hours they stipulated. I told them we were in Brooklyn, visiting my in-laws. They told us today that we had been recorded on camera coming and going through the Brooklyn Battery Tunnel, which cleared us. They didn't notify us about this. We had to call them to find out!" He rose from his chair to fetch the pad he had caused to skid off the table, but remained standing even after he'd retrieved it, hovering over his guests.

"Why don't we set up another meeting when your lab assistants can show us around?" Erika cajoled. "You need time to process everything."

"We can take both books home and review them for the next few days," Harrison added in the same tenor.

Randall bowed his head, the remorseful delinquent. "Maybe you're right. I think I need to go home." He picked up his associate's copy of *Drawn to Trouble* and handed it to Erika with unexpected delicacy. "Do you need an envelope for it?" he asked.

"No need. It will fit in the envelope with Charlene's copy," Erika assured him. She rose from her chair, retrieved the manila envelope from her bag, placed the two books inside, and tucked it back into her tote. "Safe and sound."

Harrison rose to his feet. "Wednesday early afternoon is a good time for me," he said. "Would you be free to meet then, Erika? Randall?"

"Good for me," Erika said.

"I'll pick up Owen's notes," Randall tersely agreed, already hastening to the door, his distress visibly rekindling.

* * *

"Better stay out here, sweetie," Erika cooed, stroking Jake's haunch. "You might slobber on the books." She kissed the top of his head and slipped into Harrison's study on the first floor, closing the door behind her.

Harrison was waiting for her. He had laid the books side by side on the desktop and had cleared his class's exam papers from the leather chair drawn up alongside his own. She sat down in it.

"Grace is spoiling us," she said.

He smiled. "She makes the best beef bourguignon, doesn't she? Always did." He kissed her cheek. "You don't have to help clear up afterward. You know Grace likes to run the show."

The topic was not a new one. It was still difficult for Erika to accept the concept of ever-present service. "I'm trying," she said. "It's not as if Grace tries to hide her resentment." She laughed. "She can be downright testy."

"You do love her though, right?"

"Not as much as her beef bourguignon." She opened the book nearest her and checked the author's handwritten note. "Owen Grant's copy. Shall we read the books simultaneously and compare them, page by page, as we go along? It might be a tedious process, but we'll be absorbing his ideas and looking for clues at the same time."

"It's close to four hundred pages. You think we can finish it by Wednesday?"

"Even if we can't, we'll have gotten the gist. If we don't find any clues—*overt* clues—by mid-book, I think it'll be clear we're barking up the wrong tree."

"Which brings us to Owen Grant's notes and the Dr. Seuss-ian equipment in the lab," he remarked.

"Right. Let's start with the book jackets and the text on their flaps."

They each scanned the covers of their assigned books, then together examined them side by side, looking for any subtle differences. They came up with nothing.

From the title page, they proceeded to the acknowledgements, there discovering that Hebborn had reached out to various dealers and museum people. "To see if he could locate some of his 'Old Masters,' as he called them," Erika said. "Nobody responded."

"At least not before the 1991 publication of this book," Harrison offered.

"And before the date on both of his handwritten notes," she added. "August 1992."

"If only we could track down the person or persons who finally revealed the whereabouts of those Old Masters of his," he mused.

"Another day," she said, almost officious. "At this rate we'll never get through the book by Wednesday. Remember, we're just trying to get a head start here. We probably won't get very far without Grant's notes and the assistance of Randall's lab people."

"Yes, ma'am!" he replied, in a tone generally accompanied by a military salute.

"Sorry for my impatience," she said. "I've been having twinges."

"Of regret? You think we shouldn't have taken this on?"

"I mean in my belly. It's nothing, but it makes me jumpy."

The flare of his nostrils gave away his alarm. "Oh?"

"It's nothing. I shouldn't have mentioned it."

He rose to his feet. "Let's go see the doctor."

"Haven't I been enough of a nervous ninny? Sit."

Reluctantly, he obeyed.

* * *

Two hours later they were heading into Chapter IV, "The Forging of an Artist," without having discovered so much as an inkling of a clue. With rulers and magnifying glasses, they had crept down the drawings they encountered to see if they could find the subtlest differences between the representations in each of the books: the break in a line, an added swirl, a deleted letter. No luck.

"I wonder if there could be something hidden behind the binding," Erika suggested on a whim as she closed the book that had belonged to Owen Grant and now, presumably by default, owned by Randall Gray.

Harrison, following her example, closed Charlene's book. "You do think out of the box. I'm impressed."

"You think it's possible, though? It seems like a reach."

"To think that Hebborn could have removed the binding, hidden a note, then re-glued the binding? I wouldn't put it past him." He sat back in his chair. "Have you heard of Dr. Kwakkel, the medieval book historian from Leiden University in the Netherlands?"

She could feel a mini-lecture coming on. She loved it when he shared his scholarly knowledge with her. His touch of paternalism was devoid of any threatening overtones; on the contrary, it made her feel cocooned in a shared nest.

"No, I haven't heard of him, but it's got the makings of a limerick," she said. "There was a young man from Leiden..."

He uttered his professorial laugh, a half-note lower than his usual guffaw. "I suppose Kwakkel has an unusual *cackle*," he surmised.

"Like Joe Biden—you know, from *Leiden*?" She waved her hand. "I'm sorry.

What were you about to say?"

"Well, you see," he began, after a beat, "it all started some years ago with the innovation of macro x-ray fluorescence spectrometry, a technology designed to scan Old Masters' paintings to look for hidden layers beneath the surface art. It detects traces of iron, copper, and zinc, and scientists used it in 2011 to discover a self-portrait of Rembrandt beneath a layer of another painting."

"Interesting, but how does this relate to my question about book bindings?" Erika pressed, anticipating his gentle admonition for patience, and prematurely reveling in it.

"I'm getting to that," he said, conforming to her expectations by folding his arms and affecting a touch of sternness, albeit with a sly smile.

"Sorry," she said, mugging contriteness.

"To continue: Krakkel, our Nordic professor, applies this technique of macro X-ray fluorescence spectrometry to his field in a unique manner. He scans book bindings from the fifteenth to the eighteenth centuries, and he's discovered manuscripts hidden inside them from 1300 years ago. He calls them 'stowaways from the distant past.' In fact, he believes that about twenty percent of books printed in the early modern age harbor these 'stowaways.'"

"How is this possible?" Erika asked, truly stymied.

"Fascinating, right?" He smiled broadly, abandoning his professorial role to cozy up to her eagerness, clearly a more satisfying mode of being. "After the Middle Ages, during the rise of printing press production, bookbinders commonly recycled what they considered old-fashioned handmade books by chopping up their pages and using the pieces to strengthen the bindings of their printed books."

"I never knew this!"

"Which further proves your creative instincts—to have dreamt up scanning the bindings for Hebborn's secreted notes!"

"Actually, I was thinking of asking permission to take *apart* the bindings, not X-raying them. A costly oversight. Randall's lab must contain such an X-ray device, so we can examine the bindings without destroying the books. In fact, do you think Owen Grant may have X-rayed the binding of his copy on his own?"

"We'll find out Wednesday. Think you can wait?"

* * *

Over the weekend they read Hebborn's book. Finding nothing in its first quarter to pique their sleuthing interests, they read the balance of the book more to beef up their knowledge of the author than to search for leads in finding the forged artworks his provocative letters had alluded to. The knowledge gained, apart from being interesting in itself, might turn out to be of use in the investigation—to whoever was involved with it. Simply discovering, for instance, that Hebborn had sold his works only to dealers and salesroom experts—as well as learning that he avoided bribery and undue influence when validating his fakes, relying on experts to do it for him—potentially ruled out a mare's nest of scenarios. Learning about the galleries he haunted, the men he loved, and the materials he used to perfect his deceptions all broadened their perspectives of the man and would surely inform the research to follow. Erika took extensive notes.

* * *

Late Sunday afternoon they called The Book Den on speakerphone to give Charlene and Andrea a rundown on their first meeting with Randall Gray and their independent examination of the books.

"Basically un-revelatory," Erika told Charlotte, who had answered the phone. "Regarding anything that could be deemed a secret code, that is. The book itself is an interesting read."

"You took reams of notes, I assume," Charlene said. "I get the impression you're as meticulous as Andy."

Erika laughed. "Of course. And how did your meeting with the rabbi go? Have Andy's parents come around?"

Charlene uttered a resigned laugh. "The rabbi was open to suggestion. Andy's parents regarded it as a sign of weakness. It hardened them further.

Her mother is outspoken. Her father is more passive. It's her mother who causes Andy the greatest inner turmoil."

"Andy has to be strong," Erika said. "Easy for me to say, of course."

"No, you're absolutely right," Charlene said. "Andy's distraught, but she sees now more than ever that she has to be the agent of her own destiny." She sighed. "Easy for *me* to say," she echoed. "She is sad, despite the espoused philosophy. I hope you'll give her a line of research to work on. Focusing on something constructive always takes her out of herself." She paused. "Actually, so she can be *more* herself. Does that make sense?"

"Perfect sense."

"Less fretful. I mean, she has had her really down times."

"I understand. Yes."

"The wedding hasn't been postponed, I hope," Harrison pitched in.

"Oh no, not at all!" Charlene's voice had taken on so sudden a lilt it seemed forced. "We're going full steam ahead!"

"As for giving Andy an assignment, can it wait?" he asked.

"We'll be seeing Randall again on Wednesday and reviewing Grant's notes for the first time," Erika explained. "We'll also be given access to the lab. We'll have a better idea on where to go from there. Don't worry, we'll keep Andrea busy."

"Good," Charlene said. "She'll have time to dig in before the weekend, when she's off to Earth Haven, a yoga and meditation retreat in Marlboro, Vermont. Abiding by the rules of the retreat, we'll be incommunicado. Andy was reluctant to leave me holding the bag a week before the wedding, but I insisted. She's gone there a couple of times in the past when she's been in one of her funks, and it's always helped her. Pranayama especially."

"Who?" Erika asked.

"No, *what*," Charlene corrected. "It's Sanskrit for breath control. You learn how to regulate your breath to bring focus and calm."

"Ah. Maybe *that's* what I need," Erika said.

"Who doesn't?" Harrison added.

The call ended with them setting a time Wednesday evening for a more in-depth discussion of the Hebborn project and the promise to have a meaty assignment for Andy to dig her teeth into. Harrison gave Erika a quizzical look as they rose from their side-by-side desk chairs in his study. "You were serious, weren't you?"

She boomeranged his look.

"About needing something to enhance your focus and calm," he said.

"Oh. Yes, I was."

"Aren't I enough?" he asked, the plaintiveness revealed in his eyes.

"Oh, my darling," she said, embracing him—or, more truly, the child in him. The question went unanswered.

Chapter 4

On Wednesday Harrison's classes ended at one p.m. He scarfed down his brown-bagged turkey sandwich and headed over to Randall Gray's office.

At 1:30, Erika slipped out at the tail end of an editorial brainstorming meeting, on the way grabbing a tuna on a croissant from the conference table. "I'm forgiving your truancy," her boss, Sara, cautioned her, "only if your adventure yields a compelling article for the magazine. Otherwise, I'll consider it moonlighting." Her warning was tempered by a collegial grin. "Good luck."

* * *

Erika met Harrison in the lobby of Randall's building, as planned.

"Did you have a chance to eat your sandwich?" she asked, zeroing in to deliver a peck on his cheek.

"I did," he said, smiling at her concern. "How about you?"

"Tuna—from the office smorgasbord."

"Eaten in the cab?" He picked a croissant crumb from the corner of her mouth and licked it from his finger. "My dessert. Did you bring the books?"

She patted her tote. "What do you think?"

* * *

Except for the addition of the middle-aged woman in a tailored suit sitting at the reception desk, G&G Art Consultants seemed as unpopulated as it had been on their first visit. Erika guessed the firm's main action must take place in the lab.

The receptionist ushered them to Randall's office and, with a dismissive wave from her boss, beat a hasty retreat. Randall was seated at the round conference table in the same chair he had occupied on their first visit. Erika and Harrison took this as their cue to arrange themselves as they had before. This time the table was covered in neat piles of papers.

"Owen's notes," Randall said crisply, after a perfunctory round of greetings. It was clear he was in no mood to waste time. "The books?"

Erika removed them from her tote. She handed Randall the copy that had been Owen Grant's. He took it greedily.

"I was so worried it would get lost. I shouldn't have let it out of my sight." He grabbed Erika's hand. "Not your fault, dear. I'm possessed."

"With an obligation to your friend, I imagine," Erika said, pulling her hand away. These days, an unfamiliar touch felt like a violation of the life she cradled within.

"There'll be a memorial service in two weeks," Randall announced. "The details will be listed in his obituary in next Sunday's *New York Times*. You're welcome to attend, of course. Now, let's get down to business. First, have you discovered anything you believe to be relevant in your review of the books?"

Erika launched into the rundown of their weekend, Harrison adding details. Randall appeared disappointed but unsurprised by their failure to come up with a eureka-worthy discovery.

"X-raying the bindings is an interesting idea, Erika," he said, striving for a note of enthusiasm, "but Owen covered that base himself, with no luck."

"He only examined one of the books," Harrison objected, throwing a protective glance his wife's way. "I wouldn't take anything for granted when it comes to Hebborn's contrivances. We should take a look at Charlene's binding as well." He gave the book a fatherly pat.

"That said, we're eager to see Owen's notes," Erika remarked, detached from the way the men were dancing around her ego. "And I'm anxious to see what we come up with in the lab."

"Indeed," Randall said, again reaching for her hand, more cautiously this time, as if it were a jittery kitten whose receptiveness depended on his approach. She discreetly moved her hand out of reach before his arrived. Harrison threw him a look just short of withering.

"*May* I?" he asked, sliding one of Owen's heaps of notes toward himself.

Erika realized that as she was becoming more protective of her womb's precious resident, Harrison was becoming more protective of her. Who was watching out for Harrison, she wondered? Without preface, she gave him a kiss on his cheek. His look asked the question.

"Do I need a reason?" she answered.

His grin repaired the ambient mood. "What have we here?" he asked Randall, flipping through the heap of papers before him.

"You've got Owen's notes on the text. The top three pages list the words or phrases he discovered Hebborn had circled with invisible ink. The pages below represent his attempt to deduce what words or phrases might possibly be circled in its mate—the *missing* book."

Erika reached in front of Harrison and flipped through the pages. "The infinite monkey theorem," she murmured.

"The what?" Randall asked.

"Given an infinite amount of time, a monkey randomly striking the keys of a typewriter will produce all of Shakespeare's plays," she said. "That's what Owen's exercise reminds me of. Did he have any luck?"

"No, but not for want of trying. Look at the list of Hebborn's circled words and dates. They're tantalizing."

Harrison lined up the top three pages in front of Erika and himself. A number of entries had been highlighted with a yellow marker.

"Around 2001 or 2002, Owen was concentrating on the highlighted items," Randall explained, anticipating their question. "Researching them, for lack of a better word, both intra-text and in the field. Looking for potential correlations. I can tell you a story or two. First take a look."

Erika and Harrison scanned the text segments Hebborn had circled, focusing particularly on those highlighted:

p. 72 the owner of Sea View

p. 132 the Rembrandt Room

p. 144 market value

p.228 The painting was available

p.236 summer of 1964

p.264 Christie's in-house expert

p. 296 plumed helmet

p.310 January 1970

p. 364 dealer's alias written on parcel

p. 376 sold at the Gallerie

"Just particular enough to drive one a bit mad," Erika commented.

"Knowing Hebborn from his memoir, that may have been his intention," Harrison suggested.

Randall nodded. "The note pages below list the clauses or dates or any other references Owen guessed might dovetail with the highlighted bits," he said. "To me, it all seems random, a grab bag. Let me show you an example."

He drew the pile of note paper to him and sifted through it. He plucked out a page and held it up before his guests. There was a header: *Page 132, the Rembrandt Room. Possible matches in book X.* Below it was a list of passages from the book. Two were highlighted:

p. 192 connections in the film world

p. 240 the rooms were renovated

"How did he associate these entries with the Rembrandt Room?" Erika posed. "Obviously it was not haphazard."

Randall smiled. "No, he didn't close his eyes and point his finger at any old target. Although admittedly, it did seem so to me. But there is a Rembrandt Room at the National Gallery of Art in London. In the 1980s, renovation work was done at the museum to restore some of the rooms to the Victorian style popular in the nineteenth and early twentieth century. Owen thought there was a chance that Hebborn might have circled the words in the second book to direct him to the room at the museum, which suggests that a forgery or two of his might be posing as the Master's."

"And did Owen visit the museum and evaluate the Rembrandts?"

"Up to a point. The curator allowed him to check out one or two, but did not believe there was sufficient cause to allow him wholesale access. As far as the curator was concerned, their Rembrandts were legitimately authenticated, and he considered Owen's probing an affront to the museum and to the thoroughness with which it had conducted its pre-purchase research. "

"So, that was a blind alley," Harrison concluded.

"Who knows?" Randall replied. "After all, Owen's examination of the collection was incomplete."

Erika pointed to the second reference Owen had presumably thought a plausible link with the Rembrandt Room. "What about the reference to the film world? Did Owen know a movie star who collected fine art, or more specifically, one who owned a Rembrandt?"

"Good guess, but the story's a bit more convoluted," Randall said. "There's a restaurant in Amsterdam—Restaurant d'Vijff Vlieghen—translated, The Rembrandt Room. Drawings by Rembrandt are displayed on its walls. Owen had heard about it, but had never visited it. He had been told the seats in the restaurant bear copper plates engraved with names of famous people who dined there. Names like Walt Disney, Bruce Springsteen, Kirk Douglas, Danny Kaye. Mikhail Gorbachev. First, he called the restaurant and spoke to its manager. He launched a barrage of questions about the provenance of the drawings on display. The response was immediate and conclusive. The restaurant had opened in 1939 and all of the drawings had been purchased between that year and 1957. Since Hebborn didn't begin his *career* until the 1960s, that particular line of inquiry went no further. Next, Owen asked the manager to give him a list of all the celebrities who had been honored with seat plaques. Here, the manager was not so forthcoming. The plaques were on public display, but reeling off the names to a stranger three thousand miles away seemed to him like an invasion of privacy."

"Did Owen find a way to obtain a list of those names?" Harrison asked.

"Did he actually fly to Amsterdam?"

"I have no doubt he would have—he was that driven—but he knew a curator at the Van Gogh Museum in Amsterdam. He had him visit the restaurant and jot down the names. Owen then selected out the film stars from the list and made inquiries into their art-collecting histories."

"He must have met with a bunch of road blocks," Erika surmised. "It would be difficult for an inquirer not to come across as intrusive, especially if his business is authenticating art."

Randall shrugged. "Well, he did talk to one estate manager who went on about his deceased client's collection of Andy Warhols and the like. But in any event, Owen's research along these lines came to an abrupt end just about at that point."

Harrison's brow rose. "I can't believe he tired of it."

"He didn't. His wife did."

"Oh?" Harrison instinctively turned to his wife, as if to check whether she was still by his side.

"His wife—Dorothy—had the profoundest influence on him," Randall said. "One day she cocked her head and said, 'Honey, I've lost you down the rabbit hole. Come back to me.' He packed up his notes and never looked at them again. Oh, he did continue to scavenge for the elusive second book by submitting and searching for notices in the appropriate periodicals, but his brain-teasing forays into the art world were at an end." Randall shook his head. "She waited at least a month before telling him she'd been diagnosed with stage four cancer. She didn't want him to give up his time-consuming research out of an obligation to take care of her, only out of the desire to *be* with her."

Erika's breath quickened from thinking of the almost allegorical difference between Owen Grant and her own escapist father. "What a loving couple," she said, holding back sudden tears.

Nothing escaped Harrison, whose antenna for detecting his wife's mood changes had grown keener with every passing day of her pregnancy. He refrained from reaching out to her for fear it would cause the dam to break.

"Ah, yes, but we still have Owen's notes," Randall responded, unknowingly stemming the tide. "Let's step away from the text for a moment and have a look at his study of the *artwork* in the book." He pushed the notes of textual references from his guests' range of inspection and replaced them with a compilation of another order entirely.

"This is amazing," Harrison commented after a cursory flip-through of the new papers. "You agree, darling?" he asked.

"It is," she said emphatically, with the intent of dispelling the concern still written all over his face. She knew exactly where it was coming from, and she loved him for it, but his super-sensitivity seemed to be morphing into neediness. "Looks like a study of hieroglyphics, or some kind of decrypting attempt."

They leafed through the pages with greater attention to detail. First, there were printed copies of graphics from Hebborn's book—artwork "in the likeness" of artists such as Brueghel, Piranesi, Rembrandt, Pinelli, that had been sold to identified galleries, museums, private collectors. All of the representations revealed mysterious markings that Owen had detected with the help of a video spectral computer: a mark in the shape of a teardrop embedded in a saint's robe, a sailboat lodged in the nape of a neck, signs that looked like staples, hooks, arcs. Interspersed among the drawings were pages of Owen's attempts at interpreting the markings and systematizing them into codes. His notes were nowhere near as copious as those surveying the text.

"Owen dropped his study of the artwork so he could attend to his wife," Randall offered without prompting. He rose from the table. "Time to put Charlene's book under the knife, so to speak. Let's take it to the lab." He scooped both copies of the book from the table and waited for Erika and Harrison to wrest themselves from their review of Owen's notes.

The lab, unlike the office proper, while not abuzz with activity, was at least populated by several technicians—a young man and two women of indiscriminate age absorbed in their work. Although dressed in street clothes, they all wore white gloves. Each was poised over a different appliance that made its own particular hums and ticks of work in progress. The technicians acknowledged the intruders with polite nods and minimally audible greetings.

Randall escorted his guests around the lab, introducing the technicians one by one.

Candice Hunter was a specialist in postage stamp authentication. "Candy assesses paper, color, watermark, grills, for philatelists worldwide," Randall noted, with an undertone of condescension. Candice, whose bun was as tight as her smile, dutifully explained the video machinations of her computer as it analyzed the watermarks on a German stamp purportedly of World War I vintage.

Eva Rosen, whose expertise was in the field of handwriting analysis. The video screen before Eva was clicking through one page of script after another. "You looking for the good parts?" Randall asked, suddenly jocular. Eva beamed, as if her boss had just switched on the sun.

Jeremy Young, the company's authority on anything having to do with music. "From validation of authorship to placement of historical context," Randall advised, resting his hand on the young man's shoulder. "Jerry is working with our video spectral comparator. I should add he's also our resident computer expert, our one-man Geek squad."

Jeremy, who had been tapping buttons on the imaging device, looked up and for the first time gave the newcomers a serious once-over, his focus locking on Erika. "One-man only because nobody else wants the bother," he said, his facial expression slack with reverent perusal of Erika. In her unencumbered salad days, Erika might have been something near flattered. Now, in nascent motherhood, she cringed from the visual mauling.

Harrison, glancing at the apparatus, missed both Jeremy's look and Erika's reaction. "Music. You must have some interesting stories to tell."

Jeremy, tearing his focus from Erika, returned, "I'm working on one now, actually. Claude Debussy divorced his first wife, Lily, to marry the brash Emma Bardac. Lily shot herself over it. Debussy subsequently lost a lot of his friends, and Emma was disowned by her family. One of our clients claims to have purchased a stack of letters Emma wrote to Claude during their courtship. We don't have an authenticated sample of Emma's handwriting, so I'm analyzing other elements of the documents to solidify them in historic context." He directed a cursory glance Erika's way, then turned back to Harrison and added, "I recently dealt with an issue about Erik Satie—now *there* was a character whose sublime music in no way reflects his odd ways, at least not to my knowledge. Did you know he established his own church? The Metropolitan Church of Art of Jesus the Conductor. I had the opportunity to authenticate its book of tenets, with Candice's help."

"And how did you become interested in this line of research?" Erika asked Jeremy, casting off her discomfort with him for the sake of the project at hand. "It's off the beaten track, it would seem, for someone as young as you."

She could feel him bristle from her assertion of seniority. He ironed back his hair with the palm of his hand, as if his flaxen curls had betrayed his youth. "I believe we're more or less coeval," he replied. "I might ask you the same question."

"Now, now, children," Randall intervened, smiling.

"Actually, Uncle Owen influenced my career choice," Jeremy said, recovering his sangfroid. "I have him to thank for my education, and this is how I expressed my gratitude and respect."

"Owen *Grant?*" Harrison posed.

"Who *else?*" Jeremy clipped.

Randall squeezed Jeremy's shoulder. "Jerry's dad was a fine man, but he fell on hard times. His brother, Owen, stepped in to lend a hand."

"To save the day," Jeremy amended. "He paid for my education and was there for me in every way, all the way." He shrugged off Randall's proprietary wrap by moving sideways to fiddle with the control buttons on the video spectral comparator. "And now he's gone. And here we are, more or less normalized." He knit his fingers through his thick blond hair as if he would pull out a hank of it.

"It's the way we cope," Randall said. "We move on. Explain what you can do for us, Jerry." He waved at the imaging device.

Jeremy terminated the task he was working on and set the presumptive letters from Emma Bardac on the far side of his working table. He inserted a blank paper into the device. "May I have the copy of Hebborn's book, Randall? Not Owen's copy. The unexamined one."

Randall handed him the book, and Jeremy opened it. "Page 72. I studied Owen's notes, and in his copy, this is the first page with a word cluster circled in invisible ink. Let's see if there's a corresponding cluster in the second book." He flipped open the lid of the viewing shelf and placed the book face down so that the page in question was in contact with it. He carefully lowered the lid. "Ready now." He pushed several buttons on the control panel, and a light labeled "floodlight" turned on. "If I'm not mistaken, this setting should work. My uncle ran the gamut on wavelengths—from the shortest ultraviolet to the longest infrared—and indicated the exact settings where he'd found Hebborn's invisible markings. I've got it set on nine-hundred nanometers, and as for wavelength intervals, fifteen nanometers."

"And a nanometer indicates?" Erika asked, not knowing what selection from Jeremy's smorgasbord of emotions her interruption would elicit.

"A nanometer is one billionth of a meter," he said, as solicitous as a nursery school teacher, perhaps to reestablish his own mode of seniority over her. "Light is visible to the human eye in the range of three hundred ninety to seven hundred nanometers. In the field of electromagnetic radiation, which includes visible light among others, ultraviolet light wavelengths are shorter than those of visible light, up to four hundred nanometers. Infrared light is at the opposite end of the spectrum, with wavelengths longer than visible light. Owen discovered through trial and error that the setting I've entered will do the trick. Are there any more questions?" He flashed a token look at Harrison, as if remembering his lessons on conversational etiquette, then lighted again on Erika, his attention's natural resting place. "No? Then let's begin."

Jeremy punched in the critical button and began his review, but clicked the apparatus off after only a minute and removed the paper. "No marks on this page. We can throw the corresponding-page theory out the window. Hebborn didn't make it easy for us."

Did Jeremy consider himself a member of their team, Erika wondered? Did it really matter? She tried to convince herself that he was not actually infringing on her space.

"Let's try a random page," Jeremy suggested, addressing Erika.

Was she imagining it, or did he look at her in a way that was out of the normal spectrum of interactive exchange, like infrared light? Subjective or real, it was uncomfortable. She tried to avoid eye contact.

The page revealed nothing.

"Let's try one more," Erika said. "I have a hunch."

"I second my wife's hunch," Harrison kicked in, looking narrowly at Jeremy. Harrison rarely used the term "my wife" because he thought it came across as overbearing, but he had just waved it at Jeremy like a saber. Erika wasn't a fan of such displays, but in this context it felt good. She sidled closer to him.

Jeremy took a quick intake of air, almost imperceptible, before turning to another random page and restarting the process. This time the result was positive: circled with the invisible ink revealed by the prescribed infrared wavelengths were the words "view the."

"Voila!" Randall declared. "Now what? I suspect you two should leave Charlene's book with Jerry and allow him to scan every page. How long do you predict it will take you to get the job done, son?"

Jeremy visibly balked at the term of endearment—or diminution. "The book is over three-hundred fifty pages," he fairly snapped. "I estimate it will take a good twenty hours or more. This would mean dropping all of my other projects. Give me a couple of days. I'll have it done by the weekend." His steely look softened as his eyes met Erika's.

"That will be fine," she said, looking squarely at Randall. "Can we pick up the results at your convenience?"

"I can fax the results," Jeremy offered.

"We'll want the book returned as well," Harrison said. "We'll pick up the whole shebang, if it's okay with you." There was a whiff of sarcasm in his voice that Erika guessed only she could detect.

"No problem," Jeremy said. "I can have the parcel hand-delivered to you, or I can deliver it myself, for security purposes. I'll also include duplicates of the pages with invisible ink markings in Owen's copy of the book."

Her eyes averted, Erika could not track Jeremy's gaze. "We can pick it up ourselves. You needn't go to the trouble."

"No trouble. Shall I bring it to your office—*Art News*, is it?"

"Good of you to offer," Harrison said, "but seriously—"

"Come to my office," Randall intervened. "We can touch base again. I'll make myself available any time."

"It's decided then," Erika agreed, relieved. A private encounter with Jeremy was decidedly not on her bucket list. "In the meantime, I'll contact Andrea Stein, Charlene's partner. Andrea's off to Earth Haven, a retreat in Marlboro, Vermont, this weekend. She likes to keep busy, so I'll ask her to send off a general query to select auction houses regarding Old Masters sales. Who knows, maybe we'll get lucky and a potential Hebborn forgery will turn up."

* * *

Later that evening Erika punched in the cell number Charlene had given her.

Charlene answered immediately. "What color combination do you prefer, Erika, pink and mauve or navy and canary yellow?"

"Pink and mauve. Are you knitting me a scarf?"

Charlene laughed. "We're at loggerheads about the colors of our wedding cake. You're the tie-breaking vote."

"Who won?"

"Andy did. Thank you. She needed that. She's been down lately."

"So why didn't you concede outright?"

"Because I'm tenacious—and I hate pink." She paused. "How did your meeting go with Randall Gray? Any breakthroughs?"

Erika summarized the meeting at G&G, including Jeremy's planned lab work.

"Do you want to give Andy an assignment of some kind, as we discussed?" Charlene asked. "It will take her mind off that imperious mother of hers."

"Now that the cake issue is resolved."

Another laugh, less merry. "I'll get her."

While she was waiting, Erika took another look through her and Harrison's collective notes and material for the Hebborn project, which were stowed here, in her study. Harrison was presently holed up in his own lair, preparing his lecture for the Gericault book tour.

"Hello, Erika," Andy coming on the line. "My partner is mugging a downcast look. You went with pink and mauve?"

"I did."

"It's settled, then. You and Harrison are obliged to attend our wedding. It will be quite informal."

"Only the second chairs of the Philharmonic!" Charlene chimed in from nearby.

"A string trio," Andy edited.

"Black tie?" Erika asked.

"Black jeans if you want," Andy said. "*We*, of course, will be dressed to the hilt."

"We'll be there," Erika said.

"That's great. Well, do you have an assignment I can sink my teeth into? I promise I'll be thorough."

"So I've heard."

"That's Charlene. Tooting my own horn."

"Not empty flattery," Erika assured her. "Of that, I have no doubt." She scanned her notes. "Do you have a pen and paper?"

"Yes. Fire away."

"Okay. This might give us a jump on things. If it doesn't—"

"I don't mind a little meaningless busy work. I need to be doing *something*."

"Good to hear. Well, I think you can begin by emailing a number of major auction houses in London, Rome, and New York, the most likely cities to have handled Hebborn's forgeries at one time or another. Only go for those that handle high-end consignments. In each case, try to find out the name of the manager of auction relations to address your query to. Take this down. I'm going to give you the names of about twenty-five artists Hebborn admits to have drawn under the guise of. You should ask whether any of their works were sold between 1962 and the present." She reeled off the names in her notes, ending with Gainsborough, Rubens, Titian, Rembrandt, and Corot. "Hopefully, you'll get a number of hits. Of course, you'll ask for the dates of the sales, the lot numbers, the buyers and sellers. You also should contact the oldest commercial art gallery in the world, which Hebborn dealt with quite a bit: Colnaghi and Company. In 2015 they merged with Coll and Cortés, a dealership based in Madrid, and in 2016 Colnaghi moved from Mayfair to a larger place in St. James, central London. It might be a bit difficult to track down all the pertinent archives, but wouldn't it be great if they have a sale on record that coincides with one of Hebborn's clues?"

"What's my cover?" Andrea asked. "Maybe I'll say I'm doing research on trends in collecting Old Masters vis-à-vis the concurrent socio-politico climate. For my article."

"That may well be a legitimate cover. You can reference *Art News*, and I'm sure your credentials as manager of an upscale bookshop will stand you in good stead. By the way, there'll probably be fees involved. Harrison and I are covering them."

"That's very generous."

"No problem. Truly." She kept to herself the fact that Harrison was always on the lookout for causes, however grand or humble, to ease the burden of his inherited fortune.

"Do you want to review my letter before I send it out?" Andrea asked.

"No. I trust your judgment. Anyway, this is your project. I'm your surrogate. A temp, at that."

"Okay, then I'll be back from the weekend retreat Monday night," Andy said. "Should we talk Tuesday morning?"

"By that time Harrison and I will have cracked Hebborn's code," Erika said, ending the call with a note of optimism, for Andy's sake as well as her own.

Chapter 5

Erika and Harrison sat at opposite ends of the dining room table, moving scraps of paper into various configurations. Grace, working at and around the kitchen island, was in their line of vision—as they were in hers. They could tell by her telegraphed expression as she gathered the ingredients for her heavenly shellfish stew that she was itching to sweep all their scraps into the trash can.

Erika caught her eye. "There's a method to our madness, Grace. This mess won't be here forever. It'll be gone by dinner, I promise."

"No matter to me, Miss Erika," Grace said, without malice, but also without affection. Grace had seen the grief Harrison's first wife had given him, and it might take a decade of good behavior for her to approve of his second.

Harrison was engrossed in what looked like a game of checkers with his paper bits. "I can't put them together in any way that makes sense. We must be on the wrong track. Let's rethink this."

Ever since mid-morning, when they had picked up Charlene's book and the work Jeremy had done on it, plus copies of the work Owen had done on his, Erika and Harrison had been trying to put Hebborn's text fragments into a coherent sequence. After an hour of referring to the pages themselves with no luck, Erika had gotten the bright idea of cutting out Hebborn's circled fragments so that they could be shuffled about with ease. First, she had made two copies of each of the pages on which there had been marked fragments. Next, she cut out the fragments and penciled on each either a tiny "c" to indicate it had come from Charlene's copy of the Hebborn book or "o" to indicate it had come from Owen's. As Harrison watched in awe, she distributed a complete set of cutouts to each of them, pronouncing, "Let's see what we can come up with independently."

So far they had drawn an aggregate blank.

"I'm going to try something different," Erika suddenly declared.

"What?"

"Not telling," she teased.

Grace gave her a sidewise glance.

"So far we've been merging the fragments from the two books," Erika began, to mollify Grace. "It does seem logical to integrate them, right? But Hebborn was a trickster. Let's see what happens when we work solely with the fragments from one book."

"It does seem unreasonable, but what can we lose?" Harrison said. "You want to work with the bits from Charlene's copy and I'll take the bits from Owen's?"

"Fair enough." She set aside the fragments marked with "o" and concentrated on those marked with "c." In no particular sequence, she laid the segregated scraps before her:

examine I only , call on you I to

was playing a game , the art Owen .

The truth is

Without the distraction of the more than fifty fragments from Owen Grant's copy of *Drawn to Trouble*, the fourteen fragments remaining, even out of order, made sense. It took her a few minutes to unscramble them. "Here it is," she announced. "Come around and have a look."

Harrison stood behind her, his hands on her shoulders, and peered at the statement:

I was playing a game, Owen. The truth is, I call on you to examine only the art.

He squeezed her shoulders. "Wow."

"I love the reference to Owen," she said. "It was on page thirty-one. He plucked the name from a list of British artists. Thomson and Pickersgill were among them. Clever?"

"Not as clever as you." He leaned down to kiss her.

Grace began dicing a tomato on the island countertop. Erika cocked her head toward her as a warning signal to Harrison.

"Couldn't care less," he whispered, before planting his mouth on hers in defiant passion.

Grace's dicing action intensified.

"You're such a bad boy," Erika said.

Harrison replied with an impish grin.

"Go back to your seat," Erika ordered, making fun of her maternal bent, but enjoying it. "We're going to get right down to the study of the artwork."

Harrison glanced at Grace. She was focused solely on hacking at the tomato. He took the opportunity to give Erika's breasts a sly caress before returning to his assigned place.

Erika reached across the table and took hold of his hand. "I love you," she said, defying Grace and reveling in the sound of her own voice, devoid of nurturing overtones.

For a moment they were silent, looking into each other's eyes as unfettered sweethearts, as they once had been.

* * *

Unlike the text highlights, the *representations* marked with Hebborn's invisible ink strokes were the same in each book. There were nineteen pairs in all. However, although they all matched up, Hebborn had added different symbols or glyphs on each of the thirty-eight figures.

At Erika's request, Harrison took the books to his study, where he made two copies of each of the thirty-eight pages containing the modified drawings or paintings, carefully marking each with a "c" or "o" to identify its source. When he returned, he parceled out a set to each of them.

He sat back down. "What now? I say we line up our pairs and see if either one of us detects an emerging pattern."

She agreed, and they began scrutinizing their individual sets.

After putting only four of her nineteen pairs in order, Erika asked, "Anything yet?"

"Yes. I'm looking at page two-hundred seventy-five—the 'Boucher.' In the caption, Boucher's name is in quotes, indicating it's a forgery. You got that pair in front of you?"

She sifted through her unsorted pages. "Yes, now I do. It confirms my findings."

"How so?"

"The symbols on each of the paired figures are different, but the configurations are the same."

"Exactly. On each of them, there's a diagonal line of symbols going from the upper right to the lower left. Each symbol is placed in exactly the same spot, starting from the woman's left shoulder."

"Yes. Now look at figure thirty-seven on page one-hundred eighty-four. 'A Corner of the Garden,' etc. It reads 'underpainting in the same technique as Titian.' Do you have the matched artwork?"

"Wait—yes. Ah, these symbols are in a circle. Again, the symbols are different in each, but perfectly matched."

"Or *aligned*," she said. "Which means we have to put them together somehow. Let's examine each of the matching symbols of this pair, one by one. See what we come up with."

He didn't answer. He was staring at the pictures, his eyes darting from one to the other.

"Hon?"

"Look at the outer rim of the circle of symbols on the page marked "o" for Owen," Harrison said without raising his eyes.

She cooperated. "I'm looking."

"Now, look at the page from Charlene's copy."

"Got it—oh!"

"What do you see?" he asked, almost smugly, as if he had concocted the challenge, not Hebborn.

"On Owen's copy, the *tops* of the symbols, that is, on the *outer* perimeter, are uneven, on different planes. The *bottoms*, on the *inner* perimeter, are, well, *even!* You could draw a perfect circle if you connected them!"

"And on Charlene's copy?" Harrison urged, kneading the discovery out of her.

She took a moment to verify what now appeared obvious. "The exact opposite," she declared. "On this one, the symbols on the underside of the perimeter are on varying levels. The topside is perfectly level. Here, too, you could draw a perfect circle by connecting them." She paused and then concentrated on a single symbol on the figure from Owen's copy. "I'm looking at the symbol at about three o'clock, on the lower branch of the tree."

"The symbol that looks like a petal," he said.

"Yes. Now let's look at the symbol that corresponds to that one on Charlene's copy."

They focused simultaneously.

"A teardrop," he said.

"Or an inverted petal? Put them together and you might even say they form…" She cocked her head, inviting him to finish.

"Could it be? A bifurcated *eight?*"

She smiled broadly.

"The scissors, where are the scissors?" Harrison bellowed. "Weren't they on the table?"

"When you went to make copies, Grace took them to cut up the scallions."

"Grace?" Harrison called.

"You want the scissors back, Mr. Harry?" Grace replied from the kitchen. The refrigerator door thudded shut, and she reappeared in their line of sight.

"Nail scissors would be better," Erika said. She rose to fetch them from the couple's en suite bathroom.

"I have a small pair of shears right here," Grace said, a touch of protest in her tone. "It's part of my set of paring tools."

"We can use them both," Harrison intervened. "We'll get the job done in half the time. I'll take your shears, Grace. Thanks."

When Erika returned with the nail scissors, Harrison had already cut out the circle of symbols from Owen's copy of the book. "Not bad for freehand," he had to admit, pointing to his handiwork. "I could have used a protractor, but I haven't seen one of those since ninth grade."

"Great!" Erika commended, as she returned to her seat and set about cutting out the circle from Charlene's copy. "Done," she said, several minutes later, when the task was completed. "Let's align our circles now, see if we're onto something." She slid her circle over to his, then moved around the table to sit next to him. "There, that's better."

"You do us the honors, sweetheart. Put the circles together."

"No, you," she demurred. "I love to watch your face in concentration."

"You mean like this?" He stared into her eyes.

"Yes. Go ahead, do it."

He lifted the circle she had cut out.

"Use the petals as a hitching point," she advised, before he had done a thing.

They had to laugh at her taking over, despite her charitable start.

"I mean, where *else?*" she asked, all innocence.

He laid the circles, one over the other, using the petals—their hopeful "eight"—as the guiding point of alignment. When Erika saw what the circles formed, she let out an inarticulate shriek, and Grace dropped a utensil. The circumference of their composite circle was formed from a series of letters interspersed with numbers.

Erika grabbed a pencil. Harrison handed her the lined pad at his elbow.

"What a mischievous guy," Erika said. "These letters and numbers are not all neatly bifurcated, like the number eight. Hebborn cut them at different points in the vertical plane. It would be close to impossible to have guessed his ploy with only one book in your possession."

Harrison peered down at the symbols. "It looks like a garble. Write down the symbols in a straight line. It'll be easier to analyze."

She began with their lucky charm, the number eight. The line completed, read:

8 M A N 2 N C H R I S T I E S R M C A L 1 9

"Well, there's Christie's, the auction house, loud and clear," Harrison said. "Hebborn must have experienced a moment of empathy when he decided not to make a letter salad!"

"So, shall we assume the letters and numbers are in order across the board?" Erika wondered.

"Good question. Yes, let's."

"Okay. So, I think we should work out a couple of more pairs. I think it might make it easier to figure out what the numbers and the rest of the letters represent."

"You think something will ring a bell."

"I'm hoping. Yes."

They prepared four more matching pairs. In two of them, the symbols were arranged in diagonal lines. In one, they formed another circle. All but one contained matching "petals" to fix the starting point of alignment. The one containing no such guideline—the circle—had to be rotated until the aligned symbols made sense. When they were complete, the five rows of letters and numbers, along with Erika's notes, read:

8 M A N 2 N C H R I S T I E S R M C A L 1 9 (P. 184 "same technique as Titian") - circle

M U 1 L D 9 E R S O 8 T H 6 E B Y S A M S (P.225 authentic Corot?) - line

B U N 1 Z 9 L C H R I S T 8 I E S L 3 D N (P.275 'Boucher') - line

T O N C O L N A G 7 H 3 I S 1 S U T 9 (P. 170 'Jan Breughel the Elder') - circle

C O L 1 L I N 9 S S O U 8 T H E B Y S N Y 8 C (P.89 "After a painting by Rembrandt") – line

"See how easy it is to discern things when we've got five examples in front of us?" Erika said. "It's obvious the numbers are dates."

He grinned, admiring her quickness. "And all the dates are in the nineteen-hundreds. The circles threw me off because we started reading them from a random point."

"Exactly. Let's separate out the dates."

In sequence, they read:

1982

1986

1983

1973

1988

Erika rewrote the lines of letters without the distraction of the numbers.

"Now let's extract the obvious auction houses or galleries," Harrison suggested. "From the Rembrandt look-alike, it's clear the letters NYC after Sotheby's direct us to the Sotheby's in New York City."

"It follows that the AMS associated with the Corot pair stands for the Sotheby's in Amsterdam," Erika followed up. "I wouldn't have thought of that if it weren't for the NYC." She jotted down the names, in sequence:

C H R I S T I E S R M (Erika: "Rome!")

S O T H E B Y S A M S

C H R I S T I E S L D N (Harrison: "London, of course.")

C O L N A G H I S (In unison: "The London art gallery!")

S O T H E B Y S N Y C

"Now let's write down the remaining letters in each row.," Erika said. "This is a little more puzzling."

In order, the rows of remaining letters read:

M A N N C A L

M U L D E R

B U N Z L

T O N S U T

C O L L I N S

"I guess not so puzzling, after all," Erika said.

Harrison, again lagging on the uptake, flashed her a gallant smile.

She made a conscious effort not to come off as patronizing: "I was the one taking massive notes when we first went over the text. It's not surprising certain names are more fixed in my head than yours."

"Good try, but let's face it; your reading retention outranks mine. Go ahead, don't keep me in suspense."

She smiled at his sportsmanship; adored him for it. "Well, I remember

Bram Mulder and Tan Bunzl were buyers Hebborn mentioned a number of times. So I figure the other three strings of letters represent buyers' names, too. As for 'manncal' and 'tonsut,' they emerged from the only two circle configurations. When we jotted down those two series of symbols, our starting points were random. Change those starting points and we've got Calmann and Sutton. Hans Calmann and Denys Sutton. Both buyers are cited in his book in a number of sales transactions. As for Collins, I figure we either missed seeing the name in the book, or he or she was unknown to Hebborn until a source of his clued him in on the sale after the book's publication."

"I'm more than impressed," Harrison exulted, his eyes lit with admiration.

"I love you, too. Now, where were we? We've got the buyers, the dates—dates of purchase, I assume—and the sellers."

"We need the names of the forged artists. I think our best bet is to assume the artist listed in the caption below each of the altered depictions is the most likely candidate. Anything more obtuse would be downright sadistic. Hebborn was mischievous, not cruel."

"I agree. Now, it's obvious the nineteen misauthentication disclosures Hebborn is letting us in on do not refer to the actual works above the captions. Those are noted to be either 'in the artist's collection' or 'in the style of,' or they're ones that he openly admits to having been forged."

"Therefore," Harrison stepped in, "he's almost certainly referring to drawings—or paintings, for that matter—misrepresented at the time of their sale as works of the notable artists referenced."

"Yes. The names of the artists. The names of the buyers. The names of the sellers. The dates of the sales. That's what he's given us."

"Not exactly on a silver platter, but yes."

She nodded. "So now all we have to do is figure out the other fifteen transactions. It shouldn't be hard, now that we've got the gist." After a pause, she said, "Of course, we've got to track down these works, or try to. The transactions took place over forty years ago. The art might have passed on to other owners. We've got our work cut out for us."

"Speaking of which," Harrison said, "hand me a pair of scissors. Let's see if we can get this job done by dinner."

* * *

The job was done by dinner, although to Grace's chagrin, dinner was delayed two hours.

After dinner and their apologies to Grace, they sent e-mails to Charlene and Randall indicating that they'd solved the mystery and that details would be forthcoming. Charlene shot back an e-mail telling them to wait until they could talk directly to Andrea. *As you know, I expect her back late Monday, so give us a call Tuesday morning. She'll be thrilled!*

Randall, on the other hand, called Erika's cell phone. "Tell me what you found," he demanded.

She reeled off the specifics of the nineteen sales transactions that she and Harrison had uncovered, suggesting that an unknown source may have disclosed more than half of the transactions to Hebborn post-publication. She advised that she, Harrison, and Randall, along with Charlene and Andrea, plan to set up a meeting some time the following week, after Andrea's return from her retreat in Marlboro, Vermont.

"In fact," Erika said, "why don't we get our notes to you before Andrea's return? Harrison's and my work is virtually done, and you should have a chance to study our findings before the meeting, when we'll answer any residual questions. I should tell you that the retreat's policy is to confiscate cell phones until checkout, so Andrea will be incommunicado during her stay."

"Good to know," Randall said. "And thanks, I'd appreciate the chance to look over your findings. How about tonight?"

"It's after nine, and I'm afraid we—"

"No problem. Jeremy can pick up the material. My wife and I are busy with house guests, but I'm sure the lad is available. Don't let his good looks deceive you. He's actually an inveterate loner. Give him a call and arrange a time that would be convenient for you." He rattled off Jeremy's cell phone number.

Unable to think of a good reason to refuse without causing offense, Erika acquiesced.

* * *

An hour later, Erika was standing in her lobby handing over the Hebborn material to Jeremy. Jeremy slid the Wheatleys' notes and cutouts into his small leather portfolio and tucked it under his arm.

"Is that really a Botero?" he asked, staring with undisguised awe at the zaftig bronze female figure standing on her pedestal beside the couch.

"Yes," Erika said. "It hit me the same way when I first saw it."

"And this lobby is... ...?"

Erika laughed. "Yes. The ground floor of our home."

"I'm impressed." Jeremy grinned. "You must think I'm a rube."

She shook her head. "If you are, so am I." She cleared her throat. "But I am tired, Jeremy. I don't want to be impolite, but..."

"I understand. I'll be going."

"Forgive me," she said, feeling a touch of remorse for having previously scorned him so readily without giving a thought to the cause of his social ineptitude. She laid a hand on his forearm. Jeremy gazed at her with a sudden possessive intensity. In a flash, her kindness was rescinded. She swiped away her hand and, with a staged smile, ushered him to the door.

* * *

When Erika and Harrison at last retired, they were too exhausted to navigate the hazards of sex, and they fell asleep, she spooned up against him, his body shielding hers, and hers folding him to her womb. It wasn't until Sunday brunch that they enjoyed a celebratory drink—he, champagne; she, its lookalike, ginger ale. Rested and refreshed, they withdrew to the bedroom, leaving Grace to clear up; Jake, in the lurch.

Erika lay on top of Harrison and in control of the rhythm and depth of their dovetailing: slow and shallow. He, taking her cue, lightly cupped her buttocks, withholding the pressure he longed to exert. It was a mutual exercise of restraint, until, with a wayward—or perhaps purposeful—brush of his thumbs along her crevice, they skidded toward climax. He rose up against her, and she plunged to secure him, and in a series of deep thrusts, impossible to reverse, they pulsed together, rapturously unencumbered.

Afterward, he consoled: "It's okay, my darling, it's okay."

* * *

Erika's fingers skimmed the keyboard of her desktop computer, her maternal worries dispelled, or rather buffered, by her work in progress. Interrupted by the hum of the cell phone trembling at her elbow, she was tempted not to answer it—until she saw the name of the caller.

"Hello, Randall."

"I hope I'm not interrupting dinner."

"Not at all." Her eyes wandered to her *Art News* article, poised mid-sentence on the computer screen. "How can I help you?" The corner of the screen read *8:30 PM*. Odd time to call, especially on a Sunday.

"I had to thank you directly for the material you sent me via Jeremy. Yes, you'd given me the details over the phone, but it wasn't until I'd seen your notes in person—and those cut-outs!—that I fully appreciated your ingeniousness."

"Thanks, Randall. I'll relay the message to Harrison," she added pointedly. "He's downstairs in his study. You want to speak directly to him?"

"No, that's okay." He paused. "Jeremy's a bright young man, wouldn't you say?"

"Of course," Erika replied, wondering what had prompted the non sequitur. "Why? Is there a problem?"

"No, no, it's only that I know he lacks a certain social......grace, shall we say. I wouldn't want you to judge him solely on that score."

"I don't."

"You see, Owen had a few callings in his life. Jeremy was one of them. He and Dolly never had kids of their own, and when they rescued him from his impoverished family, they doted on him. Sheltered him from life's vicissitudes, as it were."

"Thanks for the information, Randall," Erika said, puzzled. "If you have any questions about our Hebborn notes, please don't hesitate to call us."

"Certainly. I will, yes, no problem," Randall replied, his voice trailing off.

"All right, then," Erika said, before terminating the call.

Had the call been a heads-up or a half-baked catharsis? She pressed a random letter on her computer keyboard, and her dozing article came back to life.

Chapter 6

Summer was muscling into spring, forcing it into memory. Erika raised her face to the sun and tried to allow the warmth to embrace her, but she could not trick herself into yielding.

"Are you all right?" Harrison asked, standing beside her. Bill had let them off curbside in front of the Langone medical complex at First Avenue and Thirtieth Street, ten minutes early for Erika's scheduled Monday appointment at 11:30 a.m. He had driven off, under instructions to be on call for a pickup who knew when, given the unpredictable waiting-room stay.

"I was spotting this morning," Erika said. "I'm worried."

"Remember, the doctor said that's not unusual."

"That was at the beginning of the second week, and then it stopped." She lowered her gaze. "I think last night," she began, but her voice trailed off. Why finish? He must know what she was thinking.

He took her arm. "You know we did nothing to harm the baby, Erika. The medical community is not divided on this point."

She winced at the arrogance of his certainty: a jinx? "You're right," she declared, forcing herself to regain her good sense. "You know how tense I get before these visits."

He bent toward her and pressed his temple against the top of her head.

"Relax, it's a beautiful day all around," he said, before ushering her across Langone's heavily trafficked porte cochere to the revolving door.

In the lobby, they turned right and headed for the corridor that terminated at the bank of the Schwartz East elevators. They rode up to the fifth floor, where they walked the hall toward suite 5Q, the sound of Erika's three-inch high heels clacking against the marble floor, making her feel foolish for dressing up. Her tension returned.

They had been sitting for fifteen minutes alongside each other on two of the faux leather waiting room chairs arranged in rows, auditorium-style, when Erika felt a piercing cramp in her belly. She bleated in pain.

Harrison's body jerked taut, and his cell phone dropped to the floor. He grabbed her knee. "What?"

"Shh. A pain. It went away." She could feel the tears coming. "You were checking your office e-mail. Everything okay? Your teaching assistant show up?"

"Erika!" he said, looking at her closely.

The tears were flowing now. She rummaged for the tissues in her tote bag. He took the bag from her to take over the search just as she felt the rush of warm fluid between her legs. She leapt to her feet. There was a spot of blood on the chair. Panicked, she wiped it away with the hem of her skirt, as if she could make the fact of it disappear.

"Nurse!" she cried, no longer caring if she was disturbing anyone.

Harrison shot to his feet, her tote bag dangling from his wrist.

"Nurse!" Erika called out again.

The receptionist must have already buzzed the examining area because a heavyset nurse, in a controlled flurry, swung open the door to its entrance and was trotting toward Erika. She wrapped an arm around Erika's waist. "Come with me, honey," she urged, tightening her grip. She began leading Erika to the admittance door.

Erika, in fearful obedience, watched Harrison trailing after them, but the nurse turned to him without slowing her gait. "No, no, you wait here, honey. I'll come get you when we're ready."

"When?" Harrison exploded.

"Soon, dear. Be patient." She escorted Erika through the doorway, leaving him to stare helplessly at the door as it slowly closed in front of him.

* * *

"It's Erika, am I right?" the nurse asked, placing a ceramic basin on the lid of the toilet.

Erika, from an alternate universe, answered, "Yes." She felt unsteady, sick, terrified, dazed.

"Call me Peggy," the nurse said. "Let's pick this dress up, Erika. Can you hold it up?"

Erika did as she was told, and the nurse pulled down Erika's bloodied underpants as more fluid leaked from her. "All right, then, would you lower yourself—quickly!—onto the basin? We want to collect as much material as we can, honey."

Erika squatted as she was told, like a trained dog. Another cramp tore at her belly. She bent over in pain as she sloughed more of her precious "material." She screamed inwardly, ordering her malevolent body to stop, then screamed it aloud: "Stop, stop, stop!"

"Erika!" Harrison wailed outside the bathroom door.

"Go away!" she cried, just as he barged in. A woman in a white coat—Erika's doctor, Dr. Robin—grabbed Harrison's pullover shirt.

"Please, Harrison, you were asked to wait in the front room. I promise we'll get you. It won't be long."

Harrison let the doctor lead him away. He was ferociously gripping the straps of Erika's tote, as if he were hanging on to Erika herself.

* * *

Three quarters of an hour later, Erika, cleaned up and encased in a blue cotton robe, was sitting on the edge of an exam room table. Dr. Robin had asked her to lie down; she was refusing. An IV was attached to her left arm.

"I want to go home," she said, without affect. "Take me home, Harrison."

"I'd like to observe you for a while," Dr. Robin said. She placed her delicate hands on Erika's shoulders. "I want to make sure you're properly hydrated."

Harrison sat on a chair beside Erika's dangling legs. He took hold of one of her bare feet and massaged it. "You should listen to Dr. Robin," he said, his voice as laden with emotion as Erika's had been devoid of it.

"I want to go home!" Erika repeated, her emotional vacuum suddenly filled with fury. "I don't want to be here!" She pulled her foot out of Harrison's tender hold: she deserved to be punished, not petted.

"I know you're in pain," Dr. Robin said, removing her hands from Erika's shoulders, "but please understand, about twenty percent of six-to-eight-week pregnancies end in miscarriage. You mustn't be discouraged."

"My wife had invested a lot in this pregnancy," Harrison said. "It was a defining event for her."

"My baby was not a 'defining event,'" Erika said, giving him a look as if he had just dropped out of the sky. "It was a life snatched out of existence by my carelessness."

"Oh, no," Dr. Robin objected. "The cause was most likely a chromosomal anomaly, not at all unusual, and certainly not your fault."

"Giving it a name doesn't brush it off," Erika said. Her thrashing, toxic grief was keeping her body from slumping over in exhaustion.

"You're lucky, in a way," Dr. Robin said, deflecting from the central issue. "We were able to determine that you won't need a dilation and curettage. You'll just have to take it easy for a week or so."

"All that troublesome tissue was expelled from my uterus? Guess I got *something* right." She hovered at the brink of a weeping squall. "Get this tube out of me!" she barked at Dr. Robin to forestall the torrent.

Dr. Robin relented, with the proviso that Erika lie back and rest, at least until she was brought a change of clothing.

"I want everything I was wearing thrown away," Erika warned her.

"Of course, but your shoes—"

"Everything!"

With that, Erika lay back against the crackling paper sheet and stared up at the ceiling. "Will you take care of getting my things, Harrison?" She imagined a cotton sheet covering her body, as if she were dead. The thought kept her still.

Harrison kissed her expressionless face. "Of course. I'll be right outside in the waiting room. I'll make the arrangements. You rest, meanwhile."

* * *

Harrison called Grace on his cell phone. In very few words he reported what had happened, and without allowing her room to interrogate him, told her to put together a parcel of fresh clothes for Erika—"loose, casual, including underwear, sneakers." He then called Bill and in the same abrupt manner, told him to collect the parcel and drive back to Langone. "I'll meet you curbside, same place you dropped us off. Afterward, you can stay put if you're able to, or drive around. I'll call you back when we're ready to go. Please drive into the porte cochere when you pick us up."

These arrangements made, Harrison was relieved. His overriding concern was Erika's well-being. Waiting for the doctor to tell him how she'd made it through her ordeal, he realized that he'd hardly given their lost pumpkin seed a second thought. Erika would have hated him for it if she'd known.

* * *

Erika sat immobilized by despair as Bill, caught in the line-up of medical and lay vehicles, slowly crept toward her. Harrison stood alongside the bench, uselessly waving the drivers along.

At last Bill pulled up in front of them, and Harrison helped Erika into the back seat. She began to slide further in to allow him to climb in next to her.

"No," he said, pressing his hand against her knee. "I'll come around." How pitiful she looked to him in sweatpants, T-shirt, and sneakers, as if she were about to go for a jog.

In the slow-moving traffic, she felt like they were under water, pushing against an unbearably resistant sea. It was pointless to struggle. She slumped back in her seat and let her knees drop open.

At Park Avenue and Forty-sixth Street the traffic thinned and Bill surged ahead, like a racehorse breaking out of the pack. A wave of kinetic energy shot through Erika; she sensed herself running toward home, charging past Grace, taking the steps three at a time, reaching the door to her private space, and before anyone could catch her, slithering in and turning the latch, locking out the noise and babble of a ruptured universe. But when Bill finally came to a stop in front of the Wheatley residence, her damned whining body wouldn't allow her to do it, and she was forced to wait for Harrison to open the door and help her stumble out.

Just as cautiously, he escorted her to the entrance of their home, and from there, guided her to the elevator and ushered her in. On the second floor, he waited for her to step out with him, but she lied and said she wanted to get something from her study and that she would be right back down to have a cup of tea with him.

"Let me go with you," he insisted.

"Please don't treat me like an invalid," she said, strongly enough for him to back off.

She pressed the button to the third floor as her heart raced in anticipation of the awaiting solitude. Once in her study, she locked the door behind her and sank to the floor. She realized she had been holding her tote bag only as it thumped down alongside her. She pushed it away. It belonged to another life.

The blinds were drawn and the room was dark, but not dark enough. Her isolation was not deep enough. She closed her eyes, but it was useless: she knew what was on the other side of her lids. She opened her eyes. It was better to face reality than try in vain to escape it. She felt a twinge in her belly, a reminder of her failure. She wished it hurt more.

There was a knock on her door. Of course. Had she actually thought Harrison might have guessed she needed some time to herself?

"Erika?"

"Go away. Please."

"Let me in, sweetheart. I won't stay if you don't want me to."

It was pointless to make him suffer. She stood up and unlocked the door.

He waited for her to open the door, and when she didn't, he opened it himself and stepped into the room.

"Close the door," she said.

He did so. "Erika," he began.

"Don't say it. No comforting words." She leaned against the wall and slid down to the floor. She drew her knees to her chest and clasped her arms around her legs, making herself as inaccessible as she could.

He dropped down beside her.

"I want to be alone," she said.

Such a simple statement; impossible to spin, but that did not stop him from trying: he slid along the wall until at least a yard separated them. "There."

"Harrison."

"What, my love?" he asked, as if he didn't know.

"Go to work. Go see how your teaching assistant made out. Only go."

"It wasn't your fault," he said. "Do you think it was mine?"

His hale and hearty presence made the question seem disingenuous. "No, Harrison."

"Do you think maybe you're having a kind of—I don't know, a relapse of that fear that you're like your father in some way? Erika, his abandonment of his child—of *you*—in no way, *no* way—"

Her mind snagged on the word "relapse." "Do you think my failure is like a microorganism that lies dormant, and then resurfaces—like herpes?"

"I was wrong to put it like that," he said. "It's a process, that's all. For both of us."

"Process. Another clinical word."

He shook his head. "Grief. Sadness. The only words that count. I'm sorry. I get academic. But only in my speech. What's here"—he moved closer, reaching out and taking hold of her hand and pressing it against his chest—"is inexpressible in words. I hurt for you."

She grasped his hand and slapped it against her belly. "It hurts worse here."

"I know. Your pain is firsthand. Mine is through my love for you. Harder in a way because it can be questioned—misunderstood."

"Are we competing now?"

There was humor in her voice, admittedly sardonic, but it was a start. "We're not competing," he said. He kissed her hand. "We're talking."

She withdrew her hand and rewrapped her arm around her legs. "Not now. Please go now." She was looking straight ahead, impassive.

He rose slowly, defeated, but, with a hollow-sounding attempt at lightness, promised, "But not for long, darling. Not for long." He started for the door, stopped. "Will you keep the door unlocked, if only for my peace of mind?"

"As long as you respect my privacy."

"Of course."

He shut the door as quietly as possible, as if the slightest noise would cause her to recant.

* * *

Erika would not permit herself to sleep. She gave in to her selfish body only to allow it to lean its skull and spine against the wall as she went over, again and again, the day's nightmare. Reliving it kept the memory raw; healing, impossible.

There was a light tapping on the door. She didn't know how long she had been sitting there, only that the scant light in the room had dimmed. There was another tap.

"Miss Erika? May I come in?"

It was Grace. Erika had never heard the woman's supplicating tone of voice, but who else could it be? "Grace?"

"Yes, miss. Please, may I?"

A kind of dull curiosity moved her to answer, "Come in."

Grace opened the door and entered the room. She was holding a tray, bracing one side of it with her forearm. She turned the knob with her free hand and shut the door, then better secured the tray. "I've brought you some cream of tomato soup and a muffin. You need some nourishment. Would you turn on the light? You wouldn't want this old lady to trip, would you?"

Grace's gentle prodding was so uncharacteristic that it caused Erika to rise to her feet and obey, as if to the command of a hypnotist. She clicked on the wall light and took the tray from Grace. "Where should I put it?"

Grace scurried to the vanity table and pushed aside Erika's pads and pens. "Right here is good."

Erika did as she was told. Grace pulled out the chair from the vanity and reached up to touch Erika's shoulder. "Now sit and have some soup." She smoothed her scalloped white apron overlaying her starched black dress and stood there, waiting.

"I'm not hungry, Grace."

"You don't want to be hungry, but you are," Grace said, without budging.

There seemed to be no choice but to heed Grace's first prompt. Erika sat down. She had no intention of lifting the spoon provided. "Thank you." She waited for Grace to exit the room.

Grace wasn't going anywhere. She strode to the desk and dragged the chair to the vanity, placing it directly alongside Erika's. She sat down. "You must take care of yourself—for yourself as well as your husband," she said. "He loves you so. I have never seen him so distraught."

"Harrison will be fine," Erika said, staring straight ahead.

Grace shook her head. "Not if you aren't." She took Erika's hand in her own. "I haven't been very cordial to you. I apologize."

"Apology accepted," Erika said, feeling nothing.

"I have no children," Grace said. "I worked for Harrison's grandparents for fifty years. I've known Harrison all his life, and he is family to me, my only family. He is a dear man, but terribly naïve. It broke my heart to see his first wife take advantage of him. She nearly destroyed him. I was afraid you might do the same."

"I won't." She withdrew her hand from Grace's.

"I know you won't. I see how you are with him. I see how you look at him. My prejudice made me blind to this, but now I see."

Erika turned to Grace. "I'm empty, Grace. Do you see *that*?" She returned her focus to the wall.

"When tragedies occur close to us, we blame ourselves for them," Grace said, not directly responding, but on point. "You mustn't blame yourself."

"I'd like to be alone now, Grace."

"Your soup is getting cold."

Perhaps if she'd have a spoonful or two Grace would go away. She tried it. "Okay?"

"The muffin. Homemade."

Erika took a small bite. She wanted it to be tasteless, but it wasn't. "I'll have it. Will you go now?"

"I'll wait."

Erika forced herself to have a few more spoonfuls of the soup and a bite more of the muffin.

"Good girl," Grace said. "Do you know, when Harrison's grandfather passed away, his grandmother and I used to sit in this room and talk? It didn't matter about what, only that she be kept engaged." She rose to her feet. "Now, you get up and sit in the desk chair. It's more comfortable."

"I don't want to be comfortable," Erika said.

"Do it for me, then. I'm a very stubborn woman, and I don't take no for an answer. Do as I say or you'll never get rid of me."

Erika was physically and emotionally drained, and it was easier to yield than argue. She rose and waited for Grace to switch the positions of the chairs. Once Erika was reseated, Grace stood behind her and placed her hands on Erika's shoulders.

"When Harrison's grandmother was especially tense I used to massage her." She began to knead Erika's shoulders. "Like this."

"Please don't."

"Shh. Be still. Don't think."

It would be unkind of Erika to deny the favor. She sat still. Rigid. Determined not to succumb to the wicked temptation to relax and lose focus.

* * *

Harrison met Grace just outside Erika's study.

"Miss Erika tried so hard not to fall asleep," Grace answered in a whisper.

"I would have guessed that," Harrison said in like tone. "Thank you for caring for her."

Grace shook her head. "I haven't been very—" She searched for the word. "Welcoming. After—*you* know."

"I understand," Harrison said. His ex-wife's name stuck in his throat like a chicken bone. "I knew you would have come around eventually."

"Well, now I have."

"I'm grateful."

"Thank you, Master Harry. I'll leave you two alone now." She hastened off on her efficient clip to wait by the elevator.

Grace had left the door to Erika's study ajar. Harrison pushed it open and stepped into the room.

His knees buckled as he caught sight of Erika slumped over the desk chair, her hands folded under her cheek, which rested against the vanity top. She looked like a child who had fallen asleep doing her homework. Her expression was one of peaceful repose. It was imperative that he be by her side when she awakened in a state of unjustified, but predictable, remorse.

Ten minutes earlier, Grace had taken away the tray with the remnants of soup and muffin, but as he drew closer, Harrison noticed a splotch of orangey-red liquid on the vanity top, inches away from Erika's forehead. A bolt of fear struck him before he realized the liquid was not blood, but tomato soup. What if Erika awoke with a start and saw this in front of her face? He ripped his shirt out of his pants and wiped away the reminder of the morning's horror; scrubbed at the spot, like Lady Macbeth, even after there was no longer a trace of it.

He shoved the shirttail back into his pants, hiding the stain, then, slipping one arm beneath her thighs and one below her shoulder blades, he lifted her to rest against his chest. Her head rocked forward, and she uttered a thin cry, but did not awaken. Trying not to jostle her—*float, float*, he cued himself—he walked slowly out of the room and down the hall, where Grace was waiting for them at the elevator, holding open its door.

Harrison had prepared their bedroom: drawn down the bedcovers, slid the dimmer switch to its lowest setting, turned off the clock's buzzer alarm, and turned the air conditioner to its quietest mode. Very gently, he laid

Erika on the bed. He worried she might roll off the edge. This had never happened, but his long-established sense of reality had become, on this day, riddled with a fear of the unexpected. He shifted her to the center of the mattress and adjusted the pillows. Then he removed her sneakers and tucked them under the bed. She rolled over onto her side, and he used the opportunity to lift her T-shirt and loosen her bra to the least constraining hook. The sight of her innocent flesh made him weak with sadness. He kissed her back before lowering her shirt. The scent of medicinal soap clung to her body, and he thought of the unfamiliar sights and substances that had touched her today, and he hated himself for his inability to intervene.

Finally, he unfolded the cover and pulled it up to a point just above her waist, so that she wouldn't feel trapped if she woke up in the middle of the night. He stood by the foot of the bed, waiting to see if she stirred again. Only when he was convinced—or *nearly* convinced (certainty had abandoned reason)—that Erika was safely at rest, did he allow himself to leave her alone so he could wash up.

Moments later he returned from the bathroom. He had buried his stained shirt in the laundry basket. Tomorrow he would toss it in the garbage, if only to align himself with his wife, who had disposed of everything she had worn earlier in the day. To further symbolize his alliance with her—at this moment in time, ritual was his only means of expressing it—he stripped down to his shorts and redressed in T-shirt and sweatpants.

He crept into bed alongside her. There was not much room for him, since he had made sure she was in the center of the mattress. Under the covers, he lay on his back and shimmied as close as possible to her without disturbing her.

His side was almost touching her back. He turned his face so that it was inches away from the back of her head, almost nuzzling her unruly hair. It was enough for him—more than enough.

* * *

The cry pierced the silence of counterfeit reverie: "Oh God, I'm sorry!"

The sound of her own voice awakened Erika with a start. She sprang to a seated position, her back snapping into an arc, as if she'd been shot from behind.

"What?" Harrison reacted, transitioning from sleep to wakefulness. "Sweetheart, what is it?" he rasped, fully alert. He rose to a seated position almost as abruptly as she had. Her back was to him, and he could not see her face. He threw the covers off so he could slip around to see her properly. Kneeling beside her on the bed, he watched her expression of horror collapse to abject grief. He wrapped his arms around her.

"Oh, please, please." He hardly knew what he was begging for, or to what entity.

"I was on top of you, I was in control," she wept. "I saw it in a dream, the battering. Only I was inside of myself, watching our baby suffer."

He took her face in his hands. "Look at me!"

She focused on his chest.

"Look at me." He waited until she lifted her gaze to meet his. "You are besieged, I don't know by what—your history, your expectations, your hormones; it doesn't matter. What matters is that you're not being rational. Our sex had nothing to do with the miscarriage. What happened was the result of a chromosomal glitch, pure and simple. Nothing dramatic about it, except in how you configure it into the story of your life. You have to trust me on this."

She struggled to keep her gaze fixed on him. "You're disappointed in me."

"I'm disappointed the pregnancy didn't work out, nothing else! We'll try again if you want to. If you don't, we won't. My evolutionary imperative is not a factor. The species will carry on with or without my genetic input."

She tried to herd her rampant emotions into one. "I do love you, Harrison."

"I know. I'm irresistible."

They held each other tightly, and for the period of their embrace she was numbed into a passive acceptance of his argument. Yet when he drew away for a moment to the bathroom, the anesthetic effect was negated; guilt revived. By the time he returned to her side, she was steeled against his pretty talk.

"I'm going in to the office today," she said. "Don't try to coddle me."

"No, no, you have to allow yourself to heal."

She shook her head. "You don't understand, not really. My connection with that little life inside me was so fierce. I never realized how I needed it, how it—"

"Authenticated you?" Harrison suggested.

"Yes."

"So, maybe I *do* understand? A little?"

"Can you understand why I can't 'try again,' as you put it?"

"You don't want to face the possibility of ever being hurt like this again," he said. He paused. "And also," he began, but fell silent.

"What?"

"Never mind."

"What!"

He took her hands in his. "Maybe you feel if it happens again, it will prove—and of course it won't—that you're—"

"Unsuitable for motherhood," she finished for him. "Exactly. I don't want to know that."

"But it wouldn't prove anything of the kind!" he insisted.

"No, motherhood is out of the question now," she said, almost robotic. "I have to redirect myself to another purpose. I have to fully dedicate myself to work."

"You have to let yourself grieve and come out the other side," he said, taking her in his arms and alternately patting and rubbing her back, as if to resuscitate her.

She broke away from him. "I'm going to the office," she said, craning her neck to see the alarm clock. "Four-thirty. I'll stay in bed awhile longer. Will that make you happy?"

"I called *Art News* and NYU yesterday afternoon and told them we weren't coming in."

She burst into tears.

"We can compromise," he said, wiping her wet cheeks with the hem of his T-shirt. "I can bring you breakfast in bed, and then we can call Andrea Stein and clue her in on our Hebborn findings."

"Andrea was due back from her retreat in Vermont last night," she said, with a ring of enthusiasm. "We're expected to call her this morning."

The familiar pitch of involvement in Erika's voice made his breath catch. "Will you be having bacon and eggs, or French toast and sausages?" he asked, hiding his elation lest it cause a setback.

"Just coffee," she said, retreating into the pillows.

"I'm sure you'll be hungry soon," he said, his mood dipping, as he lay down beside her. "Rest now."

* * *

She woke up again at six. Harrison was not in bed. Probably preparing breakfast for her. For his sake, she would enjoy it, or pretend to.

She tried not to dwell on yesterday's events, storing them in a "recent losses" file, as if her brain were a computer. She then launched into her morning ablutions. As she was towel-drying her hair after her shower, she stared at the image in the mirror, watching the clear reflection emerge as the steam evaporated. She knew she was looking at the same un-pregnant woman from the day before, but it felt like the scene were taking place on a far-flung planet. She dropped the towel at her feet. No, it felt more like she was on the same old turf, but that she herself was different, replaced by a likeness of herself. She was reminded of the Capgras delusion, the belief that a close relative has been replaced by an exact lookalike—only in this case it was as if she herself had been replaced by an imposter.

Though there was an aura of foreign-ness about herself, she moved through her regimen like a dancer, relying solely on muscle memory. After slipping into a pair of blue jeans and a white cotton blouse, she retrieved her Hebborn material—copies of all that she'd handed over to Jeremy—along with a ballpoint pen and blank notebook from her study, then crawled back into bed with them. Her self-imposed assignment was to outline Harrison's and her findings and to suggest methods and means of inquiry pursuant to them.

Moments later, Harrison returned to the bedroom, still clad in the sweatpants and T-shirt he'd slept in and carrying a tray crowded with breakfast offerings. His face lit up when he saw her in fresh clothes, with papers and notebook on her lap. Seeing his delight, her heart leapt out to him, the spontaneity of her reaction dispelling the queasy feeling of otherness.

"What have you *got* there?" she asked, his presence a balm.

"Everything," he said. "You didn't tell me what you wanted, so I made French toast, eggs, bacon, sausages—"

"Stop. Put the tray down." She moved the Hebborn materials to the night table and then crossed her legs, lotus style. "Come sit with me. You know you'll have to eat most of this."

He placed the tray at her feet and crawled in beside her. Replicating her cross-legged position, he said, "Grace is bringing us coffee. She'll be here in a minute."

As if on cue, Grace appeared at the door, and Harrison jumped out of bed to take the tray of coffee and essential accompaniments from her. After her departure, he gingerly placed it on his night table, pushing his lamp aside to make room for it. He poured a cup for Erika and held up the creamer. "No, right?"

"Right," she said, taking the cup from him. "Thank you." She raised the cup to her lips and took a sip of the coffee, savoring it. With every ordinary move, she felt more of a piece with her body. "It's good and strong."

Harrison filled a cup for himself, leaving it on the coffee tray until he crawled back into bed. He looked at Erika, sitting beside him, calmly assessing the assorted fare. He reached for his cup, his hand shaking from tenuous relief. "What dish are you favoring?" he asked, his voice as unsteady as his hand.

"I think I'll have a little taste of everything," she said. "You'll have the rest." She glanced at him. "What's wrong? You look almost frightened."

"No, no, not at all," he said, leaning toward her to kiss her cheek and almost spilling his coffee. The fact that he did not filled him with an optimism far beyond its modest cause.

* * *

Grace knocked on their door an hour later, asking if she might clear up the remains of their breakfast. Erika said she'd help, but Grace and Harrison vetoed her. Harrison, on the other hand, insisted on being of service.

While Grace and Harrison puttered about in the kitchen, Erika collected the copies of the Hebborn findings from her night table and looked them over, then took up her pad and pen and jotted down possible strategies to find the forged art. First, of course, they must contact Andrea to see if she had heard from any of the galleries or auction houses Erika had suggested she contact. Next, they should get in touch with Greg Smith, Harrison's friend who had been of assistance in their previous pursuit of art stolen during the Cuban Revolution—their "Cuban caper," as she had called it. Greg was on the executive board of Art Loss Register, touted as the world's largest database of stolen art. If any of the art works Hebborn had referenced had at some point gone missing, Greg's research might prove invaluable.

A dull pain thrummed beneath her ribcage, like the muffled clacking of an underground train. She became conscious of it only when she put down her pen to marvel, with a kind of horror, how focused she could become on forged art so soon after a life had been stolen from her. She wondered if her body had put her bitterness on auto-pilot, expressing it as an unending ache that would keep the wound open for knife-twisting analysis even as she lumbered through her day-to-day existence.

She was staring down at her notes without seeing them, when Harrison returned from his chores.

"How's it going?" he asked, his easy tone belied by his tense posture.

She looked up. "I've been scribbling notes on where we go from here."

"That's great," he said carefully, as if his words might injure her. "Shall we call Andrea? Do you think it's too early? It's eight o'clock. Maybe I should take a shower first, give her time to start the day."

"Please don't feel like you're walking on eggshells around me," she said. "It makes me feel like I'm about to break."

"I'm sorry."

"Don't apologize either."

He smiled wanly. "Give me a hint."

"Be yourself." She set the Hebborn material aside and rose from the bed, the pain under her ribs assuaging her grief by reminding her of it. "Take a shower. We'll get down to work whenever you're ready."

Chapter 7

B y nine, she and Harrison were ensconced in his study on the first floor. They were sitting at his desk, Erika in the leather chair opposite his. Jake was sitting by her side, leaning into her, insisting she pet him non-stop, without doubt to assure him that her remoteness for the past twenty-two or so hours—an infinity in unstructured dog time—was merely a pause in the flow of mutual love, not its withdrawal.

"Don't tell Andrea or Charlene about yesterday," Erika warned Harrison, steely-eyed. "I don't want to garner any misplaced sympathy. Sympathy should be for the loss of life. *I'm* still here. People always get it wrong."

"We can't keep it a secret," Harrison said. "They knew you were pregnant."

"Thanks to you."

"I know," he said, crestfallen.

"I'm sorry. That was uncalled for. I'll tell them at some point. When it doesn't hurt as much. The pain will ease whether I like it or not."

He nodded his understanding.

Erika picked up her cell phone and realized she didn't know Andrea's cell number. She punched in Charlene's from her contacts file and activated the speaker so Harrison could be in on the conversation.

Charlene answered on the first ring with a frantic, "Did she call you?"

"What?" Erika replied, placing the phone on the desk for Harrison's benefit.

"What's wrong?"

"Andy hasn't come home," Charlene said. "No word from her. No answer when I call her. I've been calling everywhere!"

"Do you know when she checked out of Earth Haven?"

"At three-thirty yesterday, the receptionist said."

"Charlene, does she have any friends or relatives in the area?" Harrison asked. "I mean in Vermont?"

"An aunt. I called her. Nothing."

"Have you called the police?" he asked.

"They said my concern is *premature!*"

Erika reacted to the word with a quick intake of air. She pressed Jake more firmly against her leg.

"They said I have to wait another twenty-four hours before they'll get involved!" Charlene exploded. "Would you believe it?"

"We'll call our friend, John Mitchell," Erika declared with sudden fervor, her uptick of emotion latching onto Charlene's. "He's a private detective, retired from the police force. He was an amazing help with our Cuban art recovery project. He'll get right on it."

"Our wedding is less than a week away. Something's happened to her!"

"Give us all the details you know," Erika urged. "The address and number of the retreat, the name of the director. Did she drive there in a rented car?" Without waiting for an answer, the heat rising to her cheeks, she asked, "What's the name and address of the rental agency?"

Harrison reached across the desk to touch her hand. "It's okay," he whispered.

Erika slid her hand out from under. She was on a mission now. "Charlene?"

"Yes, the rental agency. Atlas. On Second Avenue, and I think Nineteenth Street. Hospitals. I haven't called the hospitals. There are so many. Where do I begin?"

"John will do all that," Erika assured her.

Charlene asked them to hold on while she fetched the information regarding the retreat. After returning, she quickly dictated them, spilling into, "I want her to walk in the door this minute so I can give her hell for not getting in touch with me!"

"We know," Harrison said.

"The detective. Do I pay him now or later?"

"Not at all," Harrison said.

"But—"

"Not a word," Harrison cut in. "It's taken care of."

"Listen to him," Erika said. "He means it."

"I don't know what to say," Charlene said.

"He told you. Not a word."

Charlene burst into tears. "Her mother blames me!" she managed to get out.

"For *what?*" Erika asked.

"For whatever happened to her daughter!" Charlene cried. "For Andy's fall from grace, and for whatever heaven-sent punishment followed!"

"You know that's insane, so get that out of your head," Erika said, her voice rising along with her need to take action. "Will you be at the book-shop today? I'll meet you there. We should talk face to face."

Harrison shot her a quizzical glance: *today?* It went unacknowledged.

"If I stay at home, I'll go crazy," Charlene said. "Yes, I'll meet you at the shop. When can you be there?"

"In about an hour," Erika said. "I'll give John a call first."

"How do I thank you?"

"By staying calm," Erika replied, disregarding her own advice.

She ended the call and began to look for John's number. "Wait!" Harrison commanded, as Erika was about to dial it.

"What?" she asked, impatient. "We can't waste time!"

"You should be resting today. Aside from the fact that you should not be getting tangled up in anything that involves trouble, and I smell trouble."

"If Andrea is in trouble, I need to help in any way I can," she said. "Maybe I can actually *save* a life!"

There was absolute silence as Erika realized the unadorned truth: the present crisis, coming the day after her own loss, connected her to it. She had to come to Andrea's aid despite the possible risks, and maybe even because of them.

Harrison slowly shook his head, a sign of reluctant comprehension. "The events are totally unrelated," he said without conviction, aware his statement was useless. Erika's decision was visceral, therefore undebatable. "I'm going to the bookshop with you," he said, saving her the trouble of a comeback. "Go ahead, call John."

* * *

There was a hand-printed CLOSED DUE TO ILLNESS sign hanging on the door of The Book Den.

"I didn't know what else to say," Charlene explained, pointing to the sign as she opened the door. "Thank you for coming. I'm a wreck."

"We wanted to be here," Erika said, falling into an embrace. She clasped Charlene tightly for support, Charlene's as well as her own.

Harrison patted Charlene's shoulder. "It's going to be all right," he assured her.

Charlene slipped out of Erika's embrace to relock the door. "Come sit."

She led them to the nook where they had last convened. Erika and Charlene seated themselves in the armchairs; Harrison perched on the stool Charlene had moved beforehand from the receptionist's area. Andrea's absence was palpable. The pause before the first spoken words marked it as a fact.

"May I offer you coffee or tea?" Charlene asked, as if she were reading from a teleprompter.

They declined. "Can we take you out to lunch in a little while?" Harrison asked. "I think it would be good for you to—"

"I'm sorry to be rude, but I don't need a diversion. I need to find Andrea!"

"Of course. Maybe we can pick up something, bring it here," he suggested, struggling to accommodate her changing mood. "Whatever you like."

"John is on his way to the retreat," Erika said, bypassing the niceties. "He asked that we text him a recent photograph of Andrea."

"Although he probably won't need it," Harrison added, his attempt to distract from the import of Erika's request only serving to highlight it.

Charlene took a deep breath and rose from the chair. "I'll be right back." As she passed Harrison, she paused and touched his shoulder. "There are no precedents for this," she said. "I'm okay with the photo and everything. I need to be participating." She glanced at Erika. "I don't know why, but I sense you understand."

Erika nodded, withholding an explanation.

Charlene continued on to the receptionist's desk, where she picked up her cell phone from the counter top. On the way back, she tapped and swiped at the device. "Here are a bunch we took two weeks ago at Macy's," she said, sitting back down. "We were picking out items for our wedding registry." She looked up. "We're an unconventional couple, but as traditional as they come," she said, breaking Erika's heart with a nostalgic smile, as if memory were all that remained. She reached out to hand the cell phone to Erika. "You want to choose one of them to send to your friend?"

"Sure," Erika said, glancing at the mosaic of photos. She enlarged one that captured Andrea standing alone in front of a display of china sets. With one hand poised palm up, Andrea was directing the viewer's attention to one of the sets, as if she were introducing a guest on a game show. She was wearing a long skirt with a floral print and a white blouse. Her hair was pulled back in a high ponytail. Erika zeroed in on her face, shown full-on. The word "lovely" hovered on the threshold of speech, but Erika left it unsaid.

"I've got one," she clipped, to lessen the sting. As efficiently as possible, she transmitted the photo to John and returned the cell phone to Charlene. Charlene kissed her fingertips then pressed them to the selected photo. Without clearing the screen, she lay the cell phone in her lap.

"I'm glad you're here," she said, focusing solely on Erika. "I mean both of you," she said, remembering to include Harrison. "I don't think I could have handled this alone."

"Charlene," Erika began. "Is there anything Andrea may have mentioned to you before she left on her trip that might explain her delay? Was she thinking of taking the scenic route back, for instance? Did she make any calls to you en route? Express any concerns about the car?"

"No," Charlene said. "No scenic routes, no weird engine sounds. No calls or texts from her of any kind."

"Memory can be perverse," Erika said. "Sometimes when we try hard to remember something, it hides from us. Then, when we direct our attention elsewhere, the memory pops up like a jack-in-the-box."

"Good idea," Harrison said, jumping up from the stool, as if inspired by the image. "I'll run out for a snack. Where's the nearest grocer or deli?"

"No," Charlene protested. "Sit down, Harrison. I'm the one whose memory needs jogging. We have a mini-kitchen in the storeroom. Do you want coffee or tea? I have corn muffins and oatmeal cookies." She grabbed her cell phone and rose from her chair. "Well?"

Harrison sat back down, defeated. "Coffee, Charlene. Black. Nothing more. Thanks."

"May I help?" Erika asked, rising. She thought not, knowing how she herself would have felt.

"Stay put," Charlene said. "I'll be back shortly. Would you like coffee or tea, Erika? I'm having green tea, but we've got herbal and raspberry, too."

"I'll have what you have."

Charlene gave a forlorn smile. "Then you'll have a cookie, too."

Erika sank back into the chair. "Yes."

Charlene headed toward the closed door at the far side of the expanse open to the public. Before she entered the private room, she looked back at her guests and paused to study them, as if she might never see them again.

"She's handling the situation pretty well," Harrison said, after Charlene had shut the door behind her. "I think your presence helps."

"We're *both* helping," Erika said, recoiling from being singled out.

"Do I stand corrected on *everything* I say?" Harrison asked, uncharacteristically peeved.

"No. You're incredibly supportive. I'm the one who's off." She looked closely at him. "You're beginning to dislike me. I can see it in your eyes."

"How do I respond to that? I don't think a simple objection will do."

"Tell me I'm delusional."

"Good answer. You're delusional."

She offered a conciliatory smile—what other option did she have?—just as a shrill cry struck the air. They leapt to their feet and took off toward the closed door. But the door swung open before they arrived, and Charlene burst from the room, holding her cell phone at arm's length, as if it had turned into a rattlesnake.

"What happened?" Erika implored.

"Look at this," Charlene said, grimacing with pain, as if the words had been gouged out of her. She flicked the hand holding the cell phone. "Take it."

Erika took the cell from her and looked down at the screen, angling it so that Harrison, standing beside her, could see it, too. On the screen there was a text message from normanstein828@gmail.com. The message had been sent a moment before:

Been trying to reach Andy with no luck. She called before she went off to VT. Sounded sluggish, like she gets when she's in one of her real low periods. Made her promise to talk to me when she got back. Where the hell is she?

Harrison stiffened. "What do you make of it?" he asked. His tone was academic, but his wide-eyed stare gave him away.

"It can't mean what you're thinking!" Charlene replied shrilly, proving that was exactly what she was thinking herself. "It's impossible! Give me back my phone!"

Erika handed her the cell. "Let's think about this," she said, learning from Harrison's mistake and maintaining a calm exterior. "I haven't known you and Andrea very long, but it's a safe guess that you're the most important person in her life. If Andrea had something important to say, why would she say it to Norman Stein—a cousin, a brother?—rather than you?"

"No reason at all," Charlene said, with a discernible note of relief. "Unless she couldn't bear facing me," she reconsidered, panic skidding back into her voice.

"I don't agree," Erika said, harnessing her composure for the purpose of calming Charlene. "Tell me who Norman Stein is, and if Andrea is close to him."

"Norman is her brother. He's an elementary school teacher. Yes, they're close. He's going to be the best man at our wedding." The corners of her mouth twitched, but she kept the tears at bay.

"Are the two in constant communication, or not so much?" Harrison asked, shifting his weight.

"Not so much," Charlene answered. "They lead divergent lives."

"Can you call him now?" Erika asked.

"He's teaching."

"Maybe he's on a break," Erika said, allowing Charlene to realize why on her own.

Charlene slapped her head with the heel of her hand. "He just texted me. Of course he's on a break." She punched in Norman's cell number and activated the speaker.

He picked up immediately. "Charlene, I'm in the staff cafeteria," he opened. "Let me run to my classroom. There's no one there."

"You're on speaker phone, Norm. With two friends who are helping me."

"I'd rather we talk privately—sorry, friends!" His panting was audible as he trotted to the classroom.

"That's okay, we understand," Harrison said.

Charlene deactivated the speaker and headed for the private room. "Please excuse me."

* * *

Charlene emerged from the room five minutes later, looking like she'd run the marathon. "Did you find out anything?" Erika asked. She and Harrison hadn't budged from the spot.

"No. Andy didn't give him a clue about what was on her mind. It was not *what* she said, but *how*, that worried him."

Erika delved right to the heart of the matter. "Charlene, do you have a hint of what Andrea might have been depressed about?"

"You mean was she thinking of leaving me? Or *worse!*" She drilled a gaze at the space before her, as if to make out—or create—an image to fill it. "No," she said, as if she had been telegraphed the answer. "No."

"Charlene, I was only asking if you had any ideas."

Charlene's eyes suddenly widened, as if she had been finger-snapped out of a trance. "I felt her," she said. "Right here, in front of me. I know it's a trick of the imagination, but it felt real." She sat back on the display table, further upsetting the arrangement of books. She looked up at her visitors with doe eyes, innocent and at their mercy. "I may be deceiving myself about Andy's state of mind. Do you think I am?"

"Of course not," Erika said, moving closer to Charlene. "You have to trust your instincts."

"You don't think she could have taken her own *life*," Charlene said, marveling almost, like a child discovering the concept of death.

"No, of course not."

"But you're not certain, are you?"

Without wavering, Erika said, "No. We can never know a person completely, can we? Even our soul mate."

"Thank you for being honest," Charlene said. "It's almost comforting. Isn't that crazy?"

"Not at all," Harrison said, coming up behind Erika and circling her waist with his arms.

Erika resisted the selfish desire to press back against him. "Do you think you're ready for that cup of tea now?" she asked Charlene. "Come, I'll help you. If we stop concentrating on this, something unexpected may come to mind. John should be checking in with us soon, and we should be ready with as many facts as possible. No holds barred with John. He can be tough."

"Sustenance is definitely in order," Harrison said, encircling Erika's waist more securely before the inevitable release.

* * *

It was time for a more aggressive approach, Erika decided. "Let's check Andrea's computer," she said, as she was helping Charlene clear the plates and mugs from the side tables in the sitting area, where she and Harrison had spent the last hour failing to nudge forth useful recollections of Charlene's without actually digging for them. "Does she have a personally dedicated computer here?"

"She has a laptop in the back room, but I don't know the password."

"Can you try to guess it?"

"You mean like they do in the movies, and always successfully? No. Andrea is hyper-sensitive about keeping things secure. She dreams up long and un-thematic passwords."

She led Erika to the back room anyway, placing the dishes she was carrying in its small but serviceable sink. Erika did the same.

"Does Andrea keep a list of her passwords somewhere?" Erika asked.

"She stores them on the cloud with a master password that unlocks all. Only she knows it. I guess we didn't plan ahead for this!" With an angry twist, she turned on the hot water full force.

"Don't worry about it," Erika said. "John will be able to access Andrea's computer files if need be."

Charlene squirted a glob of detergent, and Erika grabbed the dishcloth draped over the narrow countertop as Charlene began scrubbing the dishes with a sponge. After each item was rinsed, Charlene handed it to Erika. For a moment or two no words were exchanged.

"Exactly what 'if need be' were you referring to?" Charlene finally asked. The words sounded as much like a challenge as a question, and Erika placed the last of the dried items on the counter as she worried over her response.

"How's it going?" Harrison called from their meeting area, where he had remained after the women had turned down his offer to help.

"Be with you in a minute!" Erika answered, the sound of her own raised voice boosting her confidence. She checked herself from taking a deep breath and adding gravity to what she was about to say to Charlene. "I'm thinking John will want to know the names of Andrea's most recent contacts and what they talked about," she said, presenting an unruffled exterior. "Their exchanges may shed some light on what was troubling her when she spoke to her brother. For instance, could there have been an ex in her life who may have wanted to cause mischief by putting a crimp in your wedding plans?"

"There are no exes," Charlene shot out.

The answer had been too quick to have been deliberated. "I'm sorry," Erika said. "I didn't mean to be intrusive. I'm just anxious that you be prepared for the tough questions, however irrelevant."

Charlene placed her hands on Erika's shoulders. "My fear is mirrored in your eyes," she said. "I want to deny it, but you remind me that I can't."

Erika covered Charlene's hands with her own and said nothing. She needed to reply, yet every comforting response would be a lie. She was saved by the ring of Harrison's cell phone, jarring even from a distance. She and Charlene sprang apart and hastened to the sitting area.

"John Mitchell," Harrison mouthed as they arrived. "John, I'm putting you on speaker phone—unless you want to talk to Charlene privately." With an inquiring look, he asked Charlene the question in reverse. She shook her head, so Harrison activated the speaker and held the cell away from his ear.

"Hello, Charlene," John said. "I'm on my way to the retreat. I expect to be there in about an hour. How are you holding up?"

"You're driving and on the phone?" Charlene asked. "Hands free?" She expelled a sharp sound resembling a laugh. "What a stupid question."

"Not stupid. And yes, hands free. Let me give you an update. Before I left town, I called a couple of my guys on the inside—of the force, that is. We've put out a bunch of feelers—got a line on the municipal and local tow yards within a sizeable radius of the retreat. Same for spare parts facilities. I'm in touch with the car rental agency. There's a multi-state alert on the vehicle and license plate number. I've got a handle on area camera surveillance. You name it, I'm on it."

"I don't know how to repay you, Detective."

"Call me John. Don't worry. My boy Harrison's got it covered. Take it from me, if you object, he'll freak out."

"Hospitals!" Charlene blurted, unable to maintain the polite façade. "Did you call the hospitals? I only got to a few!"

"My wife's on that one. Don't worry, she's a pro. Quit her job at a top investment firm to work by my side."

"Is there anything we can do at our end?" Erika interjected.

"Sit tight, is all," John said. "I'll get in touch if I hear anything and when I'm about to head back. So far we haven't heard any news from the facilities we're in communication with. There's every reason to be optimistic. Questions?"

Erika touched Charlene's hand. "The text to Norman," she gently urged.

"It's irrelevant," Charlene objected, without conviction.

"Tell John that," Erika cajoled. "He's the pro."

"What are you two talking about?" John asked.

"You tell him, then," Charlene instructed Erika.

Erika squeezed Charlene's hand. "Okay."

As John listened in silence, she related the contents of Andrea's text and how it had come to light. "Thanks for this information," he said at the end of her account. "I won't misuse or overplay it, Charlene. You have my word. Is there anything else you'd like to bring to my attention?"

There was not.

"If you do, you have my cell number. Talk soon."

* * *

The threesome had barely digested the contents of Mitchell's call when the muffled ring of Erika's cell phone sounded from the depths of her tote. She dug for it, answering on the fourth ring. "Hello?" she burst out, hearing the fear in her own voice.

"It's Jeremy Young, over at G and G's. Anything wrong, Erika?"

"How did you get my number?" she shot out without thinking.

"From Randall, when he had me pick up the Hebborn material at your place. I repeat, what's wrong?"

"Sorry. I was distracted. What's on your mind, Jeremy?" She glanced over at Harrison and punched on the speaker. Harrison, the only one seated, rose to his feet and took a defensive stance, as if ready for a brawl.

"Something came up that may be of interest to you," Jeremy said, with an intimate undertone to his voice. "Remember, I was working on the Emma Bardac letters to Claude Debussy? Of course you do. Well, I determined that they are authentic, and my client asked me to inquire as to their value for insurance purposes."

"*And?*" Erika asked, finding his familiarity grating.

"Hang on. So I called my contact at Sotheby's, a classmate of mine. High school, that is, not *Harvard*," he said, pitching the name like a fastball. "He gave me a guesstimate for my client, and I asked him what was up, I mean in general."

Erika's patience was wearing thin, but it looked like Jeremy was about to come to the point. "He mentioned that a Rembrandt painting was headed onto the block. Apparently causing quite a stir, even for these jaded peddlers. It's being jammed into an upcoming auction, although the catalogue has already been printed. They've got to add an insert."

Erika's curiosity spiked. "Jeremy, have you seen the nineteen clues from Hebborn that Harrison and I came up with?"

"I have, yes."

"And are you going to tell me that this painting up for auction might relate to one of them?"

"There are elements in the provenance records, most notably the date of sale and the name of a prior owner, that jibe with one of your references," he said. "You can meet the current owner, if you like."

"When?"

"Why, today! He's come to town from Philadelphia with his wife, staying at the St. Regis. They're going to dinner and the theater, but could meet you at the hotel's Old King Cole Bar at four p.m. I told my man at Sotheby's that you're an ambitious young editor at *Art News* who'd love to do an interview with the prestigious collector. That's your cover story. I didn't want to let my guy in on your true motivation, which would make him a co-conspirator. Of course the Rembrandt is under lock and key at Sotheby's, but the owner will come prepared with a couple of hi-res photos to give you, and you can study them at your leisure. The real value will be to hear the anecdotal stuff—how he came upon the painting, and any individuals he ran across that might not be listed in the catalogue. What do you say?"

Erika looked questioningly at each of her companions. Harrison said nothing, allowing Erika to call the shots.

"You've got to strike while the iron is hot," Jeremy urged.

"Go," Charlene said. "What purpose does sitting around with me serve?"

"Who's that?" Jeremy asked. "Am I on speaker phone? Why didn't you tell me?"

"I didn't think you'd mind," Erika said. "Harrison and I are at The Book Den with Charlene Miller. Charlene is the owner of the second Hebborn book. She's as much a part of this project as we are, actually more so." She was not about to reveal the reason for their visit to the shop, if only because she felt an aura of unease when she was in Jeremy's company.

"All right. Understood," Jeremy said, clearly peeved.

"It will be problematic if the painting dovetails with one of the clues," Harrison said. "The issue would have to be taken up with Sotheby's."

"We'd cross that bridge after Erika's interview," Jeremy said curtly. "Erika, I would suggest you bring a camera, a proper one, apart from your cell phone's. It will validate your cover. I hear the collector's wife is a wannabe celebrity. She's actually the one who pushed her husband into inviting you. Play it up with her."

"We'll have to get back to you, Jeremy," Erika said, gritting her teeth. Did he think she didn't know how to conduct an interview? She held the mic against her side and whispered, "We won't leave you alone, Charlene."

"Don't be absurd," Charlene whispered back. "I'll be going home soon, anyway."

"Will you have a friend stay with you?"

"If you insist. You know Andy would want you to go. She's involved in this more than I am."

Erika held the cell away from her body.

Jeremy had apparently been speaking. "Are you there, Erika?"

"Yes, sorry. We lost the signal for a minute."

"I hope you weren't counting on bringing your husband," Jeremy said after a moment. "It would be great to have him along, and he's an art historian and all, but his presence would dilute the image we're trying to present. When does a journalist bring along a spouse on an interview?"

"How about *you*, Jeremy?" Harrison inquired. "Do *you* plan to be in attendance?"

"I'm going in my contact's stead," Jeremy declared. "As per his request. I'm serving as Sotheby's liaison. Is there a problem?"

"Not if Erika doesn't perceive there to be," Harrison said, his words chiseled in ice.

Erika again pressed the mic against her side to bar Jeremy from hearing. "It's okay only if Charlene will be with you, Harrison, or with another friend. Do you both promise me?"

They promised, and she resumed her open conversation with Jeremy to finalize plans. To Jeremy's badly concealed chagrin, Erika turned down his offer to pick her up.

* * *

Ten minutes later, Erika and Harrison walked Charlene to her apartment a few blocks from the shop. The moment Charlene turned the key and opened the door to the cozy second-floor walk-up she and Andrea shared, she burst into tears. Erika wanted to cancel her appointment, but Charlene forbade her, and before she could reverse her decision, Harrison had already called Bill to take her home to prepare her notes for her interview.

Chapter 8

John Mitchell slid into his reliable old Chevy in Earth Haven's parking area and turned the ignition key. While the engine idled, he called Harrison on his cell phone and reported that he was about to head back to New York, and that he had learned nothing critical from interviewing staff members or from examining the room Andrea had occupied. Harrison reported that Erika was home, preparing for a meeting with an art collector at the St. Regis, and that he and Charlene were waiting for her at Charlene's apartment. He gave John the address of the building, a block away from the bookshop, and John said that he would see them there in about four, five hours. "Don't leave Charlene to stew on her own," he added, although he knew Harrison and Erika well enough to realize that the advisory was unnecessary.

The call lasted three minutes. After checking in with his wife, John glanced at the dashboard clock and at his wristwatch. Both read 4:16. He noted the time and Charlene's address in the notebook he kept in the pocket of the white dress shirt beneath his lightweight outer jacket. Although he was still sharp as a whip, ten years ago the address would have been tattooed in memory. Today, at fifty-three: penciled in.

He took a sweeping glance around him before putting the Chevy in gear. The grounds of Earth Haven were meticulously cared for, but still retained a touch of willfulness. Scattered over the dense carpet of closely cropped grass were irregularly patterned stands of birch trees and sugar maples. Each group was embraced by a seemingly haphazard mix of pink wildflowers and a flower he could not name: magenta, with a thick crown of vertical petals. In the distance, partly obstructed by the trees, stood the sprawling brick main house, a kind of rustic castle, and several smaller versions, like offspring, where visitors were housed. The scene was idyllic. Someday he would like to spend time here with his wife. She was a yoga fanatic. He might finally give it a try. Why the hell not?

He shifted the car into gear and headed down the long gravel drive to the iron gate, where a guard seated in a wood-shingled booth swung open the gate remotely and waved him on his way.

The retreat was pocketed on a nine-acre parcel of land on the outskirts of Marlboro, Vermont. To connect with Interstate 91, John had to travel about ten miles on Route 9, the Molly Stark Scenic Byway. On the way to the retreat, he had marveled at the spectacular views of the Green Mountains this road afforded, and he had been tempted to stop at one of the lookout points to snap a couple of photos to show his wife and kids, but the urge had seemed disrespectful to his mission, so he had refrained. The same temptation waxed and waned on his return trip.

John had traveled about five miles along the byway when he rounded a curve and found himself headed toward a roadblock. He was forced to come to a full stop. Official vehicles facing every which way were crowded together in his lane like a schoolyard gang. Two ends of yellow security tape were tied about a car length apart to the low metal guardrail that bordered the lane. Although not visible from John's vantage point, it was easy to surmise that the tapes trailed down the embankment beyond the rail.

John felt a twinge in the pit of his stomach. The timing was all wrong, of course. These emergency vehicles were nowhere in sight an hour and a half ago, when he had passed this way himself, and Andrea Stein would have traveled this patch of Route 9 almost twenty-four hours prior to *that*. This couldn't have anything to do with her.

At either end of the cluster of vehicles, a uniformed officer was directing traffic to allow cars from opposite directions to alternate passage through the open—due north—lane. One car had just driven past John, and the officer in charge at John's end motioned for him to jump lanes and drive on. Instead, he swerved right and pulled up behind a police car. An officer jumped from the passenger side of the car, his hand on his holster, and John grabbed his wallet before the officer arrived at his door.

"Cut the engine and step out of the vehicle," the officer barked through the closed window.

John obeyed, careful not to make any abrupt movements. When they stood face to face, he explained his presence, whipping out his wallet to display his private investigator's ID. The officer was cautiously impressed but said he needed to call the jurisdiction's central office, the Windham County Sheriff's Department in Newfane, for instructions. He returned to his car to radio headquarters.

While John waited for the verdict, he stepped to the guardrail and peered down the rocky embankment. At its foot, twenty, thirty yards down, a smashed car was lying on its side. The passenger door was almost completely detached. It hung open like the lid of a sardine can. Technicians swarmed around it like hungry birds.

"I've got to check out the scene," John said, as the officer in communication with the sheriff's office returned. "My client—"

"You've got clearance," the officer said, preempting further discussion. "A lieutenant from Suffolk County, Long Island—I take it a friend of yours—called in an alert for the New York license plate involved in the accident and said you were the man to contact. My boss said he was about to give you a heads-up himself."

John's stomach dropped. "Shit."

"You're pissed? I said you could go down."

"When was the accident reported?" John asked, not bothering to clear the confusion.

"About an hour ago. The crash site was spotted from Hogback Mountain Overlook by a tourist. He called 911 about a half hour ago. Don't know how long the car's been sitting there. The techs may be able to give you an idea.

Medical examiner, too."

John's stomach hit rock bottom, right alongside Andrea Stein. "Will you do me a favor? Hold off contacting the decedent's next of kin for twenty-four hours? That'll give me a chance to talk to them. Will you pass this on to the sheriff?"

"Sure thing. Meantime, I'll call the officer in charge down at the crash site. Sergeant Terry O'Brian. Give you the thumbs up."

"Appreciate it," John said.

"Watch your step. The terrain's pretty rough. And mind the tape. Stay out of its corridor on the way down."

* * *

If the grade had been any more sheer, John would have needed mountain gear. His sneakers gave him just enough traction as he slowly made his way down the embankment to the crash site, using the jutting rock formations as stepping stones. As he descended, he toyed with the theory that someone had stolen the rental car from Andrea and that she had managed to flee unscathed. His spirits lifted as he pictured a mangled stranger at the wheel, but then plummeted as he regarded the ghoulishness of his thought. Andrea was a stranger, too, he reminded himself. Why did he feel so close to her?

He realized why as he stepped onto level ground with a mixture of relief and trepidation. Through his good friends, the Wheatleys, he was only one degree of separation from knowing her.

* * *

John was a commanding figure, and he used his stature to engender respect without being authoritative. Standing at a respectful distance, he asked Sergeant O'Brian, "Mind if I come closer?" He had already been introduced to the emergency and diagnostic personnel poring over the scene. He had not yet gotten a good look inside the car, although he had glimpsed the hem of a skirt pulled above a knee. He almost wanted O'Brian to refuse his request, as if not identifying Andrea would prolong the possibility of her being elsewhere.

"Of course," O'Brian said. "It's my understanding that's what you're here for." He pulled out a pair of latex gloves from his pocket and handed them to John. "You can take notes and photos if you like, as long as you swear not to disseminate or publish a word or an image." He beamed a collegial smile touched with the sobriety the circumstances demanded. "Otherwise we sue your ass."

The medical examiner, a fastidious-looking gentleman with thick glasses, was touching the inert figure. When he stepped back to record his observations, John was able to walk up to the gaping maw of the passenger doorway and take in an unobstructed view of Andrea Stein in her sprawl of indignity. Her upper body was jammed against the door that had been flattened by the fall. One leg was caught between the steering column and the seat; the other was stretched in front of her. Her head was twisted at an impossible angle, like an owl's, and he could see her miraculously unmarked features too perfectly, leaving no doubt about whose face it had once been.

John hesitated before taking a photograph. He knew Andrea would not have wanted to be captured in this horrific candid pose. But Charlene might demand it as proof of the event, or even to aggravate her own suffering, if only to ensure the memory would never fade.

The medical examiner shared his preliminary determination with John: as a result of the intense force of the vehicle's impact with static objects—guardrail, rocks, ground—the decedent had suffered severe body and organ impact—brain with skull; heart with sternum. He presumed the latter would be named the cause of death. The accident scene technician, a woman of small stature and formidable bearing, provided a description of what she surmised had been the vehicle's pattern of descent. She noted that the guardrail had been minimally damaged, an indication that the vehicle had more or less catapulted over it rather than driven straight into it. Because an air bag's sensors are installed in the front of the car, the fact that the driver's air bag had not deployed supported her theory.

John recorded these findings in his notebook, then broached the subject of motivation with Sergeant O'Brian. He requested that O'Brian and his team rule out suicide and foul play as precipitating causes. "If anything," he said, "I would concentrate on the latter. This 'accident' is no longer an isolated event, given the subject of my investigation: a recent homicide ruled to be a random attack that I now believe may have been premeditated. This is hypothesis on my part, with no supporting evidence, but there it is. What do you say?"

O'Brian thought for a moment and then agreed to accommodate John. "You understand this means we can't release any of the decedent's belongings either to you or to her next of kin until the case is closed. Cell phone, handbag, suitcase, anything we find of interest. We're required to maintain a strict chain of custody. In the interim, if you want to review any items, you'll have to apply for permission. All clear?"

"Absolutely."

"You would have to appear in person at the sheriff's office, and conduct your examination under our supervision."

"I get it."

"Naturally, this new slant on things will affect the coroner's examination. The body will have to be examined for injuries sustained before the accident. The inducements of intoxication and poisoning will have to be considered. You see where I'm going with this? You're not sending us on a wild goose chase, are you?"

John drew himself to his full height, making use of his ability to appear menacing. "I don't take this lightly, Sergeant. I hope you're not suggesting this is a frivolous request."

"Not at all," O'Brian said, planting his legs apart, arms akimbo.

Neither relinquishing authority, the two shook hands and exchanged cards, and John made his way back up the embankment to the privacy of his familiar old car, where he sat for a moment in respectful silence.

As he started the engine and angled into position to jump lanes and head for the highway, he decided that the kindest way to break the news of Andrea Stein's untimely death to her loved ones was face to face. That meant, of course, that he was heading for hours of brooding ambivalence about withholding information from those most justified in knowing it.

Chapter 9

Bill pulled up curbside opposite the entrance of the St. Regis Hotel on East 55th Street off of Fifth Avenue. He leaped out of the car to open the passenger door for Erika.

Erika was not up to offering her usual snappy protest.

"You okay?" Bill asked.

Erika put on her game face. "Sure. See you in an hour."

Trying to live up to her mask of confidence, she slung her bag over her shoulder before striding up the red carpeted stairs and through the revolving door into the lobby. Jeremy was planted in a plush velvet chair at the far end of the reception counter. He jumped up to greet her, much as Bill had rushed to her side. He grabbed her shoulders and kissed her European style, dallying on each cheek. As she pulled away, with no attempt to disguise her discomfort, he tried to keep hold of her with his gaze.

"They're waiting for us at the bar," he said gruffly. He took her arm to escort her more tenderly than his tone might have predicted. "You look lovely, by the way."

"Thank you," she said as neutrally as possible, slipping out of his grasp. She suddenly felt tainted by her sexuality. She checked the décolletage created by her fitted suit jacket and drew the lapels together to reduce the exposure of her cleavage.

"Where's your camera?" Jeremy asked as they passed through the elegant Astor Court Restaurant, beyond which Old King Cole, enthroned in the center of Maxfield Parrish's colorful mural, reigned over the bar and cocktail lounge area.

"I'm using my cell phone's camera," Erika said. "I do think this interview will be suitable for publication, but I'm in no mood to ham it up."

"You're the boss."

* * *

Although the adjoining Astor Court Restaurant hosted a scattering of visitors partaking of high tea refreshments, the lounge area was occupied only by a seasoned-looking bartender and three guests seated around one of the glass cocktail tables that fronted the bar. Their drinks were resting on polished wood coasters next to a single menu. Another cocktail table had been moved right up alongside the threesome's table, altering the balanced décor to accommodate Erika and Jeremy.

Two of the seated group were men, and they rose from their high-backed chairs simultaneously. They appeared to be about the same age, maybe a year or two shy of seventy, although one was decidedly more fit than the other. "Excuse us for starting without you," the more toned one said, with a nod bordering on a bow. "I'm Winston Elliot, attorney and authentication expert specializing in the Dutch Golden Age—you know the boys... Rembrandt, Vermeer, Frans Hals. Allow me to introduce my clients, George Dudley and his lovely wife Maryann."

"Mary*lou*," the woman corrected. She extended her hand, limp-wristed, as if she expected it to be kissed. "You must be the lady from the art magazine," she directed at Erika. "So happy to meet you."

Erika identified herself more specifically and extended her hand to shake with each of the group in turn.

"I'm on occasion called upon to certify an item for an auction house, gallery or individual," Elliot went on about himself. "Of course, as in this instance, I am also available to walk a client through the legal weeds, as it were, of buying or selling works of art." He pulled at the cuff of his pin-striped jacket and patted the two-eared white handkerchief peering out of its pocket as if it were a small pet. From his name to his attire, Elliot was almost too British, Erika thought. Even his accent seemed forced, as if he were a character actor not quite one with his role. The only aspect of his presentation that did not fit the mold was his pair of pointed snakeskin boots. If he wore them every day, they would qualify as a bona fide affectation.

George Dudley seemed perfectly content in his own skin as he directed Erika and Jeremy to pull up alongside him at the abutting table. He smiled affably at his beautiful young wife, who brushed against him with doting fervor in her clinging red cocktail dress, marking her territory with her pheromones, if they could be detected beneath Chanel's more universal scent.

"Erika, I know you'd like to get right into a discussion of my Rembrandt," George said, "but you and Jeremy must order cocktails first, and we should order a couple of hors d'oeuvres for the table."

"Why doesn't Erika take a few photos of us first?" Marylou suggested, finger-fluffing her strawberry blonde mane.

"After our chat," George said, softening his veto with a peck on her cheek. "I've studied the bar menu, and if there are no objections, I'll order the devilled eggs medley—bacon, truffle chive, and caviar—as well as the mac-and-cheese truffle and the eggplant with goat cheese. Are we good?"

Erika could have passed on all the selections, but she, like the rest, nodded approval.

"Take a look at the Bloody Mary variations," George said, addressing Erika and Jeremy. "Everything from 'Red Snapper' to 'Bloody Smoke.' Very creative. I'm working on the 'Mary Terranean' myself—it's got Grey Goose vodka, olive, oil, basil, oregano, you name it." He waved at the bartender, who in turn produced a cocktail waitress from behind the bar's L. The cocktail waitress was wearing a low-cut black dress and an air of efficiency. She strode briskly to their tables in her seven-inch spike heels, as if she had been born in them.

"Hi, I'm Lily. Are we ready to order?"

Jeremy hastily decided on the "Agave Maria," a Bloody Mary with tequila and peppers, and Erika refused to be overruled on her choice of the Virgin Mary. George recited his list of preferred hors d'oeuvres. As the waitress departed, Erika drew her pad and pen from her bag and launched into her interview. "How did you happen to come upon the Rembrandt?"

George took a sip of his drink. "Short version or long?"

"Whatever it takes," Erika said, leaning forward in anticipation.

"I'll take that as a long," George said. He folded his hands on the table. "Well, I should start by saying that it came about as a confluence of favorable events. My previous wife and I were touring Europe in 2008. While in Germany, we stopped by the magnificent Alte Pinakothek Museum in Munich. I went mainly to view Rembrandt's *Descent from the Cross* in person—the twisted form of Christ being lowered from the cross, the melding of awkwardness and grace. And oh, the translucence of the Lord's flesh! I was so moved. My wife was bored by it all. I think this was when I realized we were incompatible.

"In the same room hung another Rembrandt, one that I was unfamiliar with, *The Holy Family*—no, not the one with angels. This was a portrait, painted in 1634, of a contemporary couple with their infant. The title, I assume, was the master's way of flattering his patrons. I was quite taken by this portrait, and I said as much to the museum guard in my fractured German. A fellow visitor overhead me—a German fluent in English—and he took it upon himself to fill me in on the history of this couple, Maerten Soolmans and his wife, Oopjen Coppit."

"Did you know that separate portraits of this couple painted by Rembrandt were sold at Christie's for a record-breaking figure in 2016?" Elliot cut in. "The buyers, the Louvre and the Rijksmuseum in partnership, agreed to exhibit the paintings together for all time, alternating between Paris and Amsterdam."

"I do know that," George said, without looking directly at Elliot. "But in 2008 I was unaware even of the existence of those portraits." He unclasped his hands to fidget with his glass, rotating it on its coaster. "Where was I?"

"At the museum in Munich," Erika said. "Talking about *The Holy Family*."

"Yes," George said, anchoring his focus on Erika. "This gentleman told me that there was a Rembrandt portrait of the wife and the infant on pre-auction exhibit at the Scheublein auction house a hop, skip and a jump away from the museum. He said that the positioning of the mother and child, as well as the palette itself, were very similar to those I was apparently so taken with. 'If you're in the market,' he joked, 'you might have a go at it.' I said I very well might, which floored him."

"Fascinating," Erika said. "And so you purchased the painting of mother and child at auction?"

"Two days later. I had to hang around and wait for the auction. The wife continued on the tour without me. Just as well."

"Can you tell me any details about the provenance of the painting?" Erika asked, skirting the marital reference. "I know you've got the printed summary, but I'd like to hear your personal take."

"I'll give you the most recent history. In 1988, a British collector came from across the pond, as they say, to buy the painting at auction at Sotheby's. In 1999, he sold it at a private sale to Henry Rittenhouse. In 2008 Rittenhouse put it up for auction at Scheublein's in Munich, where I bought it. There was an economic global crisis going on at the time, and I suppose he had to unload it. I got it at a good price, all things considered. Ten million. And so it's come full circle, back to Sotheby's, where the bidding will start at twenty million."

"I'd say you made an investment worth ending a marriage over," Elliot suggested with a wink.

George offered a pinched smile to Erika without acknowledging the source of the comment. Erika took a sip of her Virgin Mary. "Mr. Dudley," she began.

"George—please."

"George," she said, glancing down at her notes. "I'm missing a name. Can you tell me who purchased the painting at auction in 1988?" She tried to look as blasé as possible, although her heart was racing.

"Yes. It's easy to remember. The name of a drink—Collins. Tom Collins."

"Thanks." She jotted down the name as she felt the heat rising to her cheeks. Her inner voice was screaming: *Hebborn!*

The arrival of the hors d'oeuvres provided a perfect interval for Erika to collect her thoughts. "Before we forget," George said, giving the delicacies a critical once-over, "Marylou has a manila envelope for you, Erika. It contains a couple of photos of the painting and a formal list of its dimensions and, of course, history. You want to grab it from your bag, Loulou?"

At the pet name, Marylou flashed him an adorable smile and fetched the envelope. Erika tucked it into her bag along with her notes.

"I don't suppose one of the photos is of the two of you standing in front of the painting in your home?" she said.

"No, but I can send you one," George said.

"Or we can send a professional photographer to your home."

"Good idea," George said, plucking a deviled egg from its serving dish and placing it on his plate. "Dig in." He went for a mac-and-cheese truffle as well.

Erika thought she could handle one truffle; she would think of an excuse for not eating more if pressed. "I'd like to take a look at the painting itself while it's still on exhibit at Sotheby's," she said.

"I'm going there myself," Elliot jumped in before George had a chance to respond. "I'll take you."

George eyed Elliot narrowly. It was the first time he'd looked at the man, Erika realized.

"I want to have another look before I give it my seal of approval," Elliot said, looking first at Erika and then, more slyly, at George. Erika wondered what was going on between those two.

Her thought was interrupted by a cell phone ring: a phrase from one of Chopin's preludes. Jeremy retrieved his phone from the pocket of his suit jacket. "Sorry," he said, addressing the group before speaking into the mic. "Yes?" he asked. He turned pale as he listened in silence, his lips sealed shut. "I will," he said finally, with a trace of fear in his voice. He terminated the call and slipped the cell phone back into his pocket, missing the opening on the first try. "Sorry," he repeated. He picked up his glass and rose to his feet. "Here's to our host," he offered, with forced levity. "Thank you, George, and good luck with your present endeavor!"

They clinked glasses all around and Jeremy fell back into his chair.

"Can we take time out now to have our pictures taken?" Marylou asked.

"Of course," Erika said, repressing the urge to pry into Jeremy's business. "Why don't you, George, and Elliot sit at the bar so I can include the King Cole mural in the near background?"

Elliot demurred. "I have clients who shun publicity. Their paranoia applies to themselves as well as their associates."

The Dudleys positioned themselves at the bar and Erika snapped a couple of photos of them.

"Would you send them to my cell phone?" Marylou asked, viewing them on Erika's screen.

"Of course," Erika agreed, "only don't post them on Facebook. It would be anticlimactic when one of them appears in *Art News.*"

Marylou was delighted. More so, when Erika asked her a couple of questions about her interests and aspirations. Less so, when she asked George to elaborate on his own.

They returned to the lounge area, where Erika forced down another morsel and then glanced at her watch. It read 4:55. Concern about Andrea and Charlene sprang back to the center of her thoughts.

"My driver will be waiting for me," she said. "I must run." She rose, along with the men, and made the round of handshakes. "It was wonderful meeting you," she said, already picturing herself on the way out. "I can get all of your addresses and phone numbers from Jeremy, yes?"

"Sure," Jeremy said. "Let me walk you to the door. I'm leaving myself."

They walked in silence to the exit and through the revolving door. Wordless still, they descended the red carpeted stairs to the sidewalk. Bill was waiting for Erika at the same spot he had dropped her off. Jeremy walked her to the car, glancing furtively in all directions.

"You okay?" Erika asked.

"Yes, yes. Go," Jeremy said. Shoulders hunched and head down, as if it had suddenly started to pour, he began to walk west, toward Sixth Avenue. Then he stopped and, still bowed, turned toward her. "Love you," he said, disarmingly sincere, before continuing on his way.

* * *

"I was worried about you," Harrison said, ushering Erika into Charlene's apartment. "I didn't call because I was afraid you'd be annoyed."

"You're overthinking," Erika said, not giving in to the sudden urge to fall against him with relief. "I'm fine. Have you heard from John?"

"Only to say he's on his way. How'd it go?"

She glanced past his shoulder. In the open living area beyond, Charlene was seated at a small round dining table with a scrawny young man seated opposite, clutching her hand. The two of them were staring at Erika and Harrison in mute expectation. Erika touched Harrison's arm. "Talk later," she said. She dropped her tote bag near the doorway, against the wall, and hurried past him to Charlene's side.

Without losing contact with her unnamed visitor, Charlene half-rose from her seat. "I missed you," she said. "Isn't that odd?"

"That makes two of us," Erika said. "I missed you, too."

Harrison wrapped Erika from behind. "Erika, meet Charlene's friend, Barry."

Still tethered to Charlene, Barry extended his left hand. "My apartment's one flight up," he explained, in a voice more sonorous than his gauntness had predicted.

"Oh, sorry," Charlene said, as Erika and Barry brushed fingertips. Her glance flitted from one corner of the room to the other, as if she expected something to materialize.

"How are you holding up?" Erika asked, regretting the pointless question as she uttered it: Charlene looked as if she were about to snap, or had already done so. "Can I get you tea or something?"

Charlene emitted an unearthly laugh. "That's my line, Erika. Sit down, the two of you." She shot to her feet, freeing herself of Barry's grip. "What'll it be?"

"Nothing," Barry said. "We just want to be here with you—*for* you." He turned to Erika and Harrison. "Right?"

"Of course," Erika agreed.

"Well put," Harrison said.

Charlene wrung her hands. "Not a *word* from Andy. It's as if she never existed. Why is that?" She drilled a look at Erika's forehead, as if she could pluck the answer from her brain.

As if in response, a ring sounded from the direction of a desk-table set against the far wall. Charlene leaped to her feet. "A fax!"

As the phone dedicated to the fax machine rang a second time and the fax machine began to tick forth a sheet of paper, Charlene's cell phone sang its generic lilt from the pocket of her jeans. She dug for it, activating the speaker. "Andy?" she cried, blind to the caller ID.

"This is Mrs. Fenton, the manager of Earth Heaven Retreat," the caller said, sounding flustered. "You're Charlene Miller, are you not?"

"Yes, yes!"

"I'm sending you a fax, but I wanted to explain the delay—and apologize for it. Is the fax coming through?"

"Yes!" Charlene said, approaching the desk. "Is it from Andy?"

"Please let me explain," said the caller. "First, I did want to say that I'm sorry for your trouble, and I hope that Andrea returns to you unharmed."

"What is this all about, Mrs.—Fenton, did you say?" Charlene stood over the fax machine, not daring to examine the transmission.

"Of course. Well, I believe you're aware of our policy of confiscating cell phones at check-in. As it happens, within the first hour of her arrival Friday evening, Andrea asked me to break the rules and give back her phone for a time. I turned her down, however. It would have set a bad precedent, and besides, she was honest enough to tell me the situation was not an emergency. She then asked if I would send you a fax instead. She argued that since the data to be transmitted was obtained prior to her sojourn and that there would be no exchange between herself and the receiver of the fax—the primary reason for the inception of the house rules—her request was therefore within the spirit, if not the letter, of the law."

"Yes, yes, go on!"

"I told her she should have been a lawyer, but I bent the rules for her. I suppose I'm rambling because I don't want to get to the point, which is that I handed the fax to the secretary, but it got lost in a pile of the Haven's statements and to-dos. I just unearthed it. I don't mean to make excuses, but we did have an office break-in between the hours of ten p.m. Sunday and nine a.m. Monday, when the office was unoccupied. Other than a laptop and seventy-five dollars in petty cash, no losses were incurred, but the incident did cause a bit of a kerfuffle among the staff. For years they've been urging me to beef up our security, but I've been reluctant. The move would be directly counter to our philosophy of communal trust. Have you read our mission statement?"

Charlene swiped the single sheet from the tray. "Thank you for calling," she said. "Please call again if you hear any news. I'm sorry, but I have to hang up now." She ended the call and shoved the cell phone back into her pocket.

Erika thought she'd wait for Charlene to salvage whatever was left of her equanimity before questioning her.

"What does the fax say?" Barry asked, with no such reservations.

Without responding, Charlene studied the fax. When she was done, she walked to the table and handed the paper to Erika. She opened her mouth to speak, but no words came out. Then she sat down in her chair and folded her hands on the table, as if she were waiting for her teacher to grade her work.

Erika read through the fax:

Hi Hon: Christie's NY replied to my email query. Their message concerns a Van Dyck sale in 1987 and a related incident in 1996. I forgot to forward it to the Wheatleys. It notes a head-scratching coincidence, which I'd rather not spell out in an open fax, but the Ws will understand when they see the email. Meanwhile, would you relay this sketchy info to them so they can contact Christie's ASAP if they see fit? Love you. Andy

Erika passed the paper to Harrison. To Charlene, she said, "This must be impossible for you. Do you want to keep the fax? Do you want us to take it? Tell me what we should do."

"I'll make a copy for you," Charlene said. "I want the original." She turned to Barry. "This is a mystery to you. I'll explain it later."

Barry took her hand in his and raised it to his lips. "You can tell me everything or nothing. I'm here for you."

"I know, Barry."

Harrison lay the paper on the table. "This should be …looked into," he said, searching for the suitable words.

"Of course," Charlene agreed, stiffening. "Andrea will be happy to." She snatched up the fax and marched over to the desk, where she made a copy of it using the table-top printer. "Here it is," she said, slapping the copy in the center of the table. "Take it, please!"

Harrison folded the paper and placed it in his jacket pocket.

"I'm sorry I snapped at you, Harrison," Charlene said. "I don't know what's wrong with me."

"You haven't eaten," Barry said. "That's what's wrong with you. If you guys will keep an eye on my friend, here, I'll run upstairs and heat up yesterday's chicken casserole. There's masses of it. I don't know how to make a portion for one, so if you want to invite an army, feel free."

Despite a babel of objections, Barry was determined to carry out his plan.

* * *

The sleeves of Barry's sweatshirt were slipping down his bony arms as he stood over the kitchenette sink washing the dinner dishes at his insistence. As 8:31 morphed to 8:32 on Erika's watch, which she had been checking repeatedly over the past hour, he pushed up his sleeves and raised a cup from the soapy water.

The harsh buzz generated from the ground floor stopped time in its tracks. Barry froze, cup in the air, suds creeping toward his elbow like a lazy cloud. Erika and Harrison, seated at the table with Charlene, locked gazes. Charlene restarted the flow of time by jumping up and racing to the intercom. "Detective?" she squawked into the speaker.

"Yes, it's me, John," blasted the speaker-magnified reply.

"Second floor, come up," Charlene answered before pressing the button unlocking the door to the building. She turned to Erika and Harrison. "If he had any news he would have called first," she said, preparing herself for disappointment.

Nothing, however, could have prepared Charlene for the look on John Mitchell's face as he entered her apartment. His long and lonely trip, compounded by the images of death looping in his mind like a televised disaster, had depleted him of diplomacy or the will to fake it.

"No!" Charlene cried, denying what she saw written across the stark landscape of his face.

"I'm so sorry," he said without feeling, as if he'd rehearsed the line to oblivion. "I'm so sorry."

Charlene's knees buckled, and John caught her, but only to slow her descent. He must have known she needed to crumble weightlessly into a solitary heap, out of level eyeshot of all the others. "How, how, how?" she pleaded, before grief overwhelmed curiosity and she wept uncontrollably, her body jerking and heaving as if it would escape from itself.

Erika's own grief welled to the surface, merging with Charlene's. She wanted to fall at Charlene's side and comfort her, but Barry was already on his way, and too many arms closing in would hinder Charlene from exploding despair into the infinite void.

* * *

After some time, the irreversible truth of Andrea's death found mooring, however insecurely, in Charlene's earthbound brain. Red-eyed and sobbing still, and no longer able to shape her posture in any way that hinted at a state of repose, she stood rigid before John, drawing the facts from him with a tenacity that matched death's itself. She hammered him with accusatory questions, insisting on knowing everything that was said and observed by every person at the scene of the crash. "Andrea was a great driver, so how can you say she swerved off the road? What were the weather conditions? Was there an oil slick? What are you keeping from me?"

"There's no easy way to tell you this," John began, after this final question.

"Spit it out!" Charlene cried.

"I've asked that the people in charge of the investigation rule out the possibility of foul play. My suspicions may be unfounded, but because Andrea and Owen Grant shared a common cause, I believe their untimely deaths may be related."

Charlene clung to John's hypothesis, nostrils flaring, then flung it back at him like a hand grenade. "You're having her cut open and taken apart? Where is she? When will you bring her back?"

John made a move to lay his hands on Charlene's shoulders, but she flinched. "The investigation will take some time," he said. "The medical examiner will look for indications of bruises and other signs of trauma sustained outside the time frame of the accident. A toxicology report will be submitted. All of Andrea's belongings—cell phone, suitcase, handbag—will be carefully gone over. It will be a while, Charlene. It's hard to register all this, I know."

"*Register?*" She uttered a demonic laugh.

"Nothing comes out right," he said. "Words are insufficient."

"When will I have her back?"

"Charlene, Andrea's parents are her next of kin," he said evenly. "I'm afraid—"

"No! Andy and I will be together! If her parents object, I'll fight them in court!"

"I hope you won't have to."

"Do you have photographs of her?" she suddenly veered. "Don't hold anything back from me!"

As John predicted, Charlene demanded to see every photograph of Andrea he had stored on his cell phone, although the near monomaniacal way she studied them seemed to shake him. She begged him to send the images to her cell phone, but because of his agreement with the Vermont authorities, he could not grant her request.

"I must have them," she said. "To *be* with her—to *understand!*"

Erika approached Charlene; it was okay to now, she thought. In Charlene's ear she whispered, "She's in your heart, in your head." Pulling back so she could look Charlene in the eye, she said, "You don't need a picture to be with her."

She put her arms around Charlene. She half-expected to be pushed away. She wanted so badly not to be. But their cheeks touched as Charlene returned Erika's embrace. They were wrapped in silence, alone in the room.

Charlene finally spoke. "A new life inside you," she said, her voice just above a whisper. "You should be celebrating, not here with me."

Stunned, Erika could only shake her head in denial.

Charlene understood immediately. "Oh God, I'm so sorry."

Erika, finding her voice, started to explain. "When you lost touch with Andrea, I—"

"You felt my pain as if it was yours," Charlene said. "I knew there was something between us."

"But there's no equivalence," Erika said suddenly.

"What does that even mean?" Charlene asked, almost smiling at the absurdity of parsing the states of anguish. She rested her cheek on Erika's shoulder. "It doesn't matter. They're gone."

* * *

"Do you think Charlene will be okay tonight?" Erika asked her companions. She and Harrison were seated with John behind the closed glass divider in the back of Bill's car. They had given John an account of all that had occurred in his absence, including the fax and phone call from Earth Haven.

"Barry seems like a good guy," Harrison said. "He's promised to stay by her side all night."

"I agree," John said. He grasped Erika's hand. "I'm really sorry to hear about your loss, Erika. You've got to take care of yourself. You two go home and get some rest. I'll take it from here. Charlene gave me the Steins' contact information, and I'll call them from my car. It's going to be tough breaking the news to them, and I hope they give Charlene some slack."

"I have absolute confidence in you, John," Erika said.

"As do I," Harrison seconded.

Working with the Wheatleys—translated: keeping the Wheatleys safe ranked high on John's list of priorities. "I can't emphasize enough that this has become, through accident or intent, a dangerous project, or campaign, or whatever you want to call it. I strongly suggest you cut your ties right now."

Harrison leaned forward to speak across Erika, seated between them. "I absolutely agree. Our input was limited from the start, and we've completed our findings and submitted them. We're out." He leaned back and looked at Erika. "Right?"

He watched her expression harden, holding his breath.

"On the contrary," Erika said, turning toward John. "We're in it all the way." The thrumming ache beneath her ribs had disappeared. Maybe its energy had been repurposed to stoke her resolve. "At least *I* am!"

Harrison's shoulders drooped. "Can we talk about your motivation?"

"No," she said. "You can attach a deep-seated reason to any decision and make it sound illogical. I don't have time to play that game. Are you in or out?"

Harrison shrugged. "What do you think? I'm with you. In, of course."

She was surprised—and softened—by his quick and unconditional commitment to her, despite his contrary view.

Recognizing there was no chance of a reversal, John said, "Keep in mind, my friends, I'm here for you any time you need me. You want a bodyguard, you got one."

"John, I may be determined, but I'm not a daredevil," Erika said. "I'm guessing there's a good chance that some individual or organization is tracking the course of this project and stalking everyone involved in it. I don't know why the stakes are so high, why they're willing to kill for what's in it for them, but I'm going to do my best to find out. But rest assured, I'm not planning on showing my"—she glanced at Harrison—"*our* hand. For all intents and purposes, we'll make it look like we're off the case."

"Thanks, that's good to know," Harrison said, with the barest lift in his demeanor.

"How do you plan on staying in the game while appearing to have withdrawn from it?" John asked.

"Let us worry about that, John," Erika said. "You have enough on your mind."

John shot Harrison a look of male-oriented compassion. "I'll be on my way, then," he said, going for the door handle. "Remember, you've got a standing offer of protection."

"Wait!" Erika commanded, grabbing the hem of his jacket. "We've got to discuss the cell phone!"

John sat back. "What cell phone?"

"Andrea's. We've got to check it out."

"Oh yes, for sure. I was planning on taking another trip to Vermont to examine it in person, as well as the contents of Andrea's suitcase. Is there something specific weighing on your mind?"

"Yes. Rather than bothering Charlene with the hassle of breaking into Andrea's cell phone without the password, I wonder if you can ask the Vermont crew to hack into it and send you photos of Andrea's recent emails and texts, received and sent. Charlene received a delayed fax from Andrea before you got back from Vermont. It refers to an email she got from Christie's regarding the sale of a van Dyck. I'd especially like to look at that email. There's a good chance it contains information that put her in danger."

"I'll see what I can do," John said. "Depends on how restrictive the county's rules are. I'll call them early in the morning and get back to you." He gave Erika a peck on the cheek and slid out of the car.

* * *

Harrison tried to give her a *real* kiss as they lay in bed, the two of them clad in sweatpants and tank tops. For the first time in their married life, she turned away. "Not now, darling. I'm not up to it."

"I was not planning to—"

"Of course not. I know." How could she explain that the mere stirring of desire in her belly was an affront to the tragic event it had just undergone?

Putting the idea into words, even in her thoughts, made it sound stilted. "I don't want to feel anything," she said. "I mean, in that way." She slid closer to him. "I only want to be held."

"Anything to oblige, he said, voice swollen with gratitude as he wrapped her in his arms.

Chapter 10

"You think Randall's on the level?" Erika asked, preempting the clock's wake-up alarm. She clicked the snooze button and checked the time: 6:09.

Harrison opened his eyes.

"Or maybe there's a sleeper agent at one of the auction houses?" she added. "We have to assume the worst and maintain a low profile."

"Good morning," Harrison said, slowly recovering from the lack of segue from sleep to mental acuity.

She bent toward him from her seated position and kissed his forehead. "I'm sorry I woke you up."

"Not really," he said, rising to a sitting position.

"You were awake?"

"I meant that you're not sorry you woke me up." He pulled her toward him, reveling in her animated mood.

Her smile was fleeting. "So, here's what we have to do today. Most importantly, we call Charlene to see how she's holding up, and second, we ask her permission to hand over her copy of Hebborn's *Drawn to Trouble* to Randall Gray. This will add to the appearance that we've pulled out of the investigation. Anyone keeping tabs on us will get the picture."

Chancing a rebuff, Harrison aimed his kiss for the corner of her mouth.

She did not flinch. "We should see if Randall can meet us in a public place, say for lunch, so we can bow out conspicuously," he said.

"You realize, of course, that we're jumping the gun," Erika reminded him. "It hasn't been established that Andrea's death was anything but a tragic accident."

"That's true, but John's suspicions are enough for me to act on. You know he doesn't fire off hypotheses on impulse."

"Exactly my thoughts." She stretched languidly, inadvertently exposing the sides of her breasts at the armholes of her tank top. Harrison caught the raised arm nearest him and held it still, allowing him to kiss the half-melon of flesh.

"I don't mean to disturb you, but that was irresistible," he said, letting go of her arm. "You can't fault me for being human."

"I'm sorry. That wasn't meant to entice you." She ran her hand through his thick tousled hair, wanting to bury her face in it, but resisting. "One day it will be okay again, don't you think?" she asked, sadness creeping into her voice.

"Of course," he said, wishing he could this instant make it right for her to love herself again.

"So," she said, pressing on, "do you have a couple of free hours to spend with Randall today, that is, if he's available? I know I can make the time."

"Sure," he said, hesitant, finding it more difficult than she to switch gears. "I'll make it my business to be free. You want to connect with Randall, or shall I?"

"I will. I'll call Charlene first. Let's wait until nine." Feeling a sudden chill, she thought aloud, "I hope Barry never left her side, not for a second!"

* * *

By 8:30, they had showered, dressed, and downed a Spartan breakfast of toast and black coffee. They lingered at the dining room table to strategize about the balance of their day. Erika planned to work from 10:00 to noon at *Art News*, time enough to get her article on contemporary representational art—"an oxymoron," her boss had playfully challenged—submitted to production before deadline. Harrison would conduct his seminar on the history of baroque art from 10:15 to 11:45 and ration the following seventy-five minutes to allow his six students each a private audience to sound off at least minimally to their hearts' content.

Their landline phone rang just as they were deciding where best to invite Randall Gray for lunch. Grace, puttering in the kitchen, brought the handset out to them, laying it on the table between them. The caller ID read "private caller."

Erika smiled a thank-you to Grace, picked up the device, and punched in the "talk" button. "Hello?" she directed to the mouthpiece as Grace unobtrusively returned to the kitchen area, shutting the French doors to afford them greater privacy.

"It's me. John."

Erika activated the speaker and placed the handset back on the table. "How did it go last night, John?"

"The Steins were devastated, of course. It was difficult talking to them. Andrea's father especially. He was out of control. The mother was overwhelmed by guilt. She thinks that by alienating her daughter, she set in motion the string of events leading to her death."

"I can understand that," Harrison said. "There's no basis for the claim, really, but guilt is pretty damn close to regret, and the Steins have a damn good reason to regret. Their behavior has been unreasonable."

Erika, new to the maternal-driven furies of self-reproach, felt more sympathetic. "They were trying," she said. "They met with the rabbi. Progress was being made."

"Last time I checked, they were blaming Charlene for all evil," Harrison said. His gaze landed on Erika's. "What am I saying? Who am I to judge?"

She grabbed his hand. "It's okay," she mouthed. To John, she said, "It's so early. Were you able to connect with the people in Marlboro?"

"The Windham County Sheriff's Department in Newfane, Vermont. That's the central office where Andrea's personal items are being held. I called about an hour ago and spoke to the detective handling the case. I thought he'd make me haul ass back to Vermont, but he was forthcoming as all get-out. He had his resident geek hack into Andrea's cell phone and take photos of the recent texts and emails, in- and outgoing. He emailed me the photos not five minutes ago."

"Can you send the photos to one of our cell phones?" Harrison asked.

"That's not possible. I swore there would be no data electronically transmitted. I can drop by either of your offices late afternoon, show you what I've got."

"Would you be breaking your oath if you read aloud what's on your screen?" Erika asked. "We've got a potential lunch meeting with Randall Gray, and it would be helpful to be as informed as possible. We wouldn't share any of what you tell us."

After a pause, John said, "We'll compromise. I'll tell you the nature of the transmissions without reciting them verbatim. How's that? That way I'll have a relatively clear conscience."

"Thank you!" Erika exclaimed, taken aback by the pitch of her eagerness. "The email we ought to know about before our meeting this afternoon is the one from Christie's, New York. It was sent to Andrea prior to her arrival at Earth Haven on Friday, April 23. I spoke to Andrea about sending queries to a number of auction houses on Wednesday, April 21, so Christie's reply couldn't have come before that. Can you see if you've got a screen shot of the email, John?"

"Give me a minute or two," John said. "Between April 21 and 23, you say?"

"Yes." Erika gripped Harrison's hand more tightly. "I don't know whether I'm more excited or anxious," she whispered, out of John's hearing. "Either way, I feel guilty."

"That's absurd!" Harrison returned, his whisper gravelly with stifled frustration. "Why?"

She pressed her mouth to his ear. "I'm thinking about the art, not Andrea," she said.

He freed his hand so he could hold her face and look directly at her, eye to eye. He slowly shook his head. No words were needed. She nodded; forgiven.

"I can't find it," John said, breaking the silence.

"What?" Erika asked, still focusing on Harrison.

"I don't see an email from Christie's."

"It has to be there!" Erika insisted, disengaging from Harrison. "*Christie's*—the auction house—New York branch! Did you check the Inbox *and* All Mail?"

"Erika, I also checked her texts."

"What about her spam folder?"

"Checked."

"John," Harrison intervened, "is it possible the Vermont people might have left out a page or two when they sent you the screen shots?"

"It's possible, I suppose. I'll give them a call, have them double-check the device itself. Can you wait ten, fifteen minutes? If it'll take more than that, I'll let you know right away. Good?"

"Yes," Erika agreed. "The email from Christie's has to be there, John. Andrea referred to it in a fax she composed on the evening of April 23. She was planning on having Harrison and me see it."

"Be patient," John urged. "We'll get to the bottom of this."

* * *

Erika and Harrison had not budged from their places when the phone rang again. Harrison reached for the handset and punched the Talk and Speaker buttons in rapid succession. He glanced at the caller ID and his watch. "Fifteen minutes, John. You're a man of your word."

"Did they find the email?" Erika asked, riding over Harrison's words.

"I'm afraid not," John said. "No email from Christie's."

"It can't be!"

"They even checked the Trash file, Erika."

"No, Andrea would not have deleted that email! She specifically said she was going to—oh!"

Harrison lay his hand on her thigh. "What is it?"

"Wait, wait," she said, pressing her fingers to her forehead.

"Erika?" John encouraged.

Erika sat bolt upright. "The email *was* trashed!" she declared. "Permanently deleted, I'll bet!"

"But you said," the men chorused.

"Andrea didn't delete the email," she replied. "Someone *else* did!"

Harrison gave her a wide-eyed stare. John was silent; she imagined his look matched Harrison's.

"Bear with me," she said. "John, I guess it's not possible to track down an email if it's been directed to 'delete forever,' right?"

"Not quite," John said. "Gmail and other webmail services have offline backup systems. It can take up to two months to truly delete an item. Do you want this researched, Erika? It's a long shot, but I can put in the request."

"Yes. If possible, it would help if there's a time stamp on the deletion."

"Wow!" Harrison expelled. "You're way ahead of me. Who do you think deleted the email—and *when*?"

"Beats me," John said. There was a pause on the line. "Hold on. Erika, you're not thinking what I *think* you're thinking, are you?"

"I think I am, John."

"The break-in at Earth Haven," John said, half-questioning.

"How in God's name would anyone know about that email, much less how and where to access the data?" Harrison asked. He searched Erika's face for the answer, suddenly caught on. "Randall," he said. "We dictated all nineteen of Hebborn's clues to him, and he also knew about Andrea's visit to a retreat in Marlboro, Vermont. It would have been easy to pinpoint Earth Haven."

She nodded. "To whom did he relay the information? To someone at one of the auction houses? To a dealer? Collector? To somewhere we haven't thought of? And as far as knowing about Earth Haven's policy of confiscating cell phones, anyone could have found that out. I wouldn't be surprised if it's spelled out on their website."

"You have a point," Harrison said. "From the way the director spoke on the phone, I get the feeling she's passionate about the retreat's philosophy of trust."

"I spoke to her in person," John said. "Gung-ho is an understatement. Let me grab a pen. Did the director tell you exactly when the break-in could have taken place?"

"Between ten p.m. Sunday and nine a.m. Monday," Erika said. "John, did the director tell you how many guests were enrolled in the weekend program?"

"In other words, how many cell phones would these bums have to sift through?" John rephrased. "Not that many. I was told fifteen guests had been enrolled."

"Hold on!" Harrison jumped in. "Let's assume one or more perps were able to get their hands on these cell phones. One: how could they tell which is which? Two: once they figured that out, how the hell could they crack Andrea's password? From what Charlene has told us about Andrea's attention to security, sounds like her password's ironclad. Only a pro could hack it."

John whistled. "What an innocent you are, my friend! There's an app for breaking into a cell phone's data, no matter how secure you imagine it to be. This app comes with step-by-step instructions, for Pete's sake! A motivated novice could do it."

"Count me in with the innocents," Erika stepped in, joining forces with Harrison.

"Sorry, guys. Anyway, I don't know how to answer question number one—how the perps could tell which cell phone they needed to tamper with."

"I suppose they could be stickered at check-in," Harrison suggested.

"Of course!" Erika cried. "John, when you check in with the Vermont authorities, could you ask if there's an identifying sticker on the back of Andrea's cell phone—or the residue of one?"

"Yeah, sure. Good thinking, both of you. I better get a move on. The faster I can put in a request to Andrea's webmail service, the better the chances of intercepting a command to 'delete forever' this email from Christie's—this *alleged* email from Christie's."

For efficiency's sake, Erika elided the barbed qualification. "One more thing, John, and it's important, I think you'll agree."

"Shoot."

"Can you tell the Vermont crew not to publicize the nature of their investigation, so that the public believes Andrea's death was an accident? That way, any offenders will think they're home free, maybe even let down their guard, and Harrison and I will feel less vulnerable flying under the radar."

"I agree absolutely," John said. "Later, folks. Stay safe."

Chapter 11

It started raining just as the Uber driver pulled up in front of The-Hole-In-The-Wall. Erika was not prepared, but Harrison was. He snapped open his king-sized umbrella and jumped from the café's sheltered entrance to position himself so that Erika would be fully protected when she emerged from the car.

"Thanks," she said, grabbing his arm for their scurry to the café. "I didn't check the weather forecast."

"So what else is new?" Harrison teased, reveling in the normalcy of the exchange. He shut his umbrella and kissed her cheek as they arrived at the cloistered space under the eave.

"You got here early, too," she said, as he pulled open the heavy oak door and ushered her in.

He smiled. "I was hoping we could be alone for a few minutes. What's your reason?"

"I guess the same," she said, realizing it as the words formed.

Harrison raised a hand in greeting to the coat check attendant installed in her small booth two feet from the doorway. "Hi, Maude."

"Hi, Professor," Maude returned, folding her arms on the counter. "It's been a long time." She traded smiles with Erika.

There were no outer garments to check. Erika had on a black denim jacket and jeans; Harrison, a blue blazer and corduroys. Harrison stuck his umbrella in the empty umbrella stand by the door as a waiter trotted toward them. Erika recognized Josh, the seasoned waiter who had taken their orders what seemed like a lifetime ago; in reality, a year.

"Hey, boss!"

"It's been a while," Harrison said upon his arrival. He extended his hand. "How're you doing, Josh?" The two locked hands for a fraternal pump.

"You were with this beautiful lady the last time you were here," Josh said, taking Erika's hand more genteelly, as if he were helping her step over a puddle.

"Erika is now my wife," Harrison said proudly, as if she were newly minted.

"Ah, congratulations!"

"Thank you, Josh," Harrison said. "May we sit at what used to be my table?"

"Of course!" Josh escorted them to the banquette tucked in the corner at the front of the dining room. "This will *always* be your table, folks."

"Appreciate that, Josh," Harrison said. "We're expecting a third party today."

Josh went off to fetch another place setting, leaving Erika and Harrison to slide into their leather enclosure.

"You're wearing the jacket you wore the first time we sat at this table," Erika said.

"It was raining that day, too," Harrison said.

"Do you miss coming here?"

Harrison pressed his thigh against hers. "Not really." He remembered hanging out at this table and grading papers, allowed to stay as long as he wanted. Now that he was living with Erika, he preferred holing up in his study at home, knowing that she was somewhere near, or that she soon would be.

Erika wedged her tote bag between herself and the curve of the banquette. "Charlene sounded less frantic when I spoke to her this morning," she said, thinking of Charlene's copy of Hebborn's book tucked inside her tote. "She sounded so remote, though. So hopelessly sad. I felt useless, like there was nothing for me to do or say. Do you know what I mean?"

"I do."

"Is that the way you feel about *me* now, Harrison?"

"Sometimes."

Josh arrived with the third place setting and three menu cards just as Randall Gray, accompanied by another waiter-cum-host, was rounding the turn from the coat check area.

"Am I late?" Randall asked, extending his hand, first to Erika, then Harrison.

"Not at all," Harrison said. "We were early."

Randall was clad in a black suit, white dress shirt, and gray silk tie. He looked out of place in the casual dining spot. "Cozy," he commented, seating himself in the wrought iron saloon-style side chair opposite the banquette. He pulled up closer to the round marble table-top. "Drinks, anyone?" he asked, taking the words out of Josh's mouth.

Randall ordered a gin and tonic; Erika and Harrison, the house Pinot Grigio. The small dining area was about a quarter full. Nearby, only one table was occupied: two men sipping drinks and engaged in hushed conversation. Other guests were scattered about, similarly—or seemingly—self-absorbed.

"You must be wondering why we asked you to meet us outside your office," Erika said, in a voice calculated to be overheard.

"I imagined for a change, no?" Randall said. "Why, is there a mystery?"

"No mystery. We thought we could talk more freely without interruption from personnel or phone calls from clients."

"Distractions," Randall summed up.

"Yes," Erika said. "We have very sad news. It's hard to come out with it, just like that. I mean…" It was sick, degrading Andrea's death by using it to kick off a staged conversation.

"Randall, you know Charlene Miller," Harrison said, coming to Erika's rescue.

"I never actually met her, but yes," Randall said, looking perplexed. "She's the shop owner in possession of the second copy of Hebborn's book. I thought we were all getting together this week. Why? What happened?"

"Well, her partner, Andrea Stein—"

"She was to be included at our meeting," Randall said. "Your wife told me she'd instructed her to query various auction houses." He looked to Erika for confirmation; Erika nodded. "I was told Andrea would be away for the weekend, at a retreat in Vermont. She must be back by now, am I right?"

"No," Harrison said. "I'm afraid Andrea was in a fatal car accident on her way back from the retreat. As you can imagine, her family, Charlene especially, is in a state of shock."

"Charlene and Andrea were going to be married," Erika added, giving the report dimension.

"What? I can't believe this!" Randall responded, his voice rising in pitch, drawing the attention of diners in the immediate area. He leaned across the small tabletop, his forearms flat against its surface. "One tragedy after another!"

"I know," Erika said, trapped by his looming presence.

Randall suddenly crumpled, as if the air had been let out of him. He leaned away, drooping against the back of his chair just as Josh arrived with their drinks.

"Give us a couple of minutes," Harrison requested, touching the sleeve of the waiter's white uniform jacket.

"Sure, boss," Josh answered, retreating.

Storing Randall's reaction, while seeming to ignore it, Erika said, "I brought Charlene's copy of *Drawn to Trouble* to give to you." She patted her bag. "I spoke to her this morning, and she said she wants you to keep it. She's withdrawing from the project altogether. I'm sure you can understand her change of heart."

"Who wouldn't?" Randall said quietly, avoiding eye contact.

"So," Harrison began, "now that Erika and I have played our part in getting the project off the ground, it's all in your hands, Randall."

"You sure about that?" Randall replied. He took a generous swig of his drink.

"Absolutely. I've got to concentrate on preparing for my book tour, and Erika's recently been promoted to senior editor and is up to her ears in added work." He laid a hand on her knee. "*Right*, sweetheart?" he cued.

"Right." Directing her attention to Randall, she said, "We gave Jeremy our research notes." At the word Jeremy, Randall snapped to attention; she wondered what had caused the boot-camp reaction. "I assume you received them?"

"Yes, yes," Randall said, voice distracted. "Thanks."

"Of course we're not falling off the face of the earth," she continued. "So if you have any questions, feel free to give us a call. Meanwhile, let's wrap up any issues emerging from my meeting at the St. Regis."

"Jeremy gave me a rundown on the items covered at the meeting," Randall said, as if he were reading from its minutes. "I'm aware of what transpired."

"Then I take it you've notified Sotheby's that George Dudley's Rembrandt is in all likelihood a forgery," Erika said. "I mean, you *must* have! It matches one of Hebborn's clues to a T!"

Harrison tightened his hold on Erika's knee in lieu of a verbal warning to back off. She patted his hand in reassurance.

Randall forced a laugh. "No worries. Winston Elliot lodged his suspicions about the painting's authenticity, and Dudley promptly withdrew it from the scheduled auction. Paid a hefty fine to do so, I'm told; the penalty for withdrawal is spelled out in his consignment agreement."

"Has Dudley's insurance company been notified of the painting's enormously reduced value?" Erika persisted, holding on to the subject like a pit bull. Achieving truth in the art world was as close to religion as she got.

"Good point," Randall said. "I'll follow up on that. In any case, you'll be happy to hear that Dudley plans to keep the painting hanging in his living room."

Erika was far from convinced, but she kept it to herself. She intended to pursue a few follow-ups of her own, with or without Harrison's blessing. "As for my *Art News* article," she said, "I'll go ahead with it, if the parties are agreeable."

"I don't think so, Erika," Randall demurred. "Elliot said Dudley's embarrassed as hell and would like to stay out of the limelight. His wife feels otherwise, but, pardon my French, tough shit." Randall had another go at his gin and tonic.

Harrison raised his glass. "To you and your talented crew," he directed at Randall. "Here's to success tracking down the remaining eighteen Hebborn forgeries."

Randall and Erika lifted their glasses in token assent, Erika following up with a sip of her wine.

Josh returned to the table, expectant.

"We're ready," Randall declared in no uncertain terms. "I'll have"—he scanned the menu—"the Cobb salad and a coffee—black."

Harrison and Erika ordered chicken and vegetable appetizers to share, just as they'd done the first time they'd been to the restaurant. *For tradition's sake*, their eye contact encoded.

"I don't mean to rush you folks, but I'm on a tight schedule," Randall said, as Josh headed for the kitchen.

"We wouldn't want to keep you," Harrison said. "We're headed back to our workplaces ourselves. You weren't inconvenienced, I hope."

"Not at all. I'm enjoying the break." Stopping himself short, he qualified, "Well, except for the unfortunate news. Please remember to convey my condolences to Andrea's family and Charlene."

Erika shifted uncomfortably against the leather seat. The only way to disconnect the subject of death from ordinary chatter was to change it. "As for Andrea's queries to the auction houses: I don't know if she sent them, and if she did, whether she received any answers. I can't ask Charlene to sift through Andrea's email, and now that you've got Harrison's and my notes on the forgeries, you can send out more precisely targeted inquiries."

Randall shook his head. "Is there anything you don't think of, Erika? If you ever get bored at *Art News*, you can always come work for me."

Erika flashed a demure smile. "I do like working with you. Maybe someday I'll have the chance again." She dislodged her tote from its place beside her and removed the manila envelope containing Charlene's copy of *Drawn to Trouble*. She reached across the table to hand it to him.

"Hold it for now," Randall said.

In her eagerness, she hadn't remembered that he had no place to put the book. Feeling a bit foolish, she wedged it back into her tote. "We should ask for a plastic doggie bag to protect it from the rain."

"But the rain's stopped, ma'am," Josh advised, arriving with their food.

After the painful experience she'd suffered, Harrison was acutely sensitive to anything that might remotely injure Erika's self-confidence. "For insurance, then," he said. "We'll need that plastic bag, Josh."

* * *

"You think he bought it?" Erika asked, after Randall had left the restaurant.

"You mean our alleged retirement from the project?"

"Yes." She was feeling especially conspiratorial as she slid nearer, closing the half-inch gap separating them. "We weren't too heavy-handed?"

"No, we were perfect, especially you." Her hand was resting on the table; asking to be held, he decided. He took it in both of his. "What a team we are," he said, not wasting an opportunity to remind her. "What about Randall? You think *he's* on the level?"

"I think he's hiding something. Let's plan our next move tonight. It's about time we had that consultation with our guy Greg Smith at Art Loss Register. For starters, we should ask him to try and track down the van Dyck sale in 1987 Andrea mentioned in her fax to Charlene. Meanwhile, John should be coming up with some information. " She gave a deceptively off-handed shrug. "We will see."

He drew a quick intake of breath. "The operative word here is 'we,'" he said. "Promise me you won't forget that."

"I won't," she said. "Don't worry."

Too late. He had already begun to.

* * *

Josh was right; it had stopped raining. A small kindness bestowed by the elements, but Erika was grateful. "I'm walking," she told Harrison as they stood outside the restaurant, ready to go their separate ways.

"Too far," he said. "Let me call Bill." He went for the cell phone in his jacket, but she held his wrist.

"I need a day off from being the privileged wife," she said. "Humor me."

He grinned, taking her grit as reparative. "What is it, four miles or so? That's about an hour's walk," he calculated.

"My meeting's at three-thirty. I'll make it."

They parted company, Harrison heading north for the short walk back to NYU Fine Arts; Erika, south, returning to the *Art News* headquarters downtown. She walked at a steady pace, half-engaged in observing her fellow pedestrians and avoiding the killer bikers who raced along the city's ever-multiplying bike paths, half-contemplating her next moves in the Hebborn intrigue.

She had reached Madison Avenue and 43rd Street when a woman approaching from the opposite direction caught her eye. The woman was wearing a maroon peplum jacket, black fitted skirt, and rakishly tilted black fedora. Tall and slim, she walked the pavement as if it were a runway. As their paths crossed, Erika inhaled the unmistakable scent of gardenias emanating from the woman. Typically, she found strong perfumes cloying or harsh; some had even made her sneeze. Yet after the woman walked by, the undiluted fragrance of gardenias lingered in the air, curling into memory and evoking an image of her mother kneeling in her garden as she watered her flowers. Erika had nurtured this image over the years, just as her mother had nurtured her beloved garden, so it did not come as an awakening. What did spring unexpectedly from the moment was a sudden feeling of joy at being alive to experience it. But in a heartbeat, the feeling turned on her like an auto-immune attack, transforming joy to guilt. She should not be allowed to feel happiness of any kind, she told herself—not now, not yet.

She picked up her pace, her thoughts shifting to the scheduled meeting with her fellow editors. Midway between 42nd and 41st, her cell phone rang, and she dug for it in her tote bag without missing a step. She glanced at the ID. "Jeremy?"

"I must see you," he said.

She continued walking. "We're off the project, Jeremy. You must know that."

"Bull. I know you, Erika. I see the fire in your eyes."

"What, are we on Face Time?"

"Don't joke. We have to meet. It's the only way you'll understand."

She moved from the flow of pedestrians to stand up against the display window of a high-end shoe store. "Where are you right now?" she asked.

"I'm not stalking you," he said. "I know where you had lunch with Randall. I'm nearby. Don't waste time. Where exactly are *you*?"

She told him.

"Okay," he said, "there's a supermarket right here on Lexington Avenue and 39th Street. It'll take you about five minutes. I'll meet you in the dairy section. You better come."

"Is that a threat?" Erika asked, juices flowing.

"No, an urgent plea." He ended the call.

Erika dropped her cell phone into her bag and burst into a trot, she hardly knew why, toward 39th Street.

The sprawling new-age supermarket Jeremy had led her to looked as if it had bullied its way into a community of private shops—locksmith, watch repair, bodega; immigrants who had been around long enough to define the homey character of the neighborhood. Inside, there was an escalator leading to a lower level.

"Dairy section?" Erika inquired of a man in a red uniform apron about to step onto the escalator.

"Street level, end of aisle five," the man shot back as he began his descent.

"Thanks," Erika replied to his back before setting out on her quest, made more difficult by the unexpected intersections and open spaces amid the aisles. The sprinkling of shoppers wheeling about with their carts and looking like they knew exactly where they were heading made her feel lost and alone.

When she at last reached the dairy section, at right angles to the terminus of aisle five, Erika expected to see Jeremy hovering there, drone-like, with disconcertingly eager eyes scanning the area in search of her. Instead, she saw one oddball character in pressed gray slacks, polished loafers, and a blue flannel hoodie picking packs of cheese off the display rods, turning them over to examine the reverse sides, and then hooking them back onto the rods.

Where was Jeremy? From their phone conversation, it had sounded like he was standing nearby, if not right outside the supermarket. She was about to try reaching him on his cell when she spotted a tall man with Jeremy's distinctive flaxen hair approaching from a distance. She started down the aisle. "Jeremy!" she called, waving her hand as she rushed toward him.

"Erika!" came a voice from behind.

She spun around, only to confront the cheese connoisseur, who had caught up to her. "Jeremy?" She could hardly make out the face beneath the eave of the hood. She took the liberty to pull it off his head. He had a black eye, and there were ugly bruise marks on both sides of his jaw, and an adhesive bandage had been neatly applied right beneath his hairline. "God, what *happened* to you?"

"Five stitches in the emergency room," he answered.

"I mean, who *did* this to you? Don't say you were in a barroom brawl."

"You don't think I'm manly enough to be in a barroom brawl?"

"No, I don't think you're *stupid* enough. Tell me."

"I wanted you to see me like this so you'd know what happens if you don't lay off the Hebborn project."

"We're retired from it, Jeremy."

"Spare me; it hurts when I laugh. Erika, you know I can read you like a book."

"Don't be absurd," she protested, the wheels of her mind spinning. From the discoloration of Jeremy's bruises, she knew they had not been acquired in the last few hours. She recalled his uneasiness at the St. Regis after he had received a call on his cell phone. Had he been ambushed after he'd left? What could she do to get some answers on the spot?

"Can I borrow your cell phone?" she asked, thinking quickly. "I want to talk to you, but I have to call the office to let them know I'll be late for a meeting. Maybe we can find a Starbucks or something."

It was a shameless lie, but his face lit up. "But you have a phone; I called you on it," he replied, his knit brow failing to disguise his elation.

137

"The battery ran down. I actually tried to call you back, but I couldn't. I don't want to screw up right after I've been promoted to senior editor. Please?"

"Sure." He dug his phone from the pocket of his slacks. He punched in his password and handed the device to her.

"Thanks. I'll only be a couple of minutes."

She turned her back on him to secure some degree of privacy, which she assumed he'd find reasonable, and then she meandered down the aisle to widen the space between them. Keeping within sight so as not to arouse suspicion, but far enough away for small movements to remain undetectable, she tapped the telephone receiver icon. The "Recents" screen appeared, and she scrolled to the calls from the day before. There were five. She tapped the circled "i" for each call. Only one fit the feasible time slot: an incoming call received at 4:35 p.m. from "New York, N.Y."; no name recorded. Utilizing minimum hand and body motion, she retrieved a pen from her bag and jotted the number just above her wrist so that it would be hidden by the cuff of her jeans jacket. The exercise had taken no more than two minutes.

Finally, she tapped the "Keypad" icon and entered the main number for *Art News*. When the receptionist had answered and a conversation had begun, Erika slowly turned and began her nonchalant walk back to Jeremy, timing her choreography so that he would overhear a good part of her side of the phone exchange.

"So, you'll make sure Sara gets the message, Lonnie?" Erika was saying, as she arrived at Jeremy's side. "I'll be no more than a half hour late. Yes, I understand. Bye." She ended the call and handed the cell phone back to Jeremy. "Thanks."

"No problem."

Getting right to the point, she asked, "Jeremy, are you going to tell me who beat you up?"

"No," he said.

"Because you don't know, or because you just *won't*?"

"Both. I don't know, and if I did, I wouldn't tell you. The less you know, the better off you'll be. Just keep out of it, okay?"

"Jeremy, you must know *why* you were attacked. You can at least tell me that!"

He nodded. "Simple. I told you about the Sotheby's auction, and I set up the meeting at the St. Regis. That's why." He pulled on his hood as a shopper skirting around him dealt him an unabashed stare. "Come on, let's head to a Starbucks, or anywhere you want. We'll talk more—about anything but this." He hooked his arm in hers as if he were about to escort her onto the dance floor. "Let's go." He began leading her toward the front of the store.

Without removing his arm or breaking stride, she said, "I'm sorry, Jeremy, but I'll have to take a rain check. They're not giving me any leeway. I have to get going."

He stopped dead in his tracks, causing her to lurch forward, and he slipped his arm from hers in order to face her squarely. "What's going on, Erika?"

She was about to expand on her white lie when a familiar ring pattern sounded from inside her tote bag. His jaw dropped.

"I," she feebly began.

"Don't even try. You forgot to turn it off. Bad planning."

The phone rang a few more times, then stopped.

"Aren't you curious?" he asked.

Without a word, she retrieved her cell phone and pressed the icon to view the details.

"Well?" he prodded. He was clearly struggling to keep his voice down.

"It was Harrison," she said, foolishly hoping to be rewarded for her honesty.

He took the cell phone from her and tapped onto the home screen. "I see your battery's down to a mere eighty-nine percent." He handed the cell phone back to her. She dropped it into her bag.

"Jeremy, I'm sorry, but I wanted to find out—"

His raised his hand to cut her off, and she flinched. His expression became aghast. "You thought I was going to strike you!"

"No, no," she protested. "It was an instinctive reaction!"

"Does Harrison ever hit you?" he fumed. "If he does, I'll break his—"

"Of course he doesn't!"

They were drawing curious glances from the few shoppers cruising by.

139

"Jeremy, please!" She grasped his arm: her contact, no matter what her motivation, seemed to have a calming effect on him.

"It's so frustrating," he said evenly. "Your little scheme only proves my point. You have no intention of laying off. Don't you see that I don't care what you were looking for on my phone, or whether you found it? I just don't know how to convince you." His agitation suddenly spiking, he ripped off his hood. "Take a good look at me! It'll be worse for you if you don't say you'll quit, and mean it!"

She opened her mouth to speak.

"Let me finish. This is no game. There's more to it than tracking down the Hebborn forgeries."

Of course it wasn't a game: two people had already been murdered! Nevertheless, his words gave her pause: how deeply into the sordid side of the art world might this investigation take her?

"I understand," she said. "I'll keep my nose out of it. You've convinced me."

"No, I haven't!" He pulled his hood back on. "I don't know what to do!"

"I'm going to leave now, Jeremy," she said, letting go of his arm. "I've got to get to that meeting. I promise I'll keep my word. It's hard to trust me after what I just pulled, but you've got to, and that's the end of it." She started to walk away, toward the exit.

Her release had marooned him. He rushed to her side and grabbed hold of her shoulders. "You have to repeat the promise until I believe you!" he cried, hanging onto her like she was his lifeline.

She tried to free herself. Their confrontation had finally risen to the urban threshold of alarm, and a smattering of witnesses approached to offer assistance. One shopper abandoned his cartful of groceries.

"Get your hands off her!" he bellowed, peeling Jeremy's fingers from Erika's shoulders. "Are you okay, Miss?" he asked, doting almost, as Jeremy stood stock still, in a knot of passivity, jaw locked, chest heaving.

"I'm—we're fine," Erika assured the onlookers. "We're a couple of drama queens is all. But thanks for the concern." She headed for the door before the observers, with their quizzical looks, plied for a more satisfying closure.

Jeremy, ignited by Erika's action, followed in her wake, making it through the automatic door right behind her. "Wait up!" he pleaded.

She moved away from the entrance, and he pulled up beside her. "There's nothing more to say, Jeremy." She did not want to burn her bridges, so she added, "We can talk another time, once you've calmed down." She spotted a cab parked on the opposite side of the avenue. "Taxi!" she cried, flailing her arms in the hopes of getting the driver's attention.

The pedestrian light turned red, and the wall of traffic started to advance, but the cab remained stationary. After the initial onrush there was a break in the flow, and Erika made a run for it, garnering hurled expletives en route. She looked over her shoulder as she jumped onto the curb and caught Jeremy getting set to run the same gauntlet. She hurried over to the cab, where an elderly woman was trying to maneuver herself and her three-pronged cane out of the back compartment. Erika came to her aid, hauling the woman to a safe landing. The woman showered her with thanks even as she was throwing herself onto the vacated seat.

Jeremy thrust past the woman, almost bowling her over, and flung himself at the cab door just as Erika pulled it shut. "Call me!" he shouted.

Erika gave a forceful nod. "I will!" She leaned forward in the seat. "Lock the door," she grunted at the cab driver without moving her lips, as she checked the door: it was already locked.

"Go, go! It's in the right direction, we're heading south!"

"It's a red light, lady," the driver said, uttering his first words. "Where you going?"

She recited the address for *Art News*.

Jeremy pounded his fist against the window then stepped back. He stood there, facing her as the cab pulled away. His head was bowed, so she could not see what emotion he was hiding beneath the shade of his hood.

Sitting on the edge of her seat, she grabbed her cell phone and Googled the number she'd scribbled on her arm. It was a secondary number of G&G's. She remembered Jeremy's look of alarm when he'd received that call. Had Randall or a member of his staff contacted him at the Pierre, either to threaten or warn him? She thought of the plausible scenarios the question elicited as she wiped the numbers off her forearm with the saliva-moistened corner of a tissue.

* * *

Erika told Harrison about her encounter with Jeremy, that evening as they lingered at the dinner table nursing their cups of tea. She spun her story as benignly as she could without omitting the most salient details. Her caution did not pay off.

"You mean you actually trotted over to the supermarket to meet that nut?" he asked, incredulous. "I mean, *voluntarily?*" His voice grated like sandpaper from his effort to keep Grace, clearing up in the kitchen, from making out his words. "Grace, could you give us some privacy?" he called, his tone uncharacteristically peevish.

"I'll finish up—thanks!" Erika added, squirming with embarrassment.

Grace stepped out of the kitchen, bestowed them with a look of doting indulgence, and left the dining area.

"Did you encourage him?" Harrison asked as soon as he figured Grace was out of earshot. "I bet you did."

"Are you concerned for my safety, or are you being unreasonably jealous?"

"Both. I saw the way he looked at you at the lab. A regular *colpo di fulmini,* it was."

"Speak English."

"Lightning strike!" he snapped. "Love at first sight!"

She uttered a scornful laugh. "Whatever. He's socially inept. Am I responsible for his bouts of puppy love?"

"You used to be a free spirit," he pouted.

"You mean promiscuous? Spit it out."

"Okay, yes!" he said angrily. "Maybe you're tired of me. The luster has worn off, and you're itching to move on." As soon as the words were out of his mouth, he beat the air with his hand, as if he were shooing away a fly. "I didn't mean that! I'm sorry!"

On the verge of tears, she responded only to his unedited words. "What you *really* want to say is that the luster has worn off for *you!* I lost your child, and now *you* want to move on!"

He knocked over his chair as he leaped from it. "Never!" He fell to his knees beside her and threw his arms around her waist. "I'm such a shit!"

It was stunning, she thought, how a gesture could be so overdramatic, yet so completely on the level. "Please," she said as he buried his head in her lap. "You're not a shit. Not by a long shot."

He looked up at her. "At the most stressful time in your life, I hit you with baseless accusations!" he cried.

She stroked his head. "You ought to be allowed to vent, even if it's off the wall. I've been hogging ownership of the stress. I'm the selfish one."

"Are you kidding me?"

"No," she said, "but if you want to share the warped perspective, try this: I think our old insecurities are raising their ugly heads. You feel that my guardedness means I want to be with someone else. Not true. Whereas I feel that I let you down, and that means you must want to jump ship."

"You haven't let me down. Can't you get that?"

"I'm trying."

"Try harder."

"Only if you do," she said. "Stand up."

He obeyed.

She rose from her chair. "Promise not to doubt my loyalty."

"I promise," he said. "Promise not to doubt mine—ever!"

"I do."

They embraced, slowly, drawing out the moment. She rested her head on his shoulder and closed her eyes.

"Just let it be," she crooned. "No talking now. Let it be."

The Beatles phrase echoed in hand-me-down memory, making her feel nostalgic for an era she had missed. She wondered what era she would miss at the other end of her allotted time, the thought lifting her above the present to imagine the infinite.

She fell to earth at the ring of her cell phone, lying in wait on the dining room table. She gave Harrison an affirming squeeze before breaking away to grab it.

143

"I've got news," Mitchell said, without introduction.

Erika activated the speaker. "What is it, John?"

"First, I reached Andrea's web server. Too late to abort the 'delete forever' command, but not too late to pick up the date and time of the event. One a.m., Monday, April 26."

"Within the time frame of the break-in at Earth Haven," Harrison declared. "Were you able to capture the email itself?"

"Unfortunately, no. The Christie's email address was the only means of identification."

"The time stamp of the deletion is all that's needed to prove tampering," Erika pronounced. "I suspected this, but it still comes as a surprise."

"Are you concerned about losing the contents of the email from the auction house?" Mitchell asked.

"I'm optimistic that our friend at Art Loss Register, Greg Smith, will be able to nose out the details of the van Dyck transactions that Andrea referred to in her fax to Charlene. Right, Harrison?"

Harrison tucked his hand beneath her hair and tenderly clasped the nape of her neck. "Right."

"By the way," Mitchell said, in the manner of an afterthought, "turned out there was a sticker on Andrea's cell phone with her name on it. Like you figured, Erika."

"An added convenience for the perpetrators," she said dryly. "Any other news, John?"

"Sure is. I got an eye-opening communication from the investigators in Vermont—the on-scene detective, the medical examiner, the coroner, and the like. They say their ruling may be technically inconclusive, but its probability is pushing ninety percent. Andrea's death has been officially designated as a homicide."

The formal declaration hit Erika like a rock. It was as if she was learning of Andrea's death for the first time. "What did they find, John?" she asked, as much in awe of her reaction as the cause of it.

John cleared his throat. "First, there were paint marks from an unidentified vehicle just at the point of impact. That may have been what caused Andrea's vehicle to catapult over the embankment barrier. Second, there were physical signs that Andrea was smothered by manipulated obstruction of the nose and mouth—the telltale lacerations of the lips and tongue and the slight bruising in the nose found on microscopic examination. There were a number of technical terms in the report, but that's what it boiled down to."

"It doesn't make sense to say that Andrea was suffocated before she drove off the embankment," Harrison said. "Are you implying that she was suffocated after the accident occurred? That her killer or killers actually checked her for signs of life before they left the scene?"

"Yes, and that they subsequently finished her off."

The clinical tone with which John delivered the news offended Erika. Not through any fault of his, but through the circumstances that required a certain suspension of humanity. She detected the same coolness in her own carefully modulated voice when she asked, "Have the authorities determined when Andrea's remains will be returned home, John?"

"I believe in a day or two. It's up to the Vermont crew. I did call Charlene and the Steins to tell them what's going on before the folks in charge muscle in on them to work out the details."

"Do you know if Charlene will be receiving the remains, or will she be fighting Andrea's parents for them?" Erika asked.

"Not in my job description. I hope it works out for Charlene, but who can say?"

"We'll reach out to her, John," Harrison said, massaging Erika's neck.

"I know you will. Let's keep in touch, yes? If you need my help, I'm a phone call away," John said, his tone near commanding.

"Of course," Erika said.

"Yes, lieutenant," Harrison replied.

"I should tell you the wife's planning a barbeque," John added, his tone softening. "Sometime early next month. You'll be getting a proper e-vite. She's very meticulous, that woman."

"We'll be there," Erika said, her lids drooping to half mast from Harrison's rhythmic stroking on the back of her neck. How easy, she thought, and how selfish, to yield to pleasure, even at this moment, when all she should be feeling is grief.

Chapter 12

Greg Smith, Thor look-alike, seemed out of place in Harrison's den, cluttered with academic books and papers. He should be on the ski slopes practicing for the winter Olympics, Erika thought, removing a stack of ungraded student essays from the leather armchair beside Harrison's L-shaped desk. "Please sit," she said, setting the essays on the floor.

Jake, hunkered down in one of his favorite spots under the desk, gave a grunt of acknowledgement as Erika's hands touched the floor in his line of vision. She reached into the desk's kneehole to stroke his paw as Greg sank into the buttery leather and propped his laptop case against the base of the desk.

"Glad you could make it at such short notice this morning, Greg," Harrison said, presiding from his matching armchair at the head of the desk.

"This feels like a cabal," Greg remarked, adjusting his position to best accommodate his daunting figure, shown to its best advantage in form-fitting pants and white cashmere crew-neck sweater. "I thought we could discuss your concerns over the phone, but you were so insistent, and I should say mysterious, about wanting to see me in person."

Erika took her seat in the straight-backed chair alongside Greg and across from Harrison. "We're trying to keep off the communications grid," she said, folding her hands in her jeans-clad lap. "We want whoever is calling the shots to feel secure enough to let down his guard, or at least not intensify it."

"Okay, I get that," Greg said, "but I'm still in the dark. You haven't told me what you're after. I'm flying back to London tonight, so it's best I know everything before then."

"We do appreciate your making time for us," Erika said.

"Not that big an inconvenience, guys. I'm also in town to have lunch with my brother."

When Art Loss Register consolidated its satellite offices in 2010 to its headquarters in London, Greg had moved there himself, along with two valued members of the Register's New York staff. He now had English-American dual citizenship and shuttled back and forth between London and New York with the ease of a Long Islander commuting to Wall Street. "I'm all ears," he said. "Fill me in."

Greg sat transfixed as Erika and Harrison summarized the events leading up to the present meeting, including the nineteen clues they'd found encoded in *Drawn to Mischief*. "So," he declared when they were done. "Basically, what you want from me are the details of the 1996 event at Christie's."

"Exactly," Erika said. "We'd like to know all the facts associated with the auction of Hebborn's van Dyck forgery. It's critical we know the names of all parties involved. In Andrea's fax to Charlene, she reports that there's a 'head-scratching coincidence'—her very words!—in Christie's email to her. Odds are it means there's a name or names associated with that 1996 event that Andrea recognized and was perplexed by. And that someone wanted to quash that information. Please find out the names—and everything else regarding the forgery that Harrison and I can't think of, but you can."

"You're sure about leaving out the word 'alleged'?" Greg asked. "As in 'alleged' forgery?"

"As we've shown, Hebborn himself led us to the 1987 sale of his van Dyck counterfeit," Erika replied. "He himself outed it. We also know from Andrea's fax that this painting was again put on the block, posthumously, in 1996."

"Okay, I'm convinced," Greg said. "I'm on the inside track at Christie's.

I can call them right now and they'll take us to the source. If you don't approve, we can go in the back door. I've got a link to Christie's classified database."

"Is there any other way you can access information?" Harrison asked. "We don't want to set off an alarm at Christie's."

"Look, Art Loss Register has the most comprehensive art theft archive in the world," Greg said. "I can search it now if you like, but if the van Dyck in question, pegged either as a fake or an original, has never been reported as a stolen work, then it won't turn up in our database."

"Give it a try," Harrison said. "What can we lose?"

"I agree," Erika said. "We know nothing that transpired in 1996, except that Andrea's fax tells us it should be of interest."

"Okay, here we go," Greg said. He reached for the case propped against the base of the desk. Erika and Harrison leaned forward simultaneously, as if they were about to witness a magic trick, as Greg removed his laptop from the case. He raised the lid of the device and rested it on his knees, angling it so that the lid obstructed Erika's view of the keyboard as he punched in his password. "We're in." His fingers rapidly played the keyboard as he uttered muted grunts that indicated either impediments or progress, his hosts not about to interrupt to inquire which.

At last Greg's hands shot up from the keyboard, as if he'd come to the end of a piano concerto. "You're in luck," he announced. "Christie's reported a stolen van Dyck in 1996. Seller is Anna Bunzl."

Erika issued an "Ah!" of recognition at the sound of the surname.

Greg continued undeterred. "Buyer is Alan Morell. No mention of the van Dyck being a forgery. Painting stolen en route to buyer. May have ended up on the black market. I wouldn't be surprised if it was used to launder money—maybe drug money."

"Explain that," Harrison said.

"What happens is an artwork that has been purchased with dirty money is used as collateral in a legitimate loan transaction. The money the bank hands over to the applicant is clean. In any event, the 1996 theft is listed as a cold case. I don't know if it's a matter of the authorities dragging their feet or if they reached a dead end, but there have been no entries since 1996."

"Wow," Erika commented. "Can you check its provenance to make sure this matches up with our encoded information?"

"Of course." Greg scrolled up the file to find the requested data. "Here we are. First entry in 1968, when the item was purchased by the Colnaghi gallery from a London dealer." Scrolling down a bit, he said, "Couple more sales, and here's the penultimate one: Christie's, New York, 1987. Buyer is Yvonne Tan Bunzl—the name often shortened to Tan Bunzl."

"Bingo," Harrison declared.

"Yes!" Erika seconded. "The name encoded by Hebborn! The painting must have been given to Tan's relative, Anna."

Greg smiled. "Glad I made your day, guys. Do you want me to sum up the details in this file, or do you want to take a look at the data amassed in 1996? There's a shitload of it—letters, memos, transcriptions of interviews. I can forward it as a PDF doc to you if you like. It'll save me time, and you can look over the material at your leisure."

"That would be great," Erika instantly agreed.

"Hold it!" Harrison objected. "I don't think it's wise to have this material sitting in either of our emails. I hate to sound insensitive, but we've seen where that got Andrea."

Erika was about to accuse Harrison of being not only insensitive, but *paranoid*, but held herself in check to give his statement a second's worth of consideration. "Maybe you're right," she conceded.

"Maybe?"

"Truce, guys," Greg appealed. "I'm going to pass my laptop to you and you can read the material and take notes. Any time you feel you want to review the contents of the document, or need me to interpret any of the in-house jargon, you can give me a call and I'll help you out. How's that sound?"

"That sounds perfect," Erika said.

Greg rose from his chair. "Let's switch places, Harrison. You and Erika should look over the material side by side. You got a pad and pen?"

Harrison smiled. "Always," he said, with a restorative look of affection at his obsessive note-taking wife.

* * *

Greg had long since gone off to his lunch date with his brother. After ushering him out, Erika and Harrison had returned to the study to fully digest Erika's notes on the Art Loss Register's file. The shock had not yet worn off.

"No wonder Randall didn't want this information leaked," Erika seethed. "He's in it up to his ears!"

"Let's not jump the gun," Harrison advised, maddeningly deliberate.

Erika was about to add fuel to his fire by telling him of the call from Randall's office that had produced Jeremy's angst at the St. Regis, but she held her tongue. Plans were already bubbling in her head like brew in a witch's cauldron, and she was not about to jeopardize them by setting off another of her husband's red alerts. "Well," she stated, matching his sobriety, "We can't deny that Randall's position at Christie's at the time of the 1996 incident is just not one of those neutral facts, can we?" She angled the notes to face him more squarely and hammered her finger on the list of players involved in the affair. Randall's name headed the list:

Randall Gray, Customer Support Rep

Winston Elliot, freelance authenticator/lawyer

Anna Bunzl, seller

Alan Morell, buyer

Hopkins ins agent—on behalf of Morell

Leroy Taft ins agent—on behalf of Christie's

Ship Smart Inc, driver—van Dyck transporter

"Yes, darling, I've read this list a number of times," Harrison said.

"Let's just think about this," she said. "The van Dyck—still unmasked as a fraud—was stolen in transit to its new owner, Alan Morell. Christie's insurance company and Morrell's insurance company ended up splitting the compensation to Morrell. Randall was a 'customer support representative.' Shall we guess what one of the duties of that position is?"

"Let's look it up and be sure," he suggested.

They found a lengthy description of the position on indeed.com. Among the listed duties: "managing any post-auction shipping issues."

Erika threw up her hands. "Guilty as charged! This is how I see it. Randall somehow got wind that the van Dyck was a forgery—or maybe Elliot tipped him off. Either way, Randall assigned the transport to Ship Smart and coordinated the heist," she pronounced. "The insurance payment was handed out, and then Randall, maybe with a collaborator, doubled down on the bet and sold the ersatz van Dyck as the real thing on the black market." She took a breath. "I almost wish an old painting would fall into our lap, one that we could use to entrap Elliot and Randall into trying it again. I almost feel like scouring the yard sales to see if we can come up with one."

"Mind if I play devil's advocate?" Harrison submitted, with a touch of sarcasm. "Your conclusion is a compelling hypothesis. Let's leave it at that for the moment."

"Winston Elliot was also at the meeting at the St. Regis," she impetuously revealed, if only to knock the wind out of his sails.

"Oh? Anything else you're keeping from me?" he asked, nostrils flaring.

"No," she lied.

"All right. Let's discuss where we go from here," he said, stiff-lipped.

"Tonight," she said. "I've got to get to work by one o'clock at the latest."

His eyes narrowed. "You're not planning on doing anything foolish, are you?"

"No," she said, technically escaping another lie. The plan she was hatching was foolhardy, maybe. Not foolish.

Chapter 13

Erika sat in her cramped but coveted office at *Art News*, the printout of the rough draft of her article on the history of performance art at her elbow. In ten minutes she was scheduled to meet with Sara for a critiquing, but her mind was elsewhere, as it had been all afternoon, ever since the revelatory meeting with Greg Smith. The need to act—*her* need to act—was growing more imperative with each passing minute. She had ideas. It was criminal not to put them to use.

She could not resist taking another look at the timeline she'd created to validate her emerging plan. She slipped it from beneath her *Art News* article. From the first entry to the last—"Apr 15 Owen's murder, leaving RANDALL in possession of his copy of Drawn to Trouble" to "Apr 27 call to St. Regis from RANDALL's office"—the man in charge at G&G appeared at every turn.

She pictured Harrison sitting at the desk in his study where she'd left him. She imagined him slumped over, head in his hands, sick with worry over her and her high-risk plans that no efforts of his could prevent. She felt a rush of guilt, immediately assuaged by its proof of her empathy. Harrison, she reminded herself, was not in fact moping at home. According to his schedule, texted earlier from his office at NYU Fine Arts, he should, at this moment, be lecturing a class of misty-eyed minions on the Italian Renaissance. He would survive her subterfuge.

* * *

Sara flipped Erika's article back to page two. "I'd like to see a paragraph here on the Viennese Actionists," she suggested, using her pink marker to draw a caret where she thought the insert should be. She smoothed the collar of her white silk blouse, unbuttoned just enough to demonstrate her knack of straddling rakishness and propriety. "Otherwise it looks good."

"Thanks." Erika rose from the chair opposite Sara's. She took the printout from the desk and looked down at it. She noticed her skirt had puckered up and she tugged at it; did the same with the sleeve of her cardigan. "Sara?"

"What is it, Erika?"

"I was wondering if you could, well, *cover* for me."

"This sounds intriguing."

"I'm thinking sometime soon, maybe tomorrow night."

Sara frowned. "I thought you and Harrison were doing fine. One of the few couples who—"

Erika flapped the pages of her article in the air. "It's nothing like that, Sara!"

"Glad to hear it. What, then?"

"I'll tell you one day, but not now. You have to trust me. Can you?"

"If you assure me the magazine won't be hit with a lawsuit, yes."

Erika smiled, home free. "No lawsuits, I promise. All you have to do if Harrison calls is stick to my story, that we were running behind with the issue and had to work late to make the deadline."

"Wouldn't he be calling your cell phone?"

"I'm going to shut it off. I'll tell him later it was because we didn't want to be disturbed. When you leave the office, can you forward the *Art News* number to your cell phone? That way he'll think we're still here."

"And if he asks to speak to you?"

"Tell him I'm indisposed and will call back."

Sara shook her head. "This is pretty damn devious, Erika. I hope it's worth

154

it."

"Oh, it is, Sara, it is."

* * *

Erika made the necessary calls from her study after dinner.

Jeremy answered after one ring. "Erika?"

"I hope I'm not interrupting anything," she said.

"Well, *that's* relevant! What do you want? I don't suppose you called to apologize."

Bad start. "No, Jeremy, I didn't. But I do apologize for dashing off yesterday."

"Dashing off? You left me in the lurch!"

"We don't have time for this, Jeremy. I need you to help me."

"Did your husband hurt you?" he demanded.

"Please. No. Listen to me. I'm calling you because I need you to get me into Randall's office. I remember him saying you're the computer expert, so you can help me by—"

"Are you out of your mind? Did you see what they did to me?"

"Who's 'they,' Jeremy? Do you even know? Look, I've gone over the list of questionable art transactions and the murders. They're all related, and Randall's name turns up everywhere. I'm sure it's not a one-man show, but Randall may be the ringmaster. If I get into his office, I may be able to prove that."

Silence.

"Jeremy?"

"Murders?"

She realized she'd slipped. Jeremy had not been told of Andrea's death, or at least not the questionable circumstances surrounding it. "We can't discuss this now," she said, "but you have to trust me." She deliberately softened her tone; he was such an easy mark: "I'm taking a chance on you, too, Jeremy. Trusting you."

"This is insane," he said, though he didn't sound fully invested in the sentiment. "If you're so sure of yourself, why don't you call the cops?"

"You know there's not enough evidence to seize Randall's computer. Besides, if these people think anyone is on their tail, they'll burrow deeper underground, and maybe take out a couple of curious cats on the way down. I know you get it, Jeremy," she said, preparing to reel him in. "Just like you get me."

"I don't know, Erika."

"Would you rather I try it without you? I will, you know."

His wordless sigh said it all. He was in.

"Tomorrow night. Okay? Can we make it around nine-thirty?"

"If we're going to do this, we should enter the building through the private entrance," he said. "It's a few paces west of the main entrance. I only have to punch in the password to free the lock. We got a notice they're installing a biometric feature next month. Lucky for you, because if I had to enter my fingerprints tomorrow, there'd be no covert mission. It would be better to make our entrance during security's transition from day shift to swing shift, at midnight. I'm new to this shit, but I imagine that's the time the guards will be distracted, signing off and signing in."

"I'm sorry, but I'm afraid I can't do that," Erika said. "If I'm not home by eleven or so, my husband will try to track me down."

"He's smarter than I thought."

Erika let that lie. "You'll put up with me and make it nine-thirty, then? Shall we meet at the private entrance?"

"Promptly. If you're not there, I leave."

"I'll be there," Erika said. "And Jeremy—"

"Yes?"

"As soon as we end this call, please delete it. You know, in case anyone pries."

"You're not a professional bank robber, are you? You sure cover all the bases."

"Jeremy?"

"Just joking. I'll delete the call."

After they'd signed off, Erika felt unclean. She took a self-flagellating hot shower and returned to Harrison a redeemed woman.

Chapter 14

At exactly 9:26 p.m., Erika arrived at the private entrance to the office building that housed the offices of G&G. The few pedestrians wandering the area on this unusually still and moonless night imbued the scene with the mood of an Edward Hopper painting: lonely, foreboding.

Erika, in her pantsuit and high heels, had come to this unwelcoming turf directly from the *Art News* offices, where she had been hanging out with Sara for hours in Sara's cozy office, sipping black coffee and discussing themes for future issues of the magazine. Spotting the familiar figure of Jeremy coming around the corner of Sixth and 42nd in a business suit sheathed in unzipped hoodie, Erika felt her isolation diminish, her resolve harden. "Thanks for coming on time," she said as he pulled up alongside her.

"Let's be quick," he whispered in her ear. "As we enter, hug the wall on the right and stay low, in a crouch, and make your way to the stairwell. You'll be out of camera range at that point. Got it?"

"Yes."

"I'll be ahead of you. You just have to follow me."

He punched in a series of numbers on the keyboard above the door latch. Erika heard the click of the release mechanism. At the ready, she jumped forward, ramming into Jeremy.

"Calm down. Here we go," he said. He opened the door, and as soon as Erika had slipped in, he stretched out his leg and booted the door shut behind them both.

In a frog-like position, not so easy in her heels, Erika shuffled behind Jeremy to the stairwell a few yards from the entryway. Once there, they rose to full height, and Jeremy pulled open the massive door to the stairwell and ushered her into its sterile gray interior.

"Why the hell aren't you wearing sneakers?" he asked, shutting the stairwell door.

"I'm in work attire," she said, her voice echoing in the enclosure as she began to follow him up the stairs. "We had a meeting with a potential advertiser today. I suppose I could have taken sneakers along. I guess I wanted to travel light." She removed her heels and shoved them into her tote. "I'll be fine."

They climbed the cold metal staircase without saying a word, a perverse intimacy forming as their breathing became more and more audible the closer they got to the fifth floor landing.

The long hallway outside G&G was illuminated by two low-wattage bulbs recessed in the ceiling, giving it the look of a dream on the verge of a nightmare. Jeremy inserted a key into the slot on the frame of one of the glass-paned doors. "Let's do this." He pushed open the door, and then he laid his hand on Erika's shoulder and pressed her forward.

Once they were inside, Jeremy clicked a switch on the wall panel. A smattering of office lights went on, minimally illuminating G&G's workspace. He headed for Randall's office, Erika tiptoeing behind him on bare feet.

Randall's office looked as if it had been staged by a real estate broker: not a notepaper out of alignment, not a chair off the perpendicular to its furniture's complement.

"We have to leave the room exactly like it is," Jeremy said, pushing back his hood. "Nothing out of place."

"I know," Erika said, realizing, as he uncovered his head, that she hadn't given a thought to his injuries. "The bandage is gone. You're feeling okay?"

"I'm good," he said, looking down, cheeks flushing. Erika marveled at how little it took to soften him.

"Let's start with the computer," she said, stepping around the desk to have a look at its screen. The screen was black. "Can you get into it?"

"I'm sure I can." He sat down in the desk chair and fixed her with an ardent gaze, as if he were marking the start of their shared destiny.

While he worked to get into the computer, Erika went right for the manila folders on Randall's desk, sifting through them one by one. Each contained documents associated with an individual client: descriptions of items appraised or authenticated, contracts, billing statements, names of referring agents and art experts contacted for second opinions. Winston Elliot had been called upon to support Randall's findings on two separate occasions. Erika whipped out her cell phone to photograph the pages where his name appeared, then added to her budding montage with photos of random pages with the names of experts unknown to her. She returned each folder to its original arrangement as she finished with it.

Jeremy's fingers were rapidly moving over the computer keyboard as she started in on one of the side drawers. "How are you doing?" Erika asked. "Looks like the folders represent what Randall's currently working on. May be of some use."

"I've gotten past his password, but unless you want to see a bunch of photos of his grandchildren or scan his iTunes—shit!"

"What is it?"

"Business email account. Notes on Eric Hebborn. Finances." He studied the screen more closely. "But the important files are all secured. Without their encrypted passwords, it's almost impossible to access them. Even under the best circumstances it would take hours. Sorry, the computer's a dead end."

Erika shrugged, hiding her disappointment to minimize his distress. "Thanks for trying. I'm counting on us finding something helpful in these drawers, or elsewhere. Why don't you start in the center drawer? If you see anything that links Randall with anyone or any transaction connected with the Hebborn research—or outreach—let me know."

He tapped in the commands and the screen went dark as Erika leafed through a sheaf of papers from the bottom desk drawer. "This looks more promising. Take a look at—"

Jeremy jumped to his feet. "Quick! Put the papers back and shut the drawer! I'm shutting off the light in here! Hide somewhere—under the desk!"

"What's happening?" Erika cried as she shoved the papers she was holding back into the drawer. Her question was answered by the sound of a door being opened.

"Shush!" Jeremy rasped. "Under the desk! Nobody can know you're here!"

Erika shimmied into the kneehole of the desk. Jeremy kicked her tote in after her. "Got your cell phone?" he whispered.

"Yes!"

"Turn it off and don't move. I'll be back."

Seconds later, the overhead light in Randall's office was out; the door, quietly shut. Curled up beneath the desk, she thought about the possibilities. Who was out there? A security guard on their tail? Randall? Another intruder like themselves? She fought the urge to spring out and see for herself.

"Candice!" Erika heard Jeremy exclaim. "What are *you* doing here at this hour?"

"I guess I could ask the same of you!" she heard the woman reply. The name jogged Erika's memory. This must be Candice Hunter, the philately expert she and Harrison had met in the lab on their second visit to G&G's. Erika hugged her knees in an effort to take up less space. She tried to keep calm by regulating her breaths to steady swells and releases, focusing on what was going on outside the office.

"I dropped by to catch up on the work I was doing before my sick leave," Jeremy explained.

"Ah, yes, the infamous mugging. How are you, anyway?"

"They wanted me to take it easy for a day or two and watch for signs of a concussion. I'm fine now."

"I thought I saw you coming out of Randall's office."

"I was leaving a note for him," Jeremy said. "I'm headed for the lab now. You?"

"I've just come to pick up my laptop. I stupidly left it here this afternoon, and I wanted to work on my Civil War project over the weekend. Otherwise I would have let it go until Monday." There was a long silence. "Jeremy, how come you didn't check in with security? I didn't see your name when I signed in at the front desk."

"I took a shortcut via the private entrance," Jeremy said. "When I leave, I'll make sure to register."

Did Erika detect a note of nervousness in his voice? Up to now he had been handling the situation masterfully.

"Good move," Candice applauded. "So, let's go."

Erika heard the sound of fading footfalls, then silence, then the sound of a door clanging shut. They must have gone to the lab, she reasoned. Candice should be leaving momentarily with her laptop, and Jeremy should be conveying the impression that he'd be settling in for a while. Her prediction was soon proved correct: she heard the sequential sounds of lab and main door shutting.

She waited. The minutes ticked by. Where was Jeremy? She felt as if she'd been curled up under the desk for hours, although she knew it had been less than ten minutes. The cramped position was becoming intolerable. She felt imprisoned; deterred from her mission. She had to take control.

Finally, she crawled out from under the desk and clicked on the desk lamp. Jeremy entered the room to find her pulling out the drawer she had been working on.

"I couldn't wait," she said. "What took you so long?"

"You're impossible," he said, in the lovingly resigned tone Harrison might have used. "I wanted to make sure Candice wasn't coming back to collect her effing umbrella or whatever."

Erika was already sifting through the papers she had been reviewing before Candice's arrival. "Here it is." She held out her prize without relinquishing it. "It's the sender's copy of a receipt from Ace Courier Service. The addressee is Winston Elliot, and it's dated April 24, 11:30 p.m."

"That was Saturday," Jeremy said. "I picked up your notes on Hebborn and delivered them to Randall that night."

Erika took a photo of the courier form. "Then Randall must have had our notes delivered to Elliot that same night."

"Don't jump to conclusions," he said.

"I'm not. I'm arriving at them." She flipped through the rest of the papers. "Nothing more here." She put the pile back in the middle drawer in roughly the order she found them and opened the next drawer. "One more on this side. You want to take a look in the center drawer while I do this one?"

Standing alongside her, Jeremy opened his assigned drawer. "Not much room for anything in here," he said, retrieving a store-bought wall calendar with a wildlife theme. He felt around the back of the drawer, coming up with two packs of ball point pens and an unopened bag of rubber bands.

"Unused manila folders and writing pads in this one," Erika reported. She closed the drawer and held out her hand. "Let's have a look at the calendar."

Jeremy passed it to her. "Randall occasionally refers to his software calendar, but I've heard him say this is much more reliable. Guess he's got one foot in the old school. See anything interesting?"

"Maybe. There are notations in the boxes. Mostly undecipherable, but there are names and initials—and phone numbers. I'm photographing every month. I'll study the entries later." She grabbed her cell phone from the desk and began to snap away. "What about the front cubbyholes? Anything there?"

"A bunch of perfectly sharpened pencils in one of them," he said. "Little blue paper clips in another. What now?"

"We improvise," she said, handing him the calendar to put away. She grabbed his forearm as he was about to shut his drawer. "Wait. What's that metal thing among the paper clips? A key?" She released his arm and plucked it out, turning it over in the palm of her hand. "Looks like an antique. What does it unlock, I wonder?"

"We really should get out of here, Erika," Jeremy urged, caressing the forearm she had briefly held. "Let's not push our luck."

"You can go. I'll be okay. I only have to retrace my steps and hug the wall on the left this time, yes? We'll be exiting separately, anyway, since you'll be registering with security." She began to open drawers they had already searched, looking for a secret compartment, and then began to scan the room for inspiration.

"I know you'll be okay," Jeremy said. "I'd just rather you be okay sooner rather than later."

"A few minutes more," she insisted, walking toward the built-in bookcase, a vertical line-up of shelves reserved for framed photographs and objets d'art. After using her cell phone to record each photo on the shelves for later review, she took out the key from the desk. "Any ideas, Jeremy?"

"I don't know," he said, shifting his weight. "We have to go."

Disregarding him, she pointed to one of the higher shelves and asked, "What's that box?" She stretched for it. "I'm afraid I'll drop it. Come help me."

Jeremy reluctantly obeyed. "It's an antique writing box," he said, gingerly handing it to her. "Careful with it. It was a gift from Owen. Randall treasures it."

Erika gently placed the box on the conference table. It was a gracefully shaped object made of carved rosewood and inlaid with brass. The top plate read: *L. Baines to T. Kendrick 1829.*

"It is beautiful," Erika said, more taken by the brass-embellished keyhole than by any of its other characteristics. "Let's see if it fits." She inserted the key into the slot. "Yes!" She turned the key and delicately raised the lid.

Jeremy sucked in his breath. "Oh!"

Erika extracted one of the eight rolls of bills tightly nested in the writing box, each of which was topped with a hundred-dollar bill. "I'm not about to undo this wad, so I'm guessing all the bills are of the same denomination." She hefted the thing, as if she had any idea of how to gauge its composition. "Maybe one hundred bills here, times eight rolls. Eighty thousand dollars in all. Give or take."

"Why?" Jeremy asked, more to himself than to her.

"I'm not getting clean money vibes, but let's not jump the gun."

"You think?" Jeremy asked, his disbelief revealing the depth of his naiveté.

Erika stuffed the compact cylinder back into the box and closed the lid. "I do think, yes." She locked the box. "But I may be wrong. Could you put the box back on the shelf exactly where it was?"

As Jeremy returned the writing box to its shelf, Erika placed the key back among the paper clips, positioning it as she had seen it, its shaft slightly protruding. "Thanks, Jeremy. I know you want to leave now. You go. I'll have another look around and neaten up. I'll be gone in fifteen minutes, tops."

Jeremy's clamped jaw pulsed with tension.

Erika tried a light-hearted smile. "Before you go, you better leave a note for Randall. You don't want Candice to make a liar out of you."

"You're right." There was a notepad and pen on Randall's desk. Jeremy scribbled something on the top page. "I told him I stopped by to catch up with my work, and that I was swiping a ream of copy paper for home."

"Good touch."

"I said I'd repay petty cash on Monday."

"Even better."

After he collected the paper, Erika walked Jeremy to G&G's main door. He seemed a bit unsteady, the ream of paper jammed under his arm. "You okay?" she asked.

"I'm worried about you," he said. "You sure you know what to do? Don't forget, when this door shuts behind you, it'll lock. There's no turning back."

"There's no turning back," she repeated, the words laden with more meaning than she'd intended.

* * *

Alone in the office, she riffled through Randall's desk drawers once more for good measure. Next, she searched the receptionist's drawers and the shelves of the supply closet. When she was satisfied she'd done all she could to obtain additional information within a reasonable amount of time, she restored all the areas she'd invaded to their original states. The last thing she did before exiting the premises was click off the hall lights.

The bleak stairwell was an eerie place to negotiate without a companion, Erika discovered, as she scurried down the steps in her bare feet, her bag bouncing against her hip, her hand sliding along the steel banister to guard against a fall. The image that flashed through her mind—losing her footing, clattering headlong down the brutal staircase and ending in a broken heap—created the same riotous churn of emotions as if the disaster had actually played out.

When she had at last come to the end of her solitary descent, she put her shoes back on to avoid any excessive movement of her hands and legs during the final surge, a hair's breadth out of range of the surveillance camera. She took a deep breath, pushed open the stairwell door, and dropped into a crouched position before slipping through the opening she'd provided herself. As the door swung shut, she clamped her tote bag to her side and jammed up against the left wall so hard it bruised her shoulder blades. In as compressed a form as she could mold herself, she scuttled the final few yards to the exit door.

At last, slithering up the wall like a snake, she rose to her full height, her heart pounding. She reached for the latch, tugged open the door, and sidled back into the world. The door thudding shut behind her certified her release.

The street was as desolate as it had been earlier, but in contrast to the Kafkaesque passage she had just escaped, the urban landscape glimmered with the promise of a bustling workday. Erika headed toward Sixth Avenue with the intention of hailing a north-bound cab, in the direction of home. Her eagerness to share her newfound information with Harrison outweighed her fright at the prospect of coming clean.

As she approached the corner, she was jolted by the sight immediately ahead of a man and a woman awkwardly backing out of a building's hidden entryway, not more than two yards away. The woman's knees buckled; her hand grabbed hold of the man's lapel to stop the fall.

"Do we have to stay?" the woman moaned, burying her face against the man's arm.

"Until the police come, yes," the man replied, catching sight of Erika.

Erika's next step was as unavoidable as the next breath. She took it.

166

Her eyes—she was in shock, not knowing where to look first—came to rest on the ream of paper jammed between the shoulder of the body and the base of the door.

Erika fell to her knees. "Who," she began, in a voice that must have been hers. Without warning, her gut expelled a foul-tasting liquid.

"You'll contaminate the scene!" the man cried. "Get back!" He took a handkerchief from his jacket pocket. "Here!"

Erika wiped her lips. "Thank you," she said, bewildered by her response, although *any* response would have been grotesque. She rose to her feet, but she could not step away. She could not take her eyes off Jeremy, sprawled on his back in the crypt-like enclosure. The hood of his sweatshirt was pulled toward one side and looked like Death himself might have left it behind. A small hole encircled by an ashy substance was centered on his forehead, and a pool of blood had formed by the side of his head that was untouched by the hood. His eyes were wide open, like a doll's; his features, blank, deprived of even the final millisecond of emotion.

"I've been trained in CPR," the man said. "There was no call for it. The gentleman was already dead."

The signs of violence—the black hole of the bullet's entry, the pool of blood—threw Erika into turmoil, yet on another wavelength the stillness of death transfixed her in a kind of awe. She gazed at Jeremy's right hand, palm up, fingers fanned in a graceful arc like a ballet dancer's. She marveled at its sculpted perfection, wondered why she had never noticed it in life. Studying his sneakered feet, in-toeing in final surrender, she could not help obsessing on why he had double-knotted his laces. Had he *always* double-knotted his laces? Was he anticipating an active night with her—a run for their lives?

"Listen, you don't have to stick around," the man said. "I've called nine-one-one. Frankly, you'd only complicate the incident report, and we don't want to draw it out."

Her obsessive intention suddenly shot outward. "Did you see who did this?" she cried. "Did you tell the cops which way they went? *Did* you?" She felt the bile rising again, as the image of Jeremy reaching up for the antique writing box flashed in her brain; she put the handkerchief again to her mouth.

"We didn't see anyone running away," the woman said. She stepped away from Erika. "You're getting me nervous."

Erika wished she could defy gravity, fly above the pavement, arms flapping at the speed of light, willpower transforming her into a guided missile, a drone aimed at Jeremy's killer. But the wail of sirens arose in the distance and rapidly crescendoed. Erika's muscles tensed; her visions of combat stilled. On one hand, she knew she should leave: once Jeremy's killer or killers learned that she and Jeremy had been co-conspirators, she would likely be their next victim. On the other, she wanted to hold her ground, to bear witness to whatever would happen to Jeremy's body next.

"Why aren't you leaving?" the woman persisted. "Do you *know* this man or something?"

Only when Erika heard herself reply in the negative did she realize the decision had been made.

To avoid arousing suspicion, she made a conscious choice—*self-serving bitch!*—not to look back at Jeremy as she headed to the corner. Her first few steps were slow, like walking through water, but as home beamed into her mind's view and almost within reach, her pace quickened. She was waving for a cab even before she arrived at the curb, cursing her impractical shoes and the vanity that drove her to wear them.

* * *

Once she was grounded in the back seat of a cab, her grandiose notion of physical pursuit and capture turned to thoughts of entrapment. She would draw the murderous bastard or bastards into her net. *Think, think,* she silently commanded, punching her thigh. *Start with Randall. Randall knows something. He must be pressured into giving it up.* Should she wait for Greg's input? Ask John to back her up? Schemes of cunning and deceit auditioned for precedence, convincing her one second, disappointing the next.

"Cash or credit, Miss?" the driver asked, when he pulled up in front of the Wheatley residence.

Her thoughts elsewhere, she uttered, as if through a ventriloquist, "Cash."

She paid the driver and slid out of the cab. "The door!" he shouted; she slammed it, and he drove away. Erika stood at curbside, unable to pause the stream of ideas, like a director mired in a loop of takes and re-takes. Without warning an ugly truth pitched into her thoughts: pure and undeniable, so close it had gone unnoticed. Horrified, she staggered toward the wrought-iron gate that barred entrance to her home, and with trembling fingers, managed on the second try to punch in the security code.

"Erika?" Harrison called from the balustrade above. She sat hunched over on the couch, her posture in direct contrast to the flamboyant Botero; she did not respond. She could hear him descending, taking the stairs three at a time.

"Erika?" he repeated, planting himself in the chair next to the couch. "Didn't it go well with Sara? I was worried. I called the office and she said you were busy. Are you okay?"

"I killed him," she said flatly.

"They killed your article?" he said, hearing what she knew was the most reasonable interpretation. "You mustn't take it to heart. There'll be others."

"Jeremy," she said. "I killed Jeremy."

Harrison's emotion, unlike Erika's, was betrayed by his features: panic. "You meant that figuratively, right?" he asked.

"I convinced him to meet me at G&G's tonight," she said, voice still flat. "He didn't want to, but I made him."

"What do you mean?" he asked. "Weren't you at a meeting with Sara?"

"No. I made that up. Sara cooperated. I knew Randall was tied up in some way with Andrea's murder and I wanted to search his office to see if I could find some evidence of it. I convinced Jeremy to help me, and he didn't want to."

"You already said that."

Erika squinted at him in disbelief, detecting the annoyance in his voice. Before he could pretend the words had come out wrong, she responded, her feelings rocketing to the surface: "How *can* you? Jeremy was shot in the head and left to die in a fucking doorway, and you're pissed off?"

169

"I was expressing my fear for you—and yes, anger," he said. "We were going to lay low, so now you decide to deceive me and throw caution to the wind?"

"I just told you I feel responsible for Jeremy's murder, and what rankles you is my disobedience?"

"To what extent did you have to ply your seductive wiles on that love-struck puppy?" he baited. "Like riding a bike, I suppose that's one skill you never forget." She stared at him. "Shit, I'm sorry."

"No, you're not," she said, meeting him head on. "But thank you for reminding me why I kept my plan from you. You would have given me hell about it."

"And maybe saved a life," he whipped back helplessly.

"Maybe!" she shouted. Her growing anger seemed to be saving her from caving in with remorse. Maybe that was a good thing, she thought.

"My mouth is not responding to my brain," he said. "I should leave you alone." He rose from the chair, his knees unsteady, as if he wanted to fall to them at her feet. "It'll be better later. Of course we have to talk about this. Come to bed soon, okay?"

His words sounded as hollow to her as she could tell, from his self-disgusted look, they had sounded to him.

Chapter 15

The Blue Room was one of the guest bedrooms on the third floor. It was named after the color of the girl's dress in the Mary Cassatt impressionist painting that hung above the four-poster's headboard. Over a year ago, at the start of their Cuba venture, Harrison had provided Erika shelter in this room from a criminal in the art world who had been lying in wait for her somewhere in Manhattan. Last night she had fled to the Blue Room to avoid the very person who had rescued her. The irony had crossed her mind, but she had swept it aside for matters that counted in the here and now.

She rose from the bed and grabbed her cell phone from the night table, forgetting for a moment that it was attached to the charger. Last night, before she had thrown herself on the bed in an act of mindless protocol—she had lain awake all night, never attempting the charade of trying to get a moment's peace—she had forwarded all the pictures she had taken in Randall's office to Greg Smith, asking him to search for anyone in his photos, calendar, or files with a match on the Art Loss Register database. It was 6:30 a.m., and she knew Greg could not yet have responded, but she checked anyway. Nothing. She would give him until 8:00 and then call him.

Meanwhile she would text John Mitchell. She typed out her message. When she read it over it seemed mad, outlandish at best. Without a moment's hesitation, she pressed the "send" prompt. The ping signaling John's reply came so quickly, it was as if he had been waiting for her text, fingers at the ready. *What?? Call me now.* She obliged.

"Which did I interrupt, a dream or a hallucination?" John asked.

"I'm planning a sting," Erika answered directly, in no mood for banter. "I need to know if you'll help."

There was a silence. "Before we get serious, how does Harrison feel about this?"

"Harrison knows nothing about this, and that's the way it's going to stay. He can't be involved."

"Because he'll disapprove?"

"Something like that," she admitted. "Look, John, there's been another murder. It's clear now that this is a series of related art crimes and murders. There's a cooperative effort at work here, with some individual or clan calling the shots."

"And I suppose you'll be requiring the aid of a SWAT team?" John posed in the manner of a comedic straight man.

"Yes," Erika answered flatly, killing his opening. "The FBI has a special Art Crime Team based in New York. I'm hoping my friend, Greg Smith, can bring them in."

There was another pause on the line; she took advantage of it. "As a preliminary," she said, "I need your help. Randall Gray is part of the system, and we need him to collaborate with us. We'll have to break him together."

"Erika," John at last pronounced, as if he were about to read off the Ten Commandments. "May I remind you that regarding the Hebborn intrigue, you were going to fly under the radar?"

"I plan to stay there," she replied, just as earnestly. "I only intend to pull Randall down here with me. Will you help me?"

"I suppose you'll go it alone if I don't?"

"Yes."

He heaved a sigh, clearly meant to be heard. "Where do we go from here?"

"Are you free this afternoon?" she began.

* * *

Erika had spent the night in her street clothes. After her call with John, she stripped down to her underwear and removed the floral-print silk robe from the closet. The robe belonged to Harrison's sister, Nell, the Blue Room's most frequent guest. She slipped into the robe and exited the room on the tips of her toes, as if the sound of her stirring would cause a disturbance, not the fact that she had chosen to spend a night away from her husband for the first time in their married life.

There was no protocol for retrieving an assortment of clothing from the sacred marital chamber. She was entering new territory. Harrison was sitting on the side of the bed when she stepped foot into their room. "Good morning," she said.

"I was just coming for you," he said, fidgeting with the sleeve of his T-shirt. "I figured you stayed in the Blue Room. I mean, Grace said that's where you'd gone."

"Yes. I've come for my clothes." She saw him flinch. "Not all of them. My jeans and, well, a top or two." She strode, a bit unsteady, to her closet. "Before you interrogate me, my answer is simple. I need my space for a while."

"We're not going to talk? We always talk."

"We will. Right now I need to be alone." She reached for the hanger on which her blue jeans were clipped and draped the garment over her arm, following it with two blouses and a blazer. She bent to pick up her sneakers.

He jumped from the bed. "Here, let me." But her sneakers were already in her possession when he arrived at her side. "You're so willful," he mumbled.

"One of my many flaws." She started for the door to the room.

"Are we going to have breakfast together?" he asked, starting to bristle. "I mean, exactly what are the parameters of your stand-off?"

"Off course we'll have breakfast together," she said, sounding as if she'd calculated the boundaries of her stand-off in millimeters, when in fact she hadn't a clue.

* * *

By the time she'd showered and dressed and sat through a breakfast of muffins and coffee with a side of stilted conversation, it was time to check in with Greg. She excused herself from the table. This was apparently Harrison and Grace's cue to direct pained stares at her. She tried not to take their comradely dismay to heart.

More comfortable conducting business in her office than in the Blue Room, she sat back in her desk chair and waited for Greg to pick up.

"No, it's not too early," he fairly sputtered, in answer to her opening question. "I've been awake for hours, but I haven't had a chance to review your photos. I did get your transmission off my phone and into the Register's database, like you requested."

"You sound breathless," Erika observed.

"Is it that noticeable? We've had an exciting break—historic!"

"You're not planning to keep me in the dark, are you?"

"I should. We're not publicizing the news until we've got our snitch properly enrolled in witness protection."

"You know I can keep a secret."

"No, I don't, but I'm a betting man. Seriously, this can't be leaked. You understand?"

"Absolutely."

"We've recovered two paintings stolen from the Isabella Stewart Gardner Museum!" Greg exploded, as if he'd just expelled a kidney stone.

Erika kept her voice to a whisper in answering. "Are you referring to that famous heist in 1990?"

"Yes! Rembrandt's *Christ in the Storm on the Sea of Galilee* and Vermeer's *The Concert*. The Vermeer alone is valued at two hundred million! For years, we've suspected that Robert Gentile, the Connecticut gangster now in his eighties, knew where the artworks were hidden, but he's always denied it. Well, a close associate just spilled the beans, and voila!"

There was silence on the line.

"Erika?" Greg questioned, sudden concern in his voice.

"Wait, I'm thinking."

"Erika?"

"This is amazing," she said, in hushed tone. "I was fantasizing that an old painting would fall into our lap, and here it is! This is a perfect decoy for our sting! Of course, you do need to promise not to publicize the recovery until after we've nailed the bastards."

"You lost me," Greg said.

"I'm planning something relating to the Hebborn affair. It'll involve a couple of undercover FBI guys, as well as some other minor elements to hash out—"

"Stop. Before you go on, what does Harrison think of all this?"

Harrison again? One dig at her leadership was an irritant. Two before noon raised the issue of paternalism. "Harrison doesn't know about all this, and he can't be told," she said. "You and Harrison left me out of the people-to-people trip during our Cuban venture. Now it's the other way around. I'm sure you understand."

"I think I do," he said, sardonic. "Before I agree to anything, you'll have to be more specific."

"Are you on a secure line?"

"A little late to ask, don't you think?"

She blushed. "Can we meet in an hour? It's important I clear things with you before I put the plan in motion later today."

"You work fast. Luckily, as it turns out, I catch a flight to London at five tonight. Meet me at my office. It's Saturday. We'll have the place to ourselves."

"I'm on my way," she agreed, reaching for her blazer.

* * *

Two hours after her talk with Greg, Erika was sitting in John's low-profile Chevy, parked on East 38th Street, just off the FDR Expressway.

"This is madness," John said, maybe for the third time.

"Sure," Erika agreed without conviction. He was with her; it was all that mattered.

"What if he's not home?" John asked.

"If he's not, we'll wait for him to *get* home."

She tapped in Randall's cell number. As the number rang, she silently rehearsed the message she'd leave, but the line picked up.

"What the *hell!*" Randall barked.

"Yes, it's me," Erika said, activating the speaker phone. "Are you at home?"

"What does it matter? Do you know what happened last night? No, of *course* you don't!"

"But I do, Randall."

There was a long pause, which Erika was reluctant to cut short. She allowed Randall's consternation to sink in before speaking again. "I repeat, are you at home? I'd like to talk to you face to face. It's for your own benefit. I can meet you right now at the park bench on the esplanade, directly across from your apartment building."

"How do you know where I live?"

"You can't be serious. I can find out what mayoral candidate you contributed to and probably your favorite color just by Googling you. Is your wife home?"

"No, she's out."

"She left you to grieve alone?"

John winced.

"No, she left me. Period."

"Ah, sorry," Erika said, less caustic. "I'll see you in a few minutes—and Randall?"

"What?"

"I'll be with my armed bodyguard, so don't try anything clever. Besides, there's a bunch of authority figures in on this, and they're definitely *well-positioned.*" Let him wonder: did she mean figuratively or literally? "Trust me, we've got your best interests in mind, Randall. In the long run, that is."

"Fuck you. I'll be down in five minutes."

* * *

They gave him ten.

Randall was sitting motionless on the bench, staring out at the East River, when Erika and John approached him. He reminded Erika of a George Segal sculpture, cast from a real individual and placed on a park bench, alienated from his fellow creatures and from the city itself.

"Hello, Randall," Erika said, startling him from his stony reverie. "This is Private Detective John Mitchell."

John nodded as he and Erika sat down on either side of Randall.

"Are you wired?" Randall asked.

"No," Erika said. "You want to check?"

"Yes."

Erika parted the lapels of her blazer and opened several buttons of her blouse. She gave him a good look. John did the same with his windbreaker and button-down shirt.

"Okay," Randall said. "Cover yourselves."

They did so as Randall returned his focus to the river. "We used to like this view," he said. "We used to watch the ferries come and go—and the helicopters. A few years ago, the city switched the Fourth of July fireworks from the Hudson River to the East River. The barges are right outside our picture window. It's spectacular. We always flinch when those fiery spheres expand—they seem to be heading straight for us."

"Maybe she'll come back, your wife," Erika said, with premeditated sympathy.

"No, she's gone for good," Randall said. "It's been coming for years, and I was prepared for it. But losing Jeremy …it's all over, everything."

He covered his face with his hands and his shoulders heaved as he wept, almost soundless. Randall appeared to be a broken man; primed for the taking. Good, Erika thought.

"The bastards," Randall aimed at the river, wiping his cheeks with his palms. "Jeremy was fucking harmless."

Erika placed her hand on his shoulder. "I saw him. Dead."

Randall whipped around to face her, his hips colliding with John's. "What did you say?"

Erika simply nodded confirmation. "I was in your office last night. I saw things. Took pictures."

Randall opened his mouth to object, raising his fist, but John grabbed Randall's forearm and forced it across his chest so that Randall effectively knocked the wind out of himself. "Watch it," John said.

Erika continued. "I did this because I've discovered that you were the Customer Support Representative at Christie's in 1996, the one who oversaw a shady transaction involving one of Hebborn's forgeries. You tried to suppress that information, but you failed. There have been three cold-blooded murders—Owen's, Andrea's, Jeremy's—linked to you and your gang."

"They're not my gang!" Randall objected.

There! Randall had confirmed Erika's hypothesis of a band of criminals. "Who's running you?" she pressed.

No answer.

"I saw the neat rolls of bills in your antique writing box," she prompted.

"Winston Elliot," he said, emotion depleted.

She willed her body to remain still. Pinned right up against her, he would feel any sign of tension or excitement. Determination was all she intended to convey. "He gave you the cash?" she said evenly.

Randall nodded. "He's my contact—the only one. He paid me for information, for networking, nothing more. I have a clean record and longevity in the field. I have a pedigree. I'm useful."

"You have a clean record only because the Christie's incident remains a cold case," Erika replied, presenting her hypothesis as if it were a fact etched in stone. "In fact, you've been compromised since 1996."

"My one moment of weakness," Randall admitted. "Haunting me forever." He shook his head.

"I'm listening," Erika said, marveling at his capitulation.

Randall stared across the river at the dull skyline of Queens. "Let me tell you my one mistake, a quarter of a century ago. I was working at Christie's. A masterpiece authenticated as a van Dyck was brought up for auction. I recognized it as a Hebborn forgery. I had learned how to look for one by the expert himself, Owen Grant, whose deconstruction of Hebborn's supposed Titian in 1985 had blown my mind. It's no excuse, but I was struggling at the time, and I saw an opportunity to make a buck. I told the seller of my finding, and I offered to keep quiet for a cut in the sale price. Winston Elliot was the seller's lawyer. He learned of my offer, and he threatened to expose me if I didn't agree to do a favor for him every now and then."

"Example," Erika prompted.

"The perfect mark was an ignorant but wealthy client," Randall said. "Preferably one who'd achieved his status through questionable means. Someone looking to authenticate a valuable work of art to put up for sale. I would refer this client to Elliot, who would falsely rule the work to be a forgery and then offer to reverse his findings for a sizeable fee. The mark would be sworn to secrecy to substantiate my innocence in the affair. I don't know who else was involved beyond Elliot. I was aware only that I was dealing with a bunch of scoundrels, and that every now and then I had to help orchestrate a scam for them."

Erika kept still, hoping Randall would go on. John, who hadn't said a word since his warning to Randall, continued to hold his peace, perhaps hoping the same thing.

Randall pinned his gaze on Erika. "Do you know what a relief this is? And what a horror?"

"Unburdening yourself?" Erika suggested.

"Yes. It was miserable enough, being associated with a con game. It was like an ulcer, gnawing at me all these years. But *murder*? It took a plot carried out on my doorstep to understand the lengths these thugs will go to achieve their goals. I wanted to believe Owen's murder was a random act, but after Andrea's death—and Jeremy's—I see how naïve I was!"

Erika gave a patronizing shake of her head, as if she were refuting a child's lie. "You were in denial. All along. I take it you're wracked with guilt. At least you should be."

"I am," he said.

"Good. I have a plan which will allow you to redeem yourself, and more importantly, for you to avoid jail time."

"Winston Elliot. He's my only connection. I have nothing more to offer."

"You do. Let me explain."

She cleared her throat, as if nervousness could be expelled. But before she could speak, an ear-splitting whirring sound arose from the heliport, directly in line with them and less than a quarter of a mile away.

"It'll take off in a minute," Randall said, voice raised.

Erika took the opportunity to gather her thoughts as the helicopter—bright red, "Liberty" emblazoned in white, portside—lifted off from its pad, hovered precariously over the river like a cumbersome toy, arced off in a southerly direction, and then, more quickly than Erika expected, became an anonymous speck in the sky. Time was up. She was about to test her ability to lie through her teeth.

"You remember, Randall, that we talked about x-raying the book spines to see if Hebborn had hidden any clues for us in those unlikely areas?"

"I remember, but—"

"Shh, the question was rhetorical. Just listen." She was surprising herself; doing better than expected. "Yes, that probe was unnecessary, you claimed. Owen had himself scanned the spine of his copy of *Drawn to Trouble* and had found nothing of interest. But no one had scanned the spine of *Charlene's* copy of the book, and so I decided to do just that. And what I found was truly incredible.

"I don't want to lecture you on book spines, but why not? John may find it interesting. When the spine cover is attached to the spine of the book block, it's called a tight back or flexible binding. Most paperbacks have such a spine. When they're not attached—as is the case with most hardcovers, including Hebborn's—it's called a hollow back. From the expression on your face, I can guess that you see where I'm going. Inserted in that hollow back was a narrow strip of paper containing a note in Hebborn's hand. I recognized his handwriting from the letters he wrote in the books proper. Randall, you're of course familiar with the Gardner Museum heist of 1990."

Randall started, causing his body to pop up from the bench. John pulled him back down.

"Can you name the most valuable painting stolen?" she asked in a hushed tone.

Randall was silent.

"You can speak now," Erika said.

"*The Concert*," he said, matching her muted delivery. "Vermeer. Do you mean to say—"

"Yes. The slip of paper reveals where the painting, along with a couple of others looted from the Gardner, was stashed, at least at that time. I wouldn't be surprised if knowing this information got Hebborn killed a few years later."

"Why didn't you tell me this when you handed over the deciphered codes?" Randall asked.

"Because I was saving the information for a more propitious moment," Erika answered with assurance. (Her silent comeback: *because I hadn't invented the story until today*.)

"I don't know what to say. I'm bowled over."

"Good. So you'll cooperate, yes?"

"With what?" He emitted a quivery guffaw. "Some kind of *sting*?"

"Exactly. I've got the general plan in place, but a few of the particulars need to be ironed out." (*A few?* She could hardly keep a straight face.) "With the help of the FBI, I've tracked down the alleged owner," she improvised, "and as luck would have it, he's in hot water with the mob and extremely eager to unload the painting and skip town. The deal is, he hands over the Vermeer and gets his ransom money, after which he relinquishes the remainder of the haul, no strings attached. In return, he escapes prosecution and is assigned witness protection."

"Who *is* this person?" Randall asked. His tone was casual, but his eyes betrayed ravenous curiosity.

Erika felt a curious excitement. Was this how Hebborn had felt when he was completing one of his deceptions? "To you, he's John Doe," she said. Offering a whiff of camaraderie, she smiled. "He goes by the same name to me, too. Anyway, Mr. Doe did some research on me, and I passed his test. He wants me to connect with the Gardner Museum and work out the exchange."

"Exchange?"

"The Gardner gets the painting, valued at about three hundred million. Mr. Doe gets his thirty million."

Randall did something that Erika thought only happened in cartoons: he gulped.

"You realize, don't you," she said, "that this charade will be set up to entrap your cohorts."

"I told you, my only contact is Elliot!"

"Good enough. Through him, we'll hook the big fish. Elliot will come along as the expert. You'll assist, double-check his findings. He's there to verify the painting as the real thing. You can tell him it's on my recommendation, that I met him and that I was impressed, and that the two of you can more or less name your fees. Lay it on, but not too thick."

"He'll be in on the plan?" Randall asked, incredulous.

"Of course not. To him it'll all be on the up-and-up, a legitimate transaction, one that he's bound to relay to a friend—or handler."

"You're expecting them to disrupt the exchange?"

"If we're lucky. If we're not, Elliot will just try to pull off his usual scam. If he needs a little encouragement, you'll give it to him. We'll catch him in the act, and he'll be persuaded to name names."

Randall's eyes opened wide. "They'll kill me when I walk away scot free! They'll know I cooperated with you!"

"Absolutely not. Law enforcement will see to it that you're conspicuously included in their sweep."

"I don't know. I don't know."

"Think it over, but don't take too long. I need to know by tonight." She pierced him with a stare. "You must not tell anyone about our conversation. Not your wife, to curry sympathy, not anyone in your office, not your lawyer, not your priest—not my husband! Do you understand?"

"Yes."

"We're done, then," she said. "Call me." She rose from the bench, John and Randall following suit.

As they started to separate, Erika turned to Randall. "Oh, and by the way," she said.

Randall stopped in his tracks.

"We didn't lie," she said. "We weren't wired. But, then again, we did record every word."

John smiled and patted his shirt pocket, with its contents.

"Your pen?" Randall asked weakly.

John nodded.

"Fuck you," Randall said, before walking off.

The meeting had ended with the same cursed pronouncement as it had begun. A kind of closure, Erika thought, but on a small scale. The question of whether or not her sting operation would succeed at entrapping the people responsible for Owen, Jeremy, and Andrea's deaths was wide open.

Chapter 16

"May I?" Harrison petitioned, before daring to set foot in Erika's study.

Erika punched off her cell phone, aborting its transmission to Greg's London landline. "Of course. You needn't be so formal!"

"You mean as in the manner of your reply?" He stepped into the room.

"I didn't mean it to be," she said. Except she did. Her aloofness was standing her in good stead. Her animus had all but fizzled out, but maintaining her distance allowed her to keep her secret ops mission under wraps. She spun in her desk chair to face him squarely. "What's up?"

"I was wondering if you were packing," he said, guarded.

"Packing—oh! Your lecture tour!"

"Thank you for remembering," he said, brusqueness hardly masking the hurt. "Our flight to Rome leaves at six-thirty tomorrow morning."

"Harrison, I'm so sorry. I won't be able to make it." Her regret was genuine. She had been looking forward to this trip, *before.* "I've been given a lot more assignments since my promotion, some with imminent deadlines."

"Feeble. You can do better than that."

"A break will give us time to reset," she tried.

"What, our clocks?"

"Don't make this difficult for me," she said, finger-combing her hair away

184

from her cheek.

"Why not?" he asked, gazing at her exposed temple.

"We'll be fine," she said, eliding the question. "Can you get a refund for the ticket?"

"I don't give a shit."

"Please don't leave with a bad feeling, Harrison."

"Why not? I thought I was leaving with *you!*"

"Look, I admit I was overly sensitive, but you opened an old wound—cruelly, I felt. The ten days we're apart will give us time for some soul-searching."

"I hate that expression."

"Introspection. Better?"

"Would an apology help?" he asked, waving off the issue of semantics.

"Yes, but give it time to *sink in.*"

"Sounds like you're marinating a steak." He smiled wanly. "I'll be back in ten days. Think we'll be ready to fry by then?"

He was so willing and eager to make amends—for now, at least. A part of her was tempted to pull a Sleeping Beauty on the sting operation and wake up with Harrison's mouth against hers. The part of her that was truer to her creed of self-reliance, grown fiercer in recent weeks, pushed its weaker opponent aside.

"We'll be ready to talk," she said, abandoning his cooking imagery. It was too cute to describe a marriage that might be teetering on the rocks.

Chapter 17

The first thing Harrison did after passing through airport security was grab his cell phone to call John.

"I want you to keep an eye on Erika," he demanded, on hearing John's sleepy voice.

"It's five in the morning," John rasped.

Harrison didn't give a damn. "I'll be in Europe for ten days, and Erika may be up to something. I wouldn't put it past her."

There was a pause on the line.

"John?"

"Ah—yes, I'll do that, Harrison," John replied, his voice a bit tense, like a singer caught on a note above his range.

"Are you okay, John? You know something I don't?"

"No, Harrison. We just woke up my wife—go back to sleep, hon, it's fine."

Did Harrison just hear John plant a lip-smacking kiss somewhere on his wife's face? "Are you with me, John? Are you taking this seriously?"

"Of course!" John answered, bridling. "What the hell do you think?"

"All right. You'll check in with me at least once a day?"

"Sure."

This was exactly what Erika would have been rankled about: his keeping tabs on her. He didn't care; not when he was about to put what felt like

186

a galaxy between them. "Thanks, John," he said. "I'm off to my gate. Talk soon."

He felt sick about not having knocked on the door to the Blue Room to bid Erika a proper good-bye—so what if it was 3:00 in the morning? He would not be seeing her for ten days, and what if the plane crashed and he hadn't told her he loved her? He waited until 5:30 a.m., and then he punched in the number to her cell phone. It went straight to voicemail. He waited for the prompt.

"I wanted to say good-bye," he said, trying not to overthink his tone. He did not want to make the wrong impression, not now when it was so important; maybe these would be his last words to her before the crash. "I love you," he added. So that the statement would not appear to be some kind of addendum—a polite afterthought—he said it again. "I love you, Erika. Remember."

Before going off on a pedagogic riff on what "remember" might have meant—a tendency Erika found endearing most of the time, except that this wasn't most of the time—he hung up.

I love you, he repeated inwardly, in the tone he would regret for hours not having spoken aloud.

Chapter 18

Erika lay on her back, tucked under the covers in the Blue Room's four-poster bed, refusing to wonder why Harrison had not knocked on the door to say good-bye, helplessly aware that the thought negated its premise.

She threw off the covers and sat up. She grabbed her cell phone from the night table and turned it on. It was 5:35 a.m. She and Greg still had to finalize plans for her sting operation; either that, or he had to shoot them down. She did some calculating: Greg should have arrived in London about four and a half hours ago. It was now 10:35 a.m. in London, and it was Sunday, so he was probably at home, preparing his mid-morning tea. He had given her the number of his secure landline; she prepared to call him. But the number "1" appeared in a red circle overlaying the corner of the handset icon: she had a voice message.

She listened to it, savored it more than she deemed necessary. But clinging to her impulse to call Harrison back was the need to get moving on her make-or-break talk with Greg. The alternatives were so closely aligned, and she knew that any contact with Harrison—his questions, her dodging—would impinge on her top-secret endeavor and threaten to destroy it.

Greg answered her call at once. "Good timing. I was just thinking of you vis-à-vis the director of the Gardner Museum."

"Double checking—this is a secure line?"

"Yes, and it encrypts incoming calls as well. You can't be tapped. Rest easy."

"Is it foolproof?"

"Nothing is foolproof, Erika. Where were we? The director. He approved your off-the-wall scheme; can you believe it? I don't know if he's as crazy as you or if I give the world's best pitch. We're going to have to act fast on this, or we'll sure as hell get outed. And incidentally, for our targets to believe this performance of ours, we have to invent a damn good reason why we're not simply arresting our ransomer and seizing the painting on the spot."

"I've got that covered," Erika said. She explained the scenario she had come up with at her and John's riverfront meeting with Randall. Greg was duly impressed.

"I take it the painting will be the real thing?" she prompted.

"Of course. You can bet your life that Winston Elliot, authenticator slash scumbag, would spot a fake a mile away. Vermeer's masterpiece will be in the armored vehicle."

"Armored vehicle?"

"We'll get to that. First, let's talk basics. It's vital that the staged transfer of the painting from John Doe to the Gardner Museum appears to be on the up and up. We've got an FBI agent playing John Doe, and we've got another playing the representative for the Gardner Museum. There's also the role of John Doe's lawyer, who will—convincingly, I hope—walk Doe through the legalities of the settlement. I'm getting ahead of myself."

"Certainly ahead of *me!*" Erika confessed.

"Yeah, I guess you can't tell the players without a scorecard," he quipped. "Don't worry. You'll catch on once we're underway."

"Thanks for the vote of confidence, Greg." She paused a beat. "I don't mean to jump the gun myself, but what about the cash our fictitious mob affiliate, John Doe, is demanding before he gives up the masterpiece he's been guarding for decades? I know you can't be thinking of passing out Monopoly money!"

Greg laughed. "The white and blue bills would be a real giveaway.

Seriously, the director of the Gardner is not about to take it on himself to deal in hard cash, especially since he's acting on his own, without the knowledge of his board of directors. No, the funds will be wired from the Gardner account to an account ostensibly set up by John Doe and company."

"But really just another Gardner account with a creative title," Erika guessed aloud.

"You're catching on," Greg declared with pride, as if Erika were his eager protégé.

"You were saying, about the armored vehicle?" she asked, forging ahead.

"I just decided not to supply you with any more details. The more you learn on the spot, the more believable you'll appear to be. I'll let you know when we have a firm go date."

"Before Harrison returns, please."

"I get the picture, Erika. I'll do my best."

"Oh, and one more thing, Greg."

"I know, yes, I'll look through the material gleaned from your snooping around at Randall's office. I'll get back to you about that."

"Thanks so much, but it's something else." She relayed the incident at the St. Regis and its aftermath. "I'd like you to call George Dudley. Randall told me the forged Rembrandt is hanging on Dudley's wall, but I suspect it's not. I'd like you to pretend you're an interested buyer, someone who was disappointed when the painting was withdrawn from auction."

"The object being?"

"If you ask Dudley if he'd be willing to sell it to you, he might say it's unavailable, but in the process he might drop a clue on how Elliot manipulated events. Randall let me in on how Elliot works, but the more details we can add to his MO, the better we can predict what he may be tempted to pull during the sting."

"Good thinking. What can we lose? How can I reach this Dudley character?"

Erika told him all she knew: George Dudley lived in Philadelphia, and his wife's name was Marylou. They planned to touch base the next day at 7:00 p.m. Erika's time; midnight, Greg's.

In closing, she asked, "Will you be returning to New York for the big day?"

"Of course."

"Will you be participating—I mean, on stage with us?"

"I'll be nearby," he hedged. "In the wings."

As his words were spoken, Erika was alerted to an incoming call. "John Mitchell is trying to reach me. I better take it. Shall we make it a three-way?"

"Better not," Greg advised. "Security on my phone is compromised with additional input. We're done for now. Talk tomorrow. Have a good one." He terminated the call.

"John?" she asked, switching connections: she was never certain she wasn't cutting off the caller on hold. "You there?"

"Yes, I'm here, Erika," John answered, worry in his voice.

"Is anything wrong?"

"Not yet," he said, tart. "Harrison called me from the airport. He wants me to keep an eye on you, and I don't blame him."

"You didn't—"

"No, I didn't tell him about your little covert operation, but I came close."

"Thank you, John."

"Thanks may be premature," he said. "I've decided that you'll include me in your plans, or I'll spill the beans."

Erika bit her lip.

"Well?" John nudged. "What'll it be?"

"I don't know if the director of the Gardner Museum will allow another participant," she said, embarrassed by her unmistakable whine.

"Then don't ask. I'll just crash the party."

"But who will you *play*?" she asked, tone unimproved.

"I'll play myself. Your bodyguard."

Erika reviewed her options. It was a short list.

"You have no choice," John persevered. "Harrison would sabotage the operation in a minute to keep you out of trouble."

"I know," she conceded. "So I guess you're in."

"Don't strain yourself leaping with joy," he said, the tension gone from his voice. "You know you'll feel safer with me at your side."

"I will," she said, realizing the truth as it was uttered.

* * *

In accompanying her, John would in essence be serving as Harrison's eyes and ears. Erika wondered if this would ground her or hamper her style—or both? She wished there were some mental calisthenics to train her to quit fretting over the issue. What saved her from slipping into a useless dialectic was the more compelling matter of the sting itself, now dead ahead. She felt an overpowering urge to prepare for it, yet now that she had sold the powers that be on her idea, they had taken all of the logistics out of her hands. There was nothing for her to do but wait.

She sublimated the impulse to organize into a series of activities that resembled the preparations either for the end of days or major surgery: straighten out the underwear drawer, balance the check book, finish the article on the role of the curator in shaping contemporary values, gather clothes for Goodwill. The morning sailed by on a wave of adrenalin, and it was already 1:10 by the time she ran out of tasks. She took a quick shower and threw on a pair of jeans and T-shirt, then downed a peanut butter and jelly sandwich, much to Grace's chagrin. ("We have that lovely leftover brisket, Miss Erika." "Tonight, I promise, Grace.")

She fled to her lair, where she retrieved the itinerary for Harrison's book tour from the center drawer of her desk, slipped there after they had meticulously worked out the schedule for their work-and-pleasure jaunt, ignorant of the tragedies lying in wait. Harrison's flight was due to land at Leonardo da Vinci International Airport at 8:00 p.m. CEST—Central European Summer Time. If there were no delays, he would be on the ground fifty minutes from now. He would be picked up at the airport and driven to Trastevere, the 13th district of Rome on the West bank of the Tiber River, where the American University of Rome, first stop on his whirlwind tour, would be awaiting his arrival with open arms and a bottle of Chianti. The trip from the airport to Trastevere was about forty-five minutes. Tagging on two hours for him to catch his breath, acquire a nice buzz, and be transported to the nearby bed-and-breakfast where they had made reservations for the *luna di miele*—honeymoon suite—she computed that the optimum time to phone him was 5:00 p.m., or 11:00 p.m. in Rome. She was not sure if he would want to speak to her, now that he had experienced her absence in actual fact, or what she would say to him if he *did* accept her call.

Meanwhile, she would contact Charlene.

"Erika—how are you doing?" Charlene started right in. "I've been meaning to call you." The words sounded canned.

"I've been meaning to call you, too!" Erika squawked, trying to inject life into the exchange, but turning into a parrot. "I'm okay. What about you?"

"I'm good."

"Yes?"

"Not really."

There was a break in conversation, filled with the muffled sobs of Charlene's shattered ice maiden.

"Our wedding was planned for this weekend," Charlene finally managed. "Our friends wanted to arrange a celebration—of her life, of our life together, they weren't sure what. I said no. All I want is for her remains to be released to me, without fanfare."

"Are you home? Would you like me to come over for a while? Would you like to come for a visit?"

"Another time, all right? I promised Barry I'd go see a movie with him, some darkly sad Russian saga he thinks will be cathartic. Did I tell you the Vermont authorities called me?"

"What?" Erika asked, caught off guard.

"They found a cigarette lighter under the passenger seat. They wanted to know if Andrea was a smoker. I told them no. There were fingerprints on the lighter—not hers. The rental agency thinks the lighter might have been missed by the clean-up crew between rentals. They're checking it out. I was planning on letting John Mitchell know."

"Of course," Erika said, trying to put a positive spin on the news.

The call ended on a forward-looking note of reparation and reunion, slightly forced for both of them, but phony optimism if repeated often enough transforms to the real thing, at least according to some well-respected source whose name had slipped Erika's mind.

Restless after the call to Charlene, she looked out the window of her study. What a glorious day, the sunlight forced her to observe, its abundance finding colors in bits and places easily overlooked: blue tassel on the flap of a handbag, auburn glimmer in a chestnut ponytail, sparkle embedded in limestone like shimmering eye shadow. George Seurat would have had a ball today, dotting his canvas with points of light gathered from, of all places, Madison Avenue.

The joggers were out today, in look-at-me shorts and tank tops, their bent arms churning like bars coupling the wheels of a locomotive. At the corner of 78th Street, a woman wearing a pink headband and matching shorts and top marked time in place, waiting for the light to turn green. As Erika studied her measured high-step, she found herself latching onto its rhythm, and her own heartbeat quickened when the woman surged ahead.

She suddenly knew she had to get out of the house to walk in the open air, for no other end but itself. Jake was snuggled at her feet, his face resting on one of them. She wiggled her toes, and he lifted his head and looked up at her. When she and Harrison were unavailable, Grace, or her reliable acquaintance who lived in an apartment building close by, walked Jake for them. Erika knew these walks were brief and efficient: to his favorite pee tree several yards from their front door, on to his familiar curbside spot half a block farther. Jake was old and overweight and probably fine with the short excursions, but maybe he liked pretending he was a lively pup and would prefer being dog-tired than comfortably waiting to die. Maybe Erika just needed to move.

"Take me for a walk, Jake," she said, rising from the floor.

* * *

Jake, at the end of his colorful braided leash, led the way, first to his maple tree with a circle of sod at its base, rich with new and familiar creature smells; next, to his habitual curbside spot for deposit and collection. Once

194

he had completed his rituals, he waited for Erika to take over. She dropped the sealed bag of eliminated waste into the corner trash can and led him toward Fifth Avenue, already envisioning an improvised tour of Central Park—of winding paths and swaths of green, of foot bridges and fountains, of getting lost, of finding their way, of brisk strides slowing to weaving amble, of resting on one of the benches lining the lane and bending to pet Jake, the old pup exhausted but happy to be in the world with her; she, with him.

Their outing, including Jake's bench-side snooze, went on far longer than Erika had anticipated. Still, there had been plenty of time to collect her thoughts over a cup of coffee and an English muffin before calling Harrison. She was getting ready to leave a message for him when he picked up. She repressed the urge to ask him why he'd taken so long to answer the phone.

"I was going to try to reach you again," he started right off. He sounded reserved or subdued, she couldn't tell which.

"Aha," she said, adding a little mystery herself.

"Hold on a minute, okay?"

There was a brief interval of scuffling sounds during which a composite of movie scenes looped through her brain.

"I'm here," he said.

"You retreat to the bathroom for privacy?" she asked, against her better judgment.

"What? I was in the middle of taking my jacket off!"

"I was thinking you may have company. Not that I'd blame you."

"Not that you'd blame me, or not that you'd put it past me?"

"I'm sorry, I didn't mean that." (She did.)

"You did," he said.

"How was your trip?" she asked.

"Tolerable."

"The accommodations?"

"The inn is great, only the suite is too large for a party of one."

Was he missing her, or reminding her what she was missing? "I'm glad you like it. It looked beautiful in the brochure." She felt the distance between them as if it were taffy; she didn't know if he was stretching it to pull himself farther away or tugging at it to draw her near.

"We really must talk," he said, so softly she could hardly hear him.

That was ominous. "Of course. We will." She had no idea—did not want to know, not now—whether he had any specific subject in mind. "Are you lecturing tomorrow?" she asked, swerving to neutral ground.

"You *know* I am," he said, still in that near whisper, but edging into the war zone.

She sat motionless, like an animal avoiding detection.

"Erika?"

"You must be beat after the trip and settling in. I won't keep you. Good luck tomorrow."

"Thanks," he said. "We'll talk soon." He sounded so far away. She imagined the distance between them stretched to the snapping point.

"Yes, soon," she said, not lifting a finger as the tether broke and he drifted off into space.

Chapter 19

I t was three days into Harrison's tour, Erika thought as she pulled up the trousers of her navy pantsuit. The symposium hosted by the Studio Arts College International in Florence, Italy, must be in full swing at this moment—5:00 p.m. for him; 11 a.m. for her. The conference was designed to explore the influence of mental disorder in the visual arts. Harrison's topic: four generations of madness in Gericault's family culminating in his *Les Monomanes*—Portraits of the Insane. Harrison might be holding forth even as she zipped her pants and threw on her jacket, tousled her cropped hair, and finished her what-to-wear-to-a-sting look with a conservative pair of gold stud earrings. Speaking of madness.

As she laced up her sneakers, she remembered, with a wave of remorse, how Jeremy had scolded her for wearing heels on their fateful visit to G&G's. Jeremy had lost his life bowing to her willful demands. Would this morning's exploit put any other lives in danger? She set her jaw and yanked at her laces, tying them punishingly close to the point of losing circulation.

She grabbed her tote bag and stepped out of the Blue Room, almost colliding with Grace, just arriving.

"There's a Mr. Smith asking for you at the front gate," Grace reported, narrow-eyed. "You want to check him out on the monitor?" Her look signaled that Erika might be back on probation.

Erika grabbed her tote bag and headed for the stairs leading to the lobby. "That's okay, Grace, I'm expecting him. I'm scheduled to review a bunch of art exhibitions at galleries around town. Smith's my photographer."

"And Mr. Harry?"

Erika stopped dead in her tracks. "What about him?"

"If he calls. Are you reachable?"

"My cell will be off for a while," she said. "Not to worry. Harrison and I are good."

* * *

Greg was waiting just outside the gate, his hand resting on the black canvas satchel slung over his shoulder. "All set?" he asked as Erika disengaged the lock.

"I hope so." She snapped the gate shut behind her.

"Wrong answer."

"I'm all set," she revised, tensing. There were three vehicles parked in front of her building: a stretch limo, an unmarked minivan, and its broader, taller big brother. "All for us?"

Greg offered a forbearing smile. "Yes. You're in the limo. The minivan carries a number of FBI agents who'll be in tactical gear, ready for onsite deployment. The heftier version—where I'll be—is the command center vehicle, with eyes and ears on every compartment of the armored transport that contains the Vermeer. The armored vehicle is presently in transit."

"Will the FBI agents be—"

He held up his hand. "Don't crowd your mind with details. Let's go."

He ushered her to the limo. The windows were deeply tinted, so it was not until Greg opened the rear door that Erika discovered John sitting in the back seat. She knew the FBI had done a rigorous background check on the detective and in the end had accepted him as a member of the team, no party-crashing required. But no one had told her when he was due to enter the scene. "Good to see you," she said, sliding in next to him.

"Likewise."

Greg stepped into the limo and settled into the leather seat across from Erika and John. He placed the satchel by his side. "Before I go, let me give you these," he said, zipping open the bag's side pocket. "It's a last-minute idea; came up with it this morning, in fact." He removed two small plastic bags.

John leaned in. "Ear buds," he said.

Greg handed each of them a bag. "They're the latest, virtually invisible. Can each of you insert your bud in your preferred ear?"

John had no trouble placing his; Erika, afraid she'd push too hard and lose the thing down her throat, required John's practiced hand. Greg zipped open the central section of his satchel and fiddled with a metal device sitting inside it. He pulled a headband linked to a mic nodule out of the bag and brought the mic close to his lips. "Coming through?" he asked softly. "I know it's hard to tell at such close range."

"It's working," John said; Erika nodded.

"Okay, then. I can message you if necessary. Remember, I'll be in the command vehicle with the tech team. With all the spyware secured in the transport vehicle, we'll be able to see and hear what's happening with you at all times. Questions? Make them relevant. We're on a tight schedule."

"Were you able to reach George Dudley?" Erika asked.

"Ah, the owner of Hebborn's forged Rembrandt. I spoke to his wife. The painting was not on the wall, contrary to Randall's report. She said it had been stolen. Our conversation was cut short, but my guess is that Elliot or his handlers faked a heist, split the insurance payment with Dudley, and then sold the painting at top dollar on the black market. Based on the clues surrounding the 1996 incident at Christie's, I believe that's the way they work: a profitable double-dip. If the painting's authentic, they just reverse the script and threaten to expose the real thing as a forgery. All right, now we've got to get moving. Be on the lookout."

Greg gathered his gear and took off at a trot to the command vehicle. As the limo door shut behind him, the partition between the fore and aft cabins automatically slid open, and two young men in black suits, white shirts, and black ties turned to face the rear. Scrubbed and fresh-faced, so similar in age, and both of stalwart demeanor, they could be twins, Erika thought. She almost asked them, if only to ease the knot in her belly.

The one behind the wheel addressed them. "We've given John a heads-up on our preliminary tactic. He'll relay the information to you. When the actual event transpires, try not to overplay your part."

"In other words, don't ham it up," his look-alike added. "It would arouse suspicion. Anyone want something to drink—non-alcoholic, of course?"

Erika and John declined.

"You change your mind, give us a shout-out." The partition slid shut.

Erika turned to John. "Who are these people, FBI agents?"

"Yes, I checked their credentials."

"They're straight—not posing as anyone other than themselves?"

"Correct."

The car pulled away from the curb.

"Where are we going?" Erika asked.

"I don't know. We don't have hoods over our heads, so I guess they're not hiding anything from us."

She twisted around to look out the rear window to check the convoy. "They're coming with us," she commented, more to herself than John. She turned back to face him. "I thought you were going to fill me in."

"I know we're going to be subject to a pat-down. Are you carrying?"

His directness threw her off guard. "No."

"Good. We'll be relieved of our cell phones as well. I suggest you turn yours off now."

Hands trembling—*damn it!*—she dug for her phone and shut it off. It felt like she was defusing a time bomb. She flung it back into her bag.

He touched her arm; she flinched. "It's hitting home, isn't it?" he asked. "This is not a board game. This is the real thing."

"I thought I was prepared."

He touched her arm again. This time she didn't jump. "You *are* prepared, Erika. This is your first time in the field. You're doing just great."

"Don't patronize me, John."

He grinned. "*There's* my girl. It didn't take much."

She suppressed a comeback and looked out the side window to establish her connection with the world beyond what seemed like their ever-contracting capsule. "We're heading downtown on Lexington," she said evenly. "We just passed Seventy-second Street." She pressed the control button to open the window, take in the urban air with its familiar smells. She had a wayward thought: Jake, bounding for his pee tree. The window didn't budge. She tried again. Were they really sealed in?

"Stop fidgeting with the controls," John said. "The windows are locked for our safety, not to imprison us. I heard from Charlene, by the way."

"She said she was going to call you."

"A real teaser, coming up with fingerprints on a cigarette lighter. The lighter was probably lost on a previous car rental, or dropped between rentals by someone on the dealer's clean-up squad. I wouldn't get your hopes up. Or Charlene's."

"It's hard not to," Erika said, peering out the glass barrier at what felt like a forbidden land.

* * *

Ten minutes later the convoy was lined up curbside on 38th Street, between First Avenue and the East River, illegally taking over the bike lane and then some. Randall and Elliot must have been alerted beforehand because they came marching through the swinging rear door of Randall's building and up the ramp of the building's loading dock toward the parked vehicles. Elliot brought up the rear, trailing a carry-on suitcase with a retractable handle. Both men looked dressed for the prom, minus the carnations. Elliot was wearing his pointed snakeskin boots; no surprise.

Two FBI agents in full gear jumped from the van parked behind the limo. They waited, hands resting on holstered weapons, at the top of the rise, where the ramp met the sidewalk. The limo's partition slid open, and the driver instructed Erika and John to exit the vehicle via the passenger side and take their places on either side of the agents. "Keep your hands in full view at all times," he cautioned, "or our agents will react with force. It's a matter of maintaining credibility. The show must go on, and all that. Take your bag, ma'am."

John grabbed Erika's attention with a penetrating gaze. "Remember," he half-whispered, "not everything is what it seems." He pushed open the door.

She answered with a quizzical look, but John was already moving out, and she had no option but to mutely follow his lead.

And then, she panicked: she had forgotten to warn Randall not to let on that he had met John. There was no doubt that such an unlikely meeting would arouse suspicion in a mind—Elliot's—already primed for connivance. But Randall seemed to have realized this. "Who the hell are *you*?" he aimed at John—overacting, but convincing enough to stanch Erika's fears.

"This is private detective John Mitchell," Erika said, taking her place alongside one of the FBI agents. "He's my bodyguard, and he's been vetted for this mission."

"Cocktail chat on your own time, folks," the agent on the other side of the line-up snapped. "Hands over your heads, please. Handbag at your feet. Suitcase flat on the ground."

Erika dropped her handbag on the pavement and threw up her hands. She glanced over at the agent who had just spoken. The voice had been female; a surprise. Its owner, beautiful; also off-stereotype. If she had been less attractive or dressed in Catwoman's unitard, the discrepancy between a real-life heroine and a crafted icon would not have been so blatant. In contrast, the male agent alongside Erika was the conventional composite of firefighter and Batman. Thoroughly, but with respect, he patted her down, then picked up her bag and pawed inside it. He came up with her cell phone and pocketed it. "All clear. You can put your hands down." He handed her the bag and moved on to Elliot.

Elliot was not in possession of a weapon. The agent relieved him of his cell phone and squatted in front of his carry-on suitcase.

"Careful," Elliot warned, as the agent zipped open the case. "I've got expensive equipment in there. You break it, you pay for it."

As the agent rummaged through the bubble-wrapped devices in Elliot's suitcase, Erika watched his female counterpart confiscate John's revolver and cell phone before proceeding to Randall. Randall struck a casual pose, but when he glanced over at Erika, his eyes betrayed his fear. She tried to send him a bring-it-on look of fortitude, but she could tell he wasn't moved by it. The agent dumped Randall's only confiscate-able item, his cell phone, into her pocket and waited, with the rest of the group, for her partner to complete his examination of Elliot's suitcase.

A woman carrying a small dog with a leash dangling from its collar walked out the door of the animal shelter neighboring the apartment building. A look of surprise followed by terror followed by attempted indifference flashed across her countenance like pages in a flip book.

"Nothing to see here," the female agent declared.

The woman closed her eyes for a second, as if taking the words literally, then about-faced to head toward the river—anything to avoid having to walk the gauntlet.

"Watch how you handle it!" Elliot directed at the agent zipping up his suitcase. "Don't press on it so damn hard!"

"All of you, seat yourselves in the car," the agent instructed, as if Elliot hadn't spoken. He hand-signaled the driver to pop the hood of the trunk and delivered the carry-on to its berth as Elliot looked on, shifting his weight from one foot to another, as if he had an itch it would have been unseemly to scratch.

As the agents returned to their van, Erika and her travel-mates piled into the limo, she and John returning to the seats they had occupied, Randall and Elliot taking their places opposite. Erika took a good look at Elliot, whose unsettled mood was a reminder to keep her own on course. *Steady now. Here we go.*

* * *

"Any of you know where the hell we're going?" Elliot griped, once the convoy was underway.

"To wherever they're holding the Vermeer," Randall replied, playing it cool.

"Well, *that's* enlightening! I'm having second thoughts about this," Elliot declared irritably, his British accent abandoning him with his chagrin. "I should have at least demanded my fee up front!"

"The lawyer representing the Gardner Museum will be handing you and Randall your payments on site," Erika lied.

"He *better* be!" Randall declared, playing his role with conviction. He pinned Erika with a stern look. "Why aren't you taking notes? I thought you were coming along to get a scoop for your magazine!"

"I am," she played along, "only I'm not allowed to carry any writing materials." She
wished Randall would stop flaunting his adversarial role before it aroused suspicion, especially when Elliot seemed particularly ripe for it.

Soon Elliot's question regarding their destination was answered: the limo began cruising west along 80th Street toward the majestic facade of the Metropolitan Museum of Art. At Fifth Avenue it continued on course, bearing them straight onto the paved entryway of the museum's parking garage.

Elliot was the first to react audibly. "Surely, you're kidding! Are we to be part of an exhibition? A master class, perhaps?" His acquired accent had returned.

"They must have closed part of the garage to the public," Randall mused.

Erika looked out the rear window. As expected, the escorts were right behind as the procession moved past the toll booth and up the ramp, past the crowded first and second tiers of the garage. Two FBI agents in full regalia stood at the juncture where the winding ramp leveled off at the entrance to the third tier. With nods of recognition to the limo driver and his mate, they waved the brigade through.

A large boxy-looking vehicle stood alone in the middle of the concrete expanse, like a bully in a schoolyard: clearly the armored transport that contained the Vermeer. Four FBI agents, each clutching a rifle, were stationed by its side. The agents advanced toward the convoy as it approached. With stiff-armed gestures, they signaled that the drivers park at a distance. After the three vehicles had been maneuvered into a line-up at least fifteen feet away from the transport, the agents backed off and returned to their posts.

The agent in the limo's passenger seat hopped out and threw open the rear door. "Let's move it along, guys," he requested with a pretense of camaraderie.

As the four took turns climbing out of the limo, the trunk lid floated open.

"Careful with my bag," Elliot warned, as the agent went to fetch it. "I'll take it from here."

"Be my guest," the agent said, handing the suitcase over.

Elliot extended the handle and positioned the bag for towage as Erika secretly cheered the apparent recovery of Elliot's confidence: it meant he was more likely to try something.

The agent brushed by Elliot to lead the party to the waiting transport. The closer Erika got to it, the more unassailable it seemed: steel ram bumpers, grill guards, barred windows, multiple door locks. It looked more like a mobile prison than a transport of fine art. Yet it was only when its massive rear doors were drawn open by the coordinated efforts of their FBI escort that Erika felt the full impact of the mission.

"Don't worry," came a whisper in her ear, like a jolt from her alter ego; in reality, Greg, checking in with a word of assurance. "Our eyes and ears are on you."

* * *

The agent serving as escort was the first to board the transport. He reached out to take Erika's hand to help her mount the steep step leading to its interior, but she chose to grab the sidebars on either side of the entryway instead. "Thanks," she said, to soften the rejection.

Elliot was right behind. He retracted the handle of his carry-on and hefted the bag onto the transport's steel floor, then clambered aboard. John and Randall brought up the rear. Erika found herself standing between Randall and Elliot, Elliot's suitcase tucked beside her right leg, as if it were hers.

Before them, three men sat on metal stools regarding them all with unabashed interest. Erika felt like an immigrant facing a tribunal, waiting to receive permission to enter the new world. The transport's interior was encased in steel, floor to ceiling, and beyond the silent council, a large metal table stood bolted to the floor. Next to it, a formidable-looking safe protruded from the wall, as if it had forced its way in. Further toward the front of the vehicle, a steel bulkhead separated the main area from what had to be the driver's compartment.

The FBI escort stepped forward. "Introductions," he announced. He gestured toward the nearest seated individual, a young man in sneakers, jeans, white shirt, and navy windbreaker with an FBI emblem on its pocket. The jacket was open and slightly drawn to one side, providing a good view of the firearm tucked in its holster. "You're looking at one of the two members of our art theft team on board," the escort declared. "Let's call him Agent X." He flashed a no-nonsense smile as the young man acknowledged recognition with a nod.

The portly gentleman in a pin-striped suit sitting alongside Agent X was introduced next. "This is Mr. Yardsdale," the escort began.

"Yards*dell*, the gentleman corrected, with a high-minded sniff. "But, whatever."

"Sorry. Mr. Yards*dell* is the lawyer representing the Gardner Museum. He'll be acting as its proxy in the transfer of funds—thirty million—to the account set up by the party relinquishing the artwork, going by the name of John Doe. Mr. Yardsdell will make it clear to Mr. Doe that the transfer will activate only when said work is safely in possession of the museum. Agreement papers on both sides will be signed and witnessed." To the undercover agent, aka Mr. Yardsdell, he asked, "How am I doing, sir?"

"Doing good," the poseur replied. "Doing good."

"And this is the attorney representing John Doe: Mr. Caputo," the escort announced, referring to the third seated observer, atypically slim for a mob associate, although the wide lapels of his shiny black suit jacket were a somewhat convincing counter-measure. Erika glanced at Elliot to check if he was buying the act so far. He was leaning in, a rapt and hungry look about him, causing her to conclude, at least provisionally, that he was.

The escort went on to introduce the members of what he characterized as the "incoming team," pointing to each in turn:

"Erika Shawn-Wheatley, an editor at *Art News* magazine. She helped us track down Mr. Doe and persuade him to come to the negotiating table. The only reward she requires is that we allow her exclusive rights to the story. Next, we have Mr. Winston Elliot, a highly respected art authenticator specializing in Vermeer and his contemporaries. He'll be confirming the authentication of the painting. Randall Gray, president of the G&G art consulting firm here in Manhattan, will be assisting him. Lastly, we have Private Detective John Mitchell. He's here to serve as Erika's bodyguard."

"Gotta protect her from us hot dudes," the fictitious Mr. Caputo threw in.

Eliding the remark, the presiding agent asked, "Questions?" He waited five seconds. "All right. We can admit Mr. Doe at this time. We did not want him privy to any sensitive matters that may have come up before this point." He turned to Agent X. "Give the signal, please."

Agent X pressed one of the buttons on a metal plate mounted on the wall at arm's reach. A narrow panel in the bulwark that enclosed the driver's compartment slid forward, and its occupants emerged: a man whose attire matched Agent X's, and an individual outfitted in black high-top sneakers, black tracksuit, and black ski mask that revealed, through its single opening, a set of piercing blue eyes.

"For the sake of efficiency," the agent in charge started right in, "we'll call our driver Agent Y. The man beside him is John Doe. Mr. Doe has understandably chosen to conceal his face. Now—it's all yours."

Without uttering another word, the agent brushed past Erika and company and exited the vehicle with an effortless jump. Agent X, taking over, pressed another button—this one red—on the wall plate, and the rear doors noisily lumbered shut. A brief silence followed, and then a metal scraping and snapping from outside the vehicle indicated that the final step of lockdown was being performed.

With everyone sealed in, Agent X rose from his stool and strutted toward the front of the chamber. Agent Y and John Doe stepped aside to allow him access to the wall safe's lock. At the click of the lock, he swung open the door to the safe and removed a black leather portfolio that measured about three by four feet.

Instinctively, Erika and her crew stepped closer to the table, Elliot the most aggressive of the four, halting only when his waist was in direct contact with the table's edge. He signaled for Randall to draw near. Randall acquiesced, darting a furtive glance at Erika. It caused her instant consternation: *what was that all about?*

The "lawyers," Yardsdell and Caputo, rose from their stools to join the others at ringside as Agent X lay the portfolio on the table and proceeded to unzip it.

"Wait!" Elliot cried, throwing up his hand.

Agent X froze mid-action. "What the hell!"

Elliot lay his carry-on flat on the floor and squatted in front of it. Erika felt the agents grow tense, both the obvious agents and the ones playing other parts. Elliot zipped it open and fussed about its interior before pulling out a Ziploc bag containing a small stack of white cotton gloves. He flipped shut the case and stood back up. "Help yourself," he said, unzipping the plastic bag and holding it open in front of the agent, as if he were proffering a bag of gumdrops.

"Ah, yes," Agent X replied, plucking out a pair of gloves and pulling them on. "Thank you."

"No problem," the art expert sniffed, throwing back his shoulders. "By the way, what is the ambient temperature in this cell of ours?"

"The museum dictated the rules. We've got the AC set at seventy-one degrees Fahrenheit so that the relative humidity favors optimal preservation."

"That's suitable," Elliot pronounced, as if he were handing down a judicial ruling. He directed a sober nod at the leather portfolio. "Let's see what we've got here."

The agent unzipped the portfolio and carefully lay it open, revealing a sheet of foam packing custom cut to the specifications of the case. He removed the packing sheet and handed it to Agent Y, who set it inside the safe. Then, with gloved fingers, Agent X carefully peeled away the remaining layers of protection: four sheets of parchment paper, these also cut to size.

Erika's breath caught as she beheld the unframed *Concert* adhering to its flimsy square of canvas cloth, an artifact at once immortal and subject to instant destruction: with one wrong move, it could be torn to shreds or go up in flames. She wished she could see the expressions on Elliot and Randall's faces, either admiration or avarice. It would be telling to know which, especially in light of that perplexing glance Randall had thrown her way. Was she naïve not to have considered the possibility of Randall's blowing his cover to Elliot out of fear or greed?

"Please remove the canvas from the portfolio so I can examine it properly," Elliot said, with no discernible emotion. "And give us some breathing room here. Move aside. Thank you." He leaned toward Randall and whispered something in his ear. Randall nodded in response.

The seemingly harmless exchange threw Erika's suspicions into high gear. As she stepped to the side along with her fellow cast members, leaving only the "lawyers" and John Doe with Elliot and Randall, she was inwardly bombarded. Should she tell someone about the looks she'd noticed passing between them, and risk aborting the mission? And what did those looks mean: had Randall been promised a share in the ultimate cash coup in exchange for giving Elliot a heads up? Was Erika's state of heightened awareness tricking her into seeing things that might have gone unnoticed, or into seeing things that weren't there? Though in the company of conspicuously armed federal agents, what could Randall and Elliot possibly hope to pull off in this impenetrable cocoon, beyond the predicted scam? There was no imminent threat to life and limb, so wasn't it best if she let things ride rather than abort an operation that could potentially expose a den of thieves, and worse?

The answer was expressed by her inaction, and she watched Elliot remove the tools of his trade from his suitcase and arrange them on the metal table alongside the precious canvas, then distribute his cache of white gloves to Randall and the three FBI agents role-playing as lawyers and mob affiliate John Doe.

"We have here," Elliot began, striking a pose reminiscent of a Rembrandt portrait, "a domestic scene in which members of the bourgeoisie—upper bourgeoisie, as demonstrated by the attire and accoutrements—are engaged in making music. The painting is stunning, certainly, and if by chance—highly unlikely—that it turns out to be a counterfeit"—he uttered a dismissive guffaw—"it will be a magnificent one. No painting by Han van Meegeren, the notorious Vermeer forger, could hold a candle to it."

"Move it along," the fictitious Mr. Caputo cut in. "My client and I are not here to be lectured."

"This picture's no fake," his masked cohort added gruffly.

Elliot appeared to be unfazed. "I was about to point out that van Meegeren's poorly executed forgery was given the stamp of approval by the noted twentieth century art historian, Abraham Bredius, but that it would not have gotten past *my* scrutiny." He picked up a magnifying glass from the table and turned it over in his hands. "May I remind you, gentlemen, the Gardner Museum reached out to *me*, not the other way around. You will therefore be obliged to suffer my rules. Rule number one. Do not rush me."

The agent playing Caputo threw up his hands. "Take all the time you want."

"Thank you." Elliot bent over the painting, bringing the magnifying glass very close to the canvas. "I'm looking first at the convolutions of the exposed ears, both the harpsichord player's"—he froze a moment before moving the glass several inches to the right—"and now the singer's." He stayed with the singer a bit longer. "Not bad. On a proof-of-authenticity scale of one to ten, I'd give it a six point five. Anyone familiar with the Giovanni Morelli method?" Without waiting for an answer, he continued: "Morelli was a nineteenth century art critic who studied medicine and developed a keen eye for the anatomical details unique to each artist. He was the Sherlock Holmes of authentication, and I strive to follow his example."

Elliot returned to his perusal. "I'm looking again at the singer—the position of her fingers, the posture of her wrist. Hmm. I'm rating it dead center at a five, and not a rousing one at that. Let's proceed to the stereoscopic microscope, Randall. I think I'll save the full spectroscopy for later." To the attendant trio of undercover agents, he explained, "Spectroscopy compares the wave lengths of a particular color that we want to identify to an established database, so that we can check if, say, Vermeer's natural ultramarine is indeed the color in situ—that is, on the canvas." Back to Randall: "Please prepare the painting. In my suitcase you'll find a sterile cloth that will protect the canvas from contact with the base of the device. An observation hole has been cut out in the cloth, which you will place directly over this area of tiled flooring in the painting. I will be examining the signs of aging: craquelure, pigment crystallinity, and the like."

Erika knew where this act was leading: Elliot's 'discovery' that the painting was a forgery, and his subsequent attempt to coerce John Doe and his sleazy lawyer into making a sweet enough deal for him to suppress his findings. She wondered how he planned to communicate with Doe without any of the others catching on. In writing? In whispers? His mind must be racing to come up with a convincing ploy.

She planned to save him the trouble. "Mr. Yardsdell," she began, all business-like, "may I have a word with you? I'd like to ask you a couple of questions for my magazine article regarding the transfer of funds, as well as the curatorial plans for exhibiting the Vermeer both here and abroad." She gestured toward the rear of the transport. "We don't want to disturb these gentlemen."

The bogus Mr. Yardsdell jumped to Erika's bidding almost too eagerly, as the balance of the troupe—John Mitchell and Agents X and Y—took her directive as their cue to move to the rear as well.

They carried on a brief phony conversation about the funds transfer in full voice to create the impression of journalistic legitimacy as she turned her back on the individuals huddled around the Vermeer. As John began another staged comment, Erika whispered to her companions, moving her lips so that Greg and the others stationed in the command vehicle could read them. "Keep an eye on Randall; he may have turned."

"Bring it on," Agent X whispered back. "The more the merrier. We want to smoke out as many players as possible. Any which way they come at us, we win, hands down."

"Cracks in the paint," Greg transmitted through Erika's ear bud. "Elliot's saying they're too superficial, given the age of a Vermeer painting. He's on a roll."

Great, Erika wanted to say aloud, but she held her tongue. No one but she and John knew about the ear buds, and the secret was a comfort, like an invisible friend.

"Erika, would you come here a minute?" Elliot beckoned from the far side of the examination table. "We've got a question."

Erika about-faced. "Sure thing," she replied. She took a step forward, worried John would follow her, but he allowed her to proceed alone, although he flared his nostrils in objection to their separation.

"What's up?" she asked Elliot with excruciating nonchalance as she arrived.

Elliot shrugged. "Mr. Doe says he wants to ask you a question, since you were the one who arranged this shebang."

"I didn't exactly *arrange* it," Erika demurred. "I might have had a minor—"

"Shut the fuck up!" the spurious John Doe barked. "Shit, I'm sweating like a pig in this thing."

Erika was impressed—the agent was really playing the part of an ill-mannered gangster—but then she felt her jaw drop as he tore off his ski mask and threw it to the floor. Instantly, as if by a magician's sleight of hand, a pistol was in his grasp.

She imagined the dropped jaws on the men in the rear of the cabin, including Mitchell. For a split second, she anticipated the men drawing their weapons on the aggressor before realizing that she, Randall, and Elliot, by standing across the table from him, were providing a shield for him.

A single word was pitched from Randall's throat in bewildered recognition: "*You?*"

Erika's attention snapped to Randall as the ostensible Caputo, standing two feet from the gunslinger and on the same side of the table as he lunged for him. In one movement, the hand wielding the gun whipped sideways to crack the butt against the agent's skull, and then, as the agent dropped to the floor like a rag doll, swung back to its original position.

Greg's voice, as if it were generated by her brain, softly exploded in her ear: "Fuck! He's one of them!"

Chapter 20

For a moment—he knew it would not last long—Harrison found himself seated alone at a cocktail table meant to accommodate four. If he remained relatively still, he mused, perhaps this welcome lapse of inclusion might be extended a bit longer, while the milling crowd of symposium participants and honored guests be allowed to munch their Florentine hors d'oeuvres and chat up a storm without the nuisance of engaging him.

After the presentations—his had gone remarkably well, although the students had bombarded him with follow-up questions on Gericault's madness rather than on the portraitist's ability to humanize the mad—the speakers and select guests had worked their way from the clubby lecture hall through the Baroque-renovated art gallery with its high-vaulted ceilings and frescoed walls, finally arriving in the lovely courtyard garden of the Palazzo dei Cartelloni, where Harrison now sat in welcome solitude. The sun was setting, yet even in the day's dimming, the colors of the garden, with all its varied greenery, its tidy hedges and unruly trees, were vibrant still, clinging to the fading light like a lover unwilling to part from his sweetheart's gaze. The sky, a bold spread of Titian's ultramarine streaked with azure and yellow ochre, was touched by a single daub of white-infused red earth, so pale a blush Harrison might have missed it had he been less observant.

What is it about Florence, he wondered as his gaze settled on his folded hands, resting on the table and looking like they were wrapped in thoughts of their own. The play of light here, the colors: were they really so exquisitely unique, or did the expectation of beauty impose itself on reality?

"You must try a *crostini*," came a vaguely familiar voice from above. Harrison looked up, surprised to encounter the striking figure of Aldo Fabbri pressing forward a fair young tray-bearer, his hand at the small of her back.

Harrison's love fest with Florence was instantly tarnished. "Good to see you," he said nevertheless, extending his hand to Aldo before plucking an hors d'oeuvre of bread and chicken liver pate from the waitress's tray. "Come sit down," he suggested with a near-genuine smile.

"*Certamente*," said Aldo. "But first we must request the wine—from the Fabbri vineyard, of course." Aldo turned to the waitress. "*Per favore*, a bottle of the Chianti Classico riserva," he slickly commanded, with a proprietary ogle. "As you might recall," he said, turning back to Harrison, "it's our signature wine, made from the Sangiovese grape. This year's crop"—he glanced heavenward—"*supremo!*" With a nod, he dismissed the waitress, then pulled out a chair.

"I didn't see you at the conference," Harrison said, trying not to recollect in vivid detail Aldo's play for Erika's affections at their encounter in Tuscany over a year ago. The seduction attempt had taken place when he and Erika had visited the Fabbri estate as part of their art recovery mission. Erika had not succumbed to Aldo's efforts, but her moment of hesitation had caused Harrison great consternation. *What a presumptive asshole!* he silently hurled at himself. Erika had been in the initial stages of breaking free of her mistrust in men because of what she was beginning to see in Harrison, and he had not shown her the least bit of empathy in response. "The lecture hall was rather crowded," he said, thrusting his attention to the subject at hand. "Perhaps you were hiding in the rear?"

"Alas, I arrived too late to attend the talks," Aldo said, smoothing back his coal black mane.

He's lost the golden highlights, Harrison realized. Gives the bastard a less flighty look.

"However, I did hear your talk on Gericault was admirable—ah, here's our wine," Aldo noted, at the waitress's approach.

The wine was uncorked; the glasses filled; hearty samples downed; Harrison's authentic praise begrudgingly delivered.

"To a successful book tour!" Aldo sang, raising his glass. "*Salute!*"

As they clicked glasses, Aldo cocked his head, as if at a sound in the distance. "I'm wondering. Whatever became of that woman you were with—Erika Shawn was her name, *una donna molto bella e special!* As I recall, a free spirit finding herself tethered to Puritanism, or merely conflicted by it. Either way, a pity."

"Tethered to me, if you must know," Harrison said, as coolly as his clenched jaw would allow. "As my wife."

"Ah, lucky man to have tamed her!" Aldo looked about. "But where is she? Another toast is in order!"

"Back home, in New York. Working."

"Yes?" Aldo gave him a bemused smile. "Quite a long tether, I'd say."

The mockery, however benign its motivation, immediately reawakened the fears instilled by Harrison's brilliantly deceitful ex-wife. In the conversational pause that ensued, a joyful hosanna struck the air: "Professor Wheatley!"

"What?" Harrison snapped, looking up. It was a fellow speaker, Diana Prescott, the Goya expert. "Sorry, Diana. Here, sit with us."

It was uncanny how close a likeness Diana bore to Gustav Klimt's portrait of Adele Bloch: tall, palely beautiful in a multi-colored dress, predominantly gold, her upswept black hair giving her an extra four inches. He wondered if the likeness was, in fact, purposeful. Diana, he noticed, was holding a copy of his book.

Aldo jumped to his feet and pulled out a chair for the woman. She politely nodded and then, upon seating, edged her chair closer to Harrison's. Laying the book on the table, she said, "I picked up a copy last minute. You'd already run off. You must sign it."

"Sure," Harrison said, still churlish, but softening. "Let me introduce you."

Aldo, who had brazenly reduced the distance between his and Diana's chairs as he returned to his seated position, lifted his gaze from a tour of her body and aimed it intently on her dark brown eyes, as if it had never been elsewhere.

"Dr. Diana Prescott, Aldo Fabbri," Harrison formally delivered. "Dr. Prescott teaches at—Yale, is it?"—Diana smiled her assent—"and Mr. Fabbri is a vintner of considerable note."

Fingertip handshakes were performed and first-name etiquette duly insisted on. Aldo called for another bottle of the Chianti and a glass for the "*bella donna,*" and Harrison signed Diana's copy of his book with a generic reference to the conference, along with his well-wishes. The downturn of Diana's Klimt-red lips indicated her disappointment.

A swirl of guests and servers, like a murmuration of birds, seemed suddenly to envelop the small party, plying them with small talk and garlicky finger foods, only to swoop away moments later, leaving them to their own devices. Aldo filled Diana's glass, which had been delivered along with the second bottle of wine. After refilling his own glass and topping off Harrison's, he turned to Diana and asked—leaning in and sotto voce, as if the question were too delicate to be overheard—"So, *amore mio,* what was the main gist of your talk?"

"My focus was Goya's 'Black Pictures' period, 1820 to 1823," Diana answered curtly, in lieu, it appeared, of a slap in the face. She swiveled to Harrison. "His symptoms were manifold—depression, delirium—"

"Hallucinations, weight loss," Harrison supplied.

Diana nodded. "Making it difficult to pinpoint a single cause."

"The causes, as you pointed out, were manifold as well," Harrison pitched in. He took a generous swig of his wine, emptying his glass.

"Exactly," Diana said, touching his forearm and then quickly removing it, the suddenness of the withdrawal only drawing attention to what otherwise would have been considered a harmless gesture. "There was the matter of syphilis, as well as his extensive contact with the mercury and lead contained in his paint pigments."

Harrison removed the stopper of the second wine bottle and refilled his glass. "The question is, what influence did his madness have, good or bad, on his work?" As he took a serious draw of the wine, he thought of Goya's images—*Saturn Devouring His Son*, in particular—painted on the walls of a farmhouse during that critical period. The images were transferred onto canvas fifty years later, and in the course of that project, the originals were virtually destroyed. It brought to mind how, hundreds of years before, Michelangelo's cartoon of the *Battle of Cascina* had been destroyed by over-eager copyists. More poignantly, it brought to mind how he and Erika had talked at length about the subject while on their hunt for lost art.

Harrison was about to bring this observation to light, but for no apparent reason—or none that he would admit to—he chose not to. Instead, he had another go at his wine.

Chapter 21

"Anyone else?" the assailant inquired, narrowly eying each member of his captive audience in turn.

Randall opened his mouth to speak, but shut it when eye contact was fixed on him.

"Good. Let's get rolling. Elliot, I want you to—"

Elliot froze.

"Yeah, I know your name and game, buddy," said the assailant. "So if you want to come out ahead, listen up. There's duct tape in the safe. I want you to secure this guy's wrists and ankles and take possession of his gun." He cocked his head toward the downed agent.

Elliot seemed not to have heard.

"Before he comes to and orders a Martini, okay?"

Erika ransacked her brain. How had their assailant subdued the FBI agent assigned the role of John Doe? Was the original agent dead or alive? How was it possible for an outsider to have gotten so far?

Elliot had nearly completed the task of binding the supposed Caputo's ankles and wrists with duct tape when the agent came to. "What the *fuck!*" he complained, struggling uselessly against his restraints.

"Quiet!" the instigator of the assault demanded. He was now wielding two pistols, his own and one he'd ordered Elliot to extract from the victim. One was trained on Erika, the other on the men in the rear of the compartment, poised like caged animals.

Where had Erika seen this man's face? His silky brown hair, parted in the middle, the hawkish nose? Was it an image from an old photo album, a relative long gone? Then she remembered: the photograph in Randall's office.

"Just been told this fuck's an FBI agent in the art crime division," Greg buzzed in her ear. "That's why his pic didn't show up in my data base. You're doing great, Erika. Stay calm and do what he says. You, too, John. Keep cool."

Randall, who had been complying with orders by preparing the Vermeer for transport, closed the flap of the leather portfolio.

"Zip it up," the commando ordered. "Secure the tabs with the lock—combo's eight-four-seven-three-nine."

"Hunter, what the hell's going on?" an agent bellowed from the rear. "Come to your senses, man!"

Hunter? Erika's motionless figure turned rigid as her thoughts flashed to the night of Jeremy's murder. Was it coincidence, or could it be that the traitorous agent was a relative of Candice Hunter, the woman who had been in Randall's office that night? Did she have something to do with the murder? Had she *ordered* it? Erika's impulse was to come right out with it, provoke a reaction. She decided to keep it to herself as a possible ace up her sleeve.

With the barrel of the gun in his right hand pointing directly at Erika's head, Agent Hunter swept the one clutched in his left hand over the group. Facing him, Erika could only see his stiff left arm swinging back and forth. He was almost taunting them, judging from his impish expression and pointed disregard of his colleague's entreaty.

"Elliot," Hunter said, without taking his eyes off the rear of the compartment. "Collect the weapons from the rest of the crew. Who's the clown in the gray blazer? I was holed up in the driver's cabin for act one. He wasn't part of the original cast of characters."

"Let me at him!" John roared.

"Stay the hell put, John!" Greg rasped into the ear buds. "Fuck!"

Erika heard the scuffle behind her as the agents wrestled with John.

"You can't be dumb enough to hurt anyone, you prick!" John shouted. "We're surrounded by federal agents!"

"No," Hunter replied flatly, "I'm not dumb enough to be provoked by an asshole like you, is all. However, I am willing to hurt someone"—he twirled the gun pointed at Erika's head—"if I have to. Believe me, I'd rather not have to. Hold him until he calms down, guys. Thanks." He turned to Elliot. "So, who is he?"

"He's John Mitchell, Erika's bodyguard," Elliot said, looking uncharacteristically bewildered as he stood stiffly over the duct-taped agent like a guard at Buckingham Palace. "I guess he came on late in the game. He's unarmed. I saw your agents confiscate his weapon and his cell phone with my own eyes."

"Good for you. Go collect the arms from the other three." He eyed his fellow agents. "I know I don't have to prove to you that I mean business. Slowly remove your weapons from your holsters and toss them—gently!—to the center of the floor." He waited for them to comply, then had Elliot deposit the guns in the safe. "You can secure their ankles and wrists now," he told Elliot. "They won't give you any trouble, will you, gentlemen? Step away from the door. I need room to exit." He tapped Erika on the shoulder with the gun. "No fidgeting."

Elliot approached the foursome with the duct tape. As soon as he drew close, Agent X lunged at him, pinning him in a headlock. The rolls of duct tape went flying.

"Bad idea," Hunter said coolly. He took careful aim with the gun cradled in his left hand and shot. Agent X uttered a blood-curdling cry, releasing Elliot in order to grab hold of his own injured leg.

"Don't gawk, Elliot," Hunter said. "Use the tape to make a tourniquet and get on with it. I haven't got all day."

Trembling, Elliot did as he was told.

"No sweat, guys," Hunter cajoled. "If you cooperate, believe me, in a couple of hours you'll be looking back on this as a bad dream. Elliot?"

Elliot was securing the tourniquet. "What?"

"Keep working, but listen up while I explain. You're the only one who's in the dark, Elliot. This whole thing was arranged to catch you in the act of working a deal. Every inch of the place is rigged with spyware, like on a reality show." He glanced up as if he were addressing an unseen entity. "How do I look? I hear fluorescents are not that flattering." Back to Elliot, he said, "There was no arrangement with the Gardner Museum. The Vermeer had already been recovered. Your authentication services were not needed. The thirty million ransom payoff was a fiction, a closed circuit exchange. The idea was to have you incriminate yourself and then encourage you to get off the hook by giving up the particulars on some of the higher-ups." He paused. "That brings us to right now. I am about to walk away with a painting valued at three hundred million dollars. If you prove yourself a friend, you'll get a nice payoff. Your first taste of non-fiction. Do you trust me, Elliot?"

"Do I have a choice?" he asked weakly, the alpha dog vanquished.

"Yes. You can choose to get wasted. Now, your friend here, the snitch"—he flicked his head toward Randall—"is going to help me out, too, except his only reward will be my promise not to stick him with a fatwa. Am I making my point? Are we on the same page?"

"Yes," Elliot said, looking at Randall in bewilderment, as if he'd never seen him in his life.

Randall nodded blankly, as if he were unsure he'd been included in Hunter's query.

The three agents and John had been secured. They sat on the floor, arms behind their backs, legs drawn up to their chest, except for the injured Agent X, whose legs were stretched out in front of him.

"Ready, now," Hunter said. "Here we go. Elliot, the safe is unlocked. Grab a gun if you need it. Don't get close to these guys; they're pros. At seventeen hundred hours, you can turn them loose." He glanced at the ceiling. "You get that? I get a sniff of one of you people on my tail before that, your girl's history. The snitch, too."

"Why do you need *me* along?" Randall objected.

"As insurance. And because I can't have you flipping my boy Elliot. You're my boy, right, Elliot?"

The instruments of Elliot's trade were lined up on the metal table, uselessly at the ready. Elliot gave them a hard stare, as if to reclaim his identity from them. "Right," he replied.

Now that his potential attackers had been neutralized, Hunter no longer needed a spare body to act as a shield for him. He moved to the side of the table where Erika stood and shoved the gun he was holding in his left hand into his waistband. "Grab the portfolio," he commanded her.

The portfolio was leaning against the side of the table. She clutched its handle and lifted it to her side, her knees buckling with the weight of it: not its poundage, that was negligible, but the weight of responsibility thrust upon her. She feared for the life of the painting as much as for her own. Her palm felt like it was on fire.

With a hand gesture, Hunter directed Randall to move up alongside Erika, then for the two of them to march to the rear, he following behind. The faces of the bound captives twisted with unspoken curses as Hunter skirted around them to get to the wall-mounted control panel and press the critical button.

As the door slowly opened, Elliot watching the bound men, Hunter positioned Erika and Randall for a quick departure. When he, Erika, and Randall were down the steps and standing on the floor of the garage, Hunter began to shut the door. It had almost closed when one of the captives managed to throw his body against it in an attempt to hurl himself out of the vehicle. Erika tensed, ready to act: she imagined the agent coming at Hunter like a human cannon ball. Once he hit, the gun would fly out of Hunter's hand, and she would make a dive for it. No sooner had her thought gelled than Hunter put a bullet in the daredevil's leg, wedged in the now-widening door space. The leg twitched back with an accompanying roar from the victim, not of pain but anger—*at the damn leg for retracting*, Erika thought. She imagined disabling Hunter with a swift film-worthy blow, furious at her own inability to do it.

Without a word referencing the event, Hunter slammed the door shut and secured the lock. He prompted his hostages forward toward the door to the museum, a nondescript entry found on each level of the garage. Keeping a tight grip on his weapon, he shifted it to his jacket pocket and ordered his hostages to precede him into the building.

A museum security guard sat at a small table in a nook just inside the doorway. He picked up his scanner wand from the table, ready to probe any handbags or backpacks. Erika's tote bag was back in the transport vehicle. The only visible item of interest was the portfolio containing the Vermeer masterpiece. The guard requested that she open it. As she began to, Hunter whipped out his gun and, in the same accomplished manner with which he had dispatched his colleague, knocked the guard senseless. He propped the man upright in his seat so that it appeared he had fallen asleep, then re-concealed his gun and urged his charges forward into the museum proper.

They entered an open area, an anteroom to the galleries. On their left was a check-in desk and a table exhibiting a sampling of museum store gifts. The woman at registration called them over.

"Keep moving," Hunter ordered. "I'm hugging your backs, so don't try anything heroic."

The woman at registration, clearly distraught, hailed a museum guard stationed nearby. He made no move to come to her aid.

And then, as she was nudged into the first room of the modern art wing, Erika's earbud received a message, broken up by static.

"I'm coming," Greg began. "Hunter won't recognize—transmitted your pics—got the museum's camera feed—museum guards told not to inter-fere—if you're hearing say oh god—take—"

"Oh god," she muttered under her breath.

The response was static. Had Greg heard her reply?

"God's not going to help," Hunter said. "Head for the staircase. We're going down."

As they reached the first floor and ordered to march on through the European Sculpture galleries and on to Medieval Art, Erika was tempted to make a run for it. There were more visitors than on the upper levels, and she thought she could escape into the crowd more easily. On the other hand, she had seen Hunter inflict violence without batting an eye, and she did not want to put the lives of innocent bystanders in jeopardy. She had no choice but to comply, and wait for her chance.

They were almost at the main entrance of the museum.

"Slowly now," Hunter said, so close behind them that Erika could feel his breath on her neck. "We're going to walk out of here and down the staircase to the street. It's a long way down, so don't try anything, or you'll find yourself tumbling down head first. Go."

On her tentatively paced descent, with her precious parcel held high so it would not come into contact with the concrete steps, Erika scanned the scene below, looking for possible options of escape. There were several taxis pulled up curbside; in front of them, a black limousine idled, its tailpipe coughing up a pale gray stream of exhaust. When they were just a few steps from street level, the limo's horn sounded four syncopated beats, as if in Morse code.

"That's me," Hunter said.

Suddenly—without warning, and almost sending Erika sprawling down the remaining steps—Randall, with a primal yawp, rose up at her side. He flung himself at Hunter, lifting the younger and burlier man off his feet and throwing him to the sidewalk. Hunter landed face down, one leg draped against the last step, his attacker sitting astride his lower back.

The limousine screeched off, almost colliding with a passing bus.

Randall had created the opportunity; she had to take it. She lay the portfolio on the sidewalk—gingerly, even at the pinnacle of danger—and knelt on top of Hunter, digging her knees into his shoulders. Hunter struggled to free himself as she bent lower, her head almost touching his, her knees pressing harder against him.

And then she saw the hand reach for the handle of the portfolio. "No!" she screamed, stretching for it, just as another pair of talon-like hands clamped under her arms and lifted her straight up in the air, like an eagle carrying off its prey.

Chapter 22

"I believe they'd like us to leave," Diana suggested, drilling Harrison with another of her searching looks that thus far had not garnered a response in kind.

Harrison looked about him. The crowd had thinned to near zero, and the nearest catering staff member was pitching him a smile of impatience capped by an arched brow. Aldo had long since gone off to pursue more receptive game, since it was clear Diana was not in the market, or at least not in his. "Send my love to your wife," had been his parting words to Harrison.

Harrison directed a nod of understanding to the impatient staff member and addressed Diana: "Yes, let's go." He lifted his glass and drank the remaining drops. There were three empty bottles on the table, and although his speech was not slurred, he suspected his thinking was. "Where are you staying? Can I offer you a lift?"

Diana smiled. "Thanks, but I'm at the Hotel de Medici. I can walk there." She picked up her wine glass. It was empty; she blushed and put it down. "Would you like to join me for a cocktail? They've got a lovely bar lounge."

Harrison remembered it well. It's where he and Erika had quarreled after their encounter with Aldo Fabbri. "I'm staying at the de Medici myself," he said. "We can walk together. Do you want to pick up your materials? I left mine in the lecture hall."

"They were locking up when I left the hall," Diana said. "We can pick up our slides and things tomorrow morning, when we stop by for our breakfast send-off." She flashed him a coquettish smile, no doubt provoked by the contiguous placement of the words "our" and "breakfast."

"Sure," Harrison said. He rose to his feet. He felt ever-so-slightly tipsy.

* * *

As they walked the charming but irregular cobblestone streets of Florence, Diana, in her strappy stiletto heels, held onto Harrison's arm for the ostensible purpose of maintaining her footing. She did not let go even after they had entered the carpeted terrain of the Hotel de Medici. Quite the contrary. She gripped him yet more firmly as she attempted to guide him toward the lounge bar while crooning, "What an elegant chandelier," as if she hoped to distract him from her assertiveness.

"Yes, it is, but I think I'll head up to my room," Harrison demurred, gently exerting an opposing force by steering her toward the bank of elevators.

As the elevator door opened, Diana finally released him, only to chore-ograph a breast-brushing-up-against-arm move that might have been considered accidental had there not been more than ample room. They were alone in the elevator. Diana pressed the third floor button; Harrison, the fifth.

"It was terrific meeting you," Diana said, reaching up with both hands to pluck the clips from her Klimt-inspired bouffant hairdo. "Ah, that's better," she said, as a mass of wavy black hair cascaded down her back. "It was beginning to give me a headache."

The elevator stopped at the third floor. The doors parted.

"It was terrific meeting you, too," Harrison said. "See you in the morning."

Diana made no move to exit the elevator. Instead, she pressed the button that kept the doors open. "I think this is the scene where the gentleman, after a moment of required hesitation, follows the woman out of the elevator."

"Wrong movie," Harrison said, fascinated by her hair. It was truly magnificent.

Diana gave him a curious look. "I don't understand. We're over four thousand miles from home. Life is beautiful. *We're* beautiful. Why not?"

This requires some thought—no, it doesn't. "Diana," he said, "what is the one thing about your husband you would not tolerate his losing? The one irreplaceable thing. Think it over."

"I don't have to. *I'm* the one irreplaceable thing about him." She laughed. "This is amusing. What's the one thing about you your wife wouldn't tolerate losing? What's the deal breaker for her, I wonder? Your teeth? You do have a great smile."

Harrison laughed, flattered despite the message he was about to communicate. "You want to know?" he asked. "Right now I'm number one on her shit list. I'm feeling lonely and rejected, pie-eyed and horny. I'm standing in front of a beautiful woman who has invited me to fuck her, and my wife would never be the wiser. I say no thanks and I have no regrets. That's it. The one thing."

"But she wouldn't be the wiser, you said."

"Exactly the point."

Diana shook her head. "This reminds me of Schrödinger's cat experiment. Don't ask me why."

"I won't," Harrison said. "Let's just say goodnight and free up the elevator."

Diana removed her finger from the button. "You'll never know what you're missing," she said, blowing him a kiss as she scooted out the door.

* * *

Harrison was not given to brooding, but alone in his hotel room, he sat on the edge of the bed and brooded. He missed Erika terribly, and the incident with Diana had made him realize what an ass he'd been, jealous and petulant at a time when Erika was most vulnerable. What he had feared on some atavistic level of being was that Erika, when it came to extra-marital sex, was given to acting on impulse. Seeing this acted out in the flesh made him realize how unfounded his fear had been.

Adding dimension to his guilt, he had hired John to keep an eye on

227

her without her knowledge. Yes, he had been worried that Erika would place—or *further* place—herself in harm's way, but he should not have taken precautions underhandedly. Independence and honesty were of utmost importance to Erika, and he had crossed her on both counts. He must call her and tell her about John. First, though—and here he knew he was messing with his new rules—he would call John, give him hell for not having gotten in touch with him with an update this afternoon.

But both John's and Erika's phones went straight to message center. He needed to speak to them directly, soon. He would try again in an hour. No—fifteen minutes.

Chapter 23

Erika twisted around to take a look at who'd lifted her off Hunter's back as if she weighed no more than a rag doll. The powerhouse was wearing FBI gear. Beside him stood the person who had grabbed the portfolio handle.

"Greg!" she cried in relief, as her feet hit the pavement.

Before she had a chance to process the situation, the situation changed, as if time had contracted outside her: a swarm of FBI agents had surrounded Hunter, guns drawn, while another was handcuffing his hands behind his back. Another agent shouted at the gathering crowd to move off, and the circle of onlookers began to widen, like a dilating pupil.

The agent who'd handcuffed Hunter felt for the turncoat's gun and retrieved it from the tracksuit's jacket pocket. "You can get off him now," the agent advised Randall, still sitting astride Hunter like a cowboy. "You pre-empted us, man. We were waiting in ambush, see?" He pointed toward the garage entrance. "Great job!"

Hunter writhed beneath Randall. "Fuck!"

Randall's right hand pressed against Hunter's pants pocket. "Wait! His cell's vibrating!"

"Grab it!" Erika shouted, in chorus with Greg and the attending agent.

Randall reached into Hunter's pants pocket and extracted the cell phone while the agent dug the barrel of his gun into Hunter's cheek. "Not a sound!" He took the cell from Randall and passed it to one of the agents on guard. "Press 'accept' and listen. Don't talk. Don't terminate."

The receiving agent held the cell to his ear. He nodded to his mate. Seconds later he made a slashing sign across his neck to indicate the call had ended. The gun butt was removed from Hunter's cheek, leaving a circular indentation.

"Caller female," said the agent holding the phone. "Number listed as 'private.'"

"What'd she say?"

"'You coming?' That's it. She waited, then cut out."

"Run the cell over to command. They'll triangulate the position of the caller off of the cell phone towers, no sweat. On the double—go!" He hoisted Hunter to a seated position on the third step of the museum staircase. The cheek that had hit the sidewalk was abraded, but had not bled. "More comfortable? Now, you want to make this easier on us by telling us who the lady is? And where she's at?"

"Go to hell. I need a cigarette."

"Fuck you, man. Talk, and I'll think about it."

Hunter made no response, slumping into a private gloom.

Greg sidled up to Erika. "Probably the wife," he said in hushed tones. "I got an earful from the agents riding with me."

"Is her name Candice, by any chance?" Erika asked, in full voice.

Hunter sat up.

"How did you know?" Greg asked, stunned himself.

"It's a long story." Fixing Hunter with a direct gaze, she said, "Thanks for letting me know you're a smoker. I may have found a lighter you lost."

Hunter blanched, but remained silent.

Greg's knuckles were turning white from his grip on the portfolio handle. "I've got to get this to the transport vehicle—now!"

He marched into the garage flanked by two of the armed FBI agents, just as John Mitchell, along with three more agents, emerged from the garage with a handcuffed Winston Elliot in tow and Erika's tote bag slung over his shoulder. Two ambulances, sirens wailing, pulled into the garage entrance, and two police cars drew up curbside, their signature siren-pitch in jarring dissonance. Within minutes, Agent Hunter and Winston Elliot had been delivered to a police car and driven off for interrogation.

"Let's get out of here," John said, grabbing Erika's elbow. "I've got us officially dismissed, at least for the time being." He handed her the bag. "Your cell phone's in there." He ushered her toward the curb, away from the nexus of activity.

"How did you pull it off?" she asked, still in disbelief at having witnessed him strolling out of the garage with Elliot at gunpoint.

"Not without help, that's for sure," he said. "We'll talk. First, let's get a move on." He jumped into the street to hail an oncoming cab.

"Let's go to my place," she suggested. "We can talk there."

"Anywhere but here," he said, as the cab pulled up in front of him.

* * *

Grace eyed John as if he were a stray dog Erika had found in a muddy ditch. "John *who?*" she asked suspiciously, a guard dog herself.

"John Mitchell," Erika repeated. "John is a private investigator," she added cordially, pretending she had not detected the hostility in Grace's manner.

"A friend of the *family*," John punched, in no mood to humor her.

"John and I have a legal matter regarding the art magazine to discuss," Erika said. She forced a smile. "Not as serious as it sounds, but we'll need a few minutes to ourselves. We'll be in the living room."

"Will your friend be staying for dinner?" Grace asked stiffly.

"No can do, ma'am," John answered for Erika.

"Coffee or tea?" Grace dutifully persisted.

"Thanks, Grace," Erika said. "I'll take it from here."

They went into the living room, where Erika shifted restlessly in the oversized armchair. "Speak!" she commanded.

John, catty-corner to her on the couch, raised the glass of red wine she'd provided. "First a toast. To survival."

She clicked his glass with hers and took a token sip. "Well? How did you do it?"

John took a more generous swig and set his glass on the coffee table. "When Elliot was packing up his instruments, the agent acting as the lawyer Yardsdell wriggled back to back with me and undid the tape binding my wrists. By the time Elliot spotted what was going on, it was too late for him to grab one of the weapons from the safe. Mine was already drawn."

Erika sat forward. "What? But yours was confiscated!"

John shook his head. "Not mine. The FBI confiscated the weapon they planted on me that morning to impress Elliot. They left me with my own. Clever, right?"

"I'm impressed! If I could whistle, now would be the time."

John smiled. "One of the few ideas you didn't dream up yourself, eh?"

Erika was about to demur, but suddenly remembered that she hadn't checked her cell phone since mid-morning. She dug for it in the tote bag she'd dropped beside her on the floor and turned it on. "Harrison tried to reach me five times," she said after checking. "No voice message—why didn't he text?"

John shrugged. "Same thing here," he said quietly.

"What? What's going on here? Harrison tried to reach you five times, too? Why's your face turning red? What are you hiding from me? *John?*"

Grace appeared at the entrance to the living room as John was opening his mouth to speak. From his sheepish expression, it didn't look like an adequate answer was on its way.

"There's another gentleman to see you, Miss," Grace said, with a subtle stress on the word *another*. "Greg Smith—the photographer from this morning, as I recall."

John gave Erika a quizzical look.

Grace, missing nothing, eyed John narrowly before returning her attention to Erika. "Shall I unlock the gate?"

"Please," Erika replied. "Show him up."

Soon Greg had joined them. "Your cell was off, so I took a chance and ran over," he said, planting himself on the couch alongside John. "I'm flying back to London later tonight, so I won't be long." He smiled. "A lot's gone on, so I'll talk fast."

"May I offer you a drink?" Erika asked.

"Thanks, no. Ah, before we go any further, what was that all about—where you nailed Hunter for being a smoker?"

"Right." An image of Andrea flashed in Erika's mind, redirecting her thoughts. She turned to John. "Do you think you can forward a set of Agent Hunter's fingerprints to the Vermont team investigating Andrea's death? See if there's a match with those found on the cigarette lighter recovered from her rental car?"

"Good move, Erika," John declared. "I'll have the FBI or the cops from the local precinct get those prints to the proper authorities ASAP."

"Out of my bailiwick," Greg commented, "but kudos to you, Erika."

"How are the injured men doing?" John asked, swinging the conversation to the day's central focus. "When you returned the Vermeer painting to the transport vehicle, you must have seen them being loaded into the ambulances."

"I did, yes. They were alert and bearing up nicely. Tough guys."

"What's been happening since then?" Erika asked. "Did the FBI track down the woman who called Hunter?"

"Within minutes. Triangulating the position off the cell phone towers is much faster than in the old days—i.e., last week."

"I'm guessing it's Candice," Erika said. "Am I right? Where was she?"

"Yes, and she was calling from Kennedy Airport. Last I heard, airport security was attempting to intercept her, and the FBI was on its way. How the hell did you guess who she was, anyway?"

"From the name Hunter." Erika recounted her experience at Randall's office the night Jeremy was killed. "I'm guessing Candice alerted her husband—or *someone* in her cabal—to waylay Jeremy and end his meddling for good. He'd already been put on notice with a severe beating."

"Erika," Greg said, sitting forward, "do you know anything about this woman?"

"Other than that she's a philatelist? No."

"To begin with, her maiden name is 'Volkov.'"

"Now, *there's* a show-stopper!" John declared, giving words to Erika's dropped-jaw response.

"Her parents defected from Russia in 1976," Greg went on. "Her father's a math teacher. Her mother, now hear this, is a museum curator. Some place in the Midwest that features international crafts and such. I *told* you I got an earful from those teammates of Hunter's!"

After its initial shock, Erika's brain was racing full throttle. "Was the couple planning to flee the country with the Vermeer?" she asked, already breathless. "Did the FBI check the manifest on all flights leaving for Russia—or anywhere in the Federation—Belarus, Ukraine—God, how many republics *are* there?" Oh, how she wanted to share this—*all* this—with Harrison!

"It's the first thing the agents thought of," Greg said. "In fact, Aeroflot is leaving today for a non-stop flight to Moscow. That's what the FBI's betting on." He rose from the couch. "Erika, I don't know the upshot of it all—or not yet, anyhow. We each have our sources of information and we'll share them as they become known. Meanwhile, I'd better get my act together before I miss *my* flight. I'll show myself out."

He gave Erika a quick bear hug, John, a hand-pump, and took off before a feasible objection could be raised. John adjusted his position on the couch, making himself more comfortable—or, by the looks of it, less uneasy. "I forgot to ask Greg about the earbuds. Think he wants them back?"

"I'll ask him the next time we speak," she replied curtly. "What's going on with you and Harrison, John?"

John's glance fell to his lap. "What do you mean?"

"As a private eye, I would think you'd be better at this. It's obvious you're keeping something from me."

"I *am* usually better at this. You put me off balance, you and Harrison, being friends and all."

"Now you sound like you're having to choose sides." She was beginning to feel sick to her stomach. "Is Harrison planning to leave me?"

"Of course not! What makes you think that?"

"We've had our problems."

"Listen, Erika. Harrison texted me not to open my mouth until he's had a chance to speak to you directly. The issue has nothing to do with wanting to leave you. Get that idea out of your head. The man's crazy about you, for god's sake." He gave her a smile of encouragement. "Maybe just crazy, period."

Erika looked down at her cell phone. "Something's going on with him. I could hear it in his voice the last time we spoke. I have to try calling him. Will you excuse me?" She rose from the chair. "I'll be right back."

John leapt to his feet. "No, no, I'll get going. I kept my wife in the dark about today's agenda, and I want to get back to her. By the way, what's up with your housekeeper? Why does she hate me?"

"She doesn't hate you. She's over-protective."

"Of whom?" He waved off the question. "Never mind. There's been far too much drama for one day." He smiled. "But you can see me to the door. *I* may need protection—from *her*."

* * *

Erika tried calling Harrison, but his cell phone was either shut off or in a dead zone. She sat at the desk in her study—her lair—to devise a plan. About what, she was unsure, only that action was required.

Surely, the success of the day's operation, which she had played a major role in devising, had gone a ways toward restoring her sense of—what was it?—*usefulness*. The loss of her baby was still painful to the touch, but her sense of failure had been distilled, somehow. It no longer defined her. Maybe it was true, from evolution's point of view, that the sole purpose of conjugation was the preservation of the species. Did that mean it had to be her sole purpose as an individual? Wasn't it true that the peacock's tail was a thing of beauty in itself? Could she help it if she missed the curve of Harrison's thigh, the tautness between his legs, the swoon of their coming together? Could such a wonder not be appreciated solely for itself? And did not her yearning for his company override all missteps and lapses—his; hers?

She could not sit still. Being both exhausted and exhilarated from the day's events must be contributing to her restlessness, as well as her shameless curiosity—this admission was extracted like a rotten tooth—about what Harrison was *up to* so far from home.

At this thought, she grabbed the itinerary from the desk drawer; scanned it; computed on her fingers that in roughly ten hours Harrison would be checking in at the Radisson Blu Hotel in Berlin, probably to unwind—more finger calculating—before heading over to the Berlin University of the Arts for the opening session of the two-day conference on French painters of the Romantic era. She switched on the desktop computer, logged into American Airlines, checked the flights to Berlin, found the one best aligned with Harrison's itinerary, and, after fetching her AMEX card from her wallet, purchased a round-trip ticket, returning to New York on the same flight from London as his. She'd worry about the intervening hops later, once she had joined him.

Grace was passing by the open door to the master bedroom as Erika was packing her suitcase. The housekeeper stopped dead in her tracks. "Where are you going, Miss?" she asked, making no effort to conceal her alarm. "Are you moving out? You can't do that!" Quickly adding, after hearing her own voice, "I'm sorry for being so bold."

Erika dropped her folded shirt into the suitcase and turned to Grace. "*Are* you?"

Grace gave her a puzzled look, either because she didn't understand the reference or because it was the first time she'd ever heard Erika answer her with anything resembling a retort.

"Never mind, Grace," Erika said, already feeling guilty. "It's just that I thought we had become friends. You were so understanding, so kind, when I—" The words would not come out. "I thought you liked me."

Grace stepped into the room, but kept a formal distance from her. "Oh, but I *do* like you!" she protested. "I only thought that maybe you had gone off on him somehow—Master Harry, I mean. After your troubles and all. And when you—I'm sorry, it's not my place to bring it up—but when you moved into the Blue Room—"

236

"Stop, please, Grace. Am I to be on parole for the crimes of Harrison's ex-wife forever? I'm not leaving Harrison. I love him, *whatever* Room I'm in—Blue, Pink, Purple, you name it. Can you understand that, once and for all?"

Grace took a step closer. "May I give you a hug, Miss?"

"Of course!" Erika said. She initiated the embrace, careful not to exert too much pressure on Grace's frail frame. "Before you ask," she said, releasing her, "in a few hours I'm flying out of Kennedy to join Harrison on his book tour. I'll leave a note with the flight number and name of the hotel. If Harrison calls, don't tell him. I want it to be a surprise."

Grace grinned from ear to ear. Erika realized that it was the first time she was seeing more than just the tips of Grace's teeth.

* * *

Bill answered his cell phone almost immediately when Erika called to request a ride to the airport. "I know it's short notice," she said, "so I can contact Uber if it's inconvenient for you."

"I'm actually meeting your husband's flight in about two hours, give or take," Bill replied, somewhat surprised. "I can swing by for you now, no problem."

It took her a moment to process. "What do you mean, you're meeting his flight? Is there something wrong? Is he sick?"

"Oh, no, I don't think so!" Bill answered, suddenly tense. "Although when my wife picked up the phone, she said he sounded a little, well, jumpy is all."

"Did he tell you why he was returning early?"

"I didn't think it was my place, and he didn't offer."

"Please come get me, Bill. I'm canceling my flight, so whenever you're ready."

"Do I understand you correctly?" Bill asked, hesitant. "You want to come along for the ride?"

"Yes!" Erika cried, unable to hold back her emotion, an unfamiliar admixture of excitement and dread.

Chapter 24

Before approaching its entrance, Erika took a moment to gaze at the impressive building, tucked in on one of the side streets of West Chelsea. She had been here a number of times since her reunion with Harrison at JFK nearly three months ago, but only for task-related purposes: to consult with the plumber, choose a wall color, accept delivery of tufted leather benches, re-angle track lighting. Now, an hour before the art gallery's 6:00 p.m. grand opening, she stood silently in awe, undisturbed.

"This is nothing short of a miracle," Sara marveled from behind, ending the reflective moment.

Erika spun around to greet her boss. "Glad you could make it," she beamed, leaning in for the obligatory kiss.

Sara flashed her a quizzical look. "You think I'd miss this? Sorry for being unfashionably early, but that's how excited I am!" She waved her hand in an all-inclusive flourish. "This is stunning. Did Harrison change the façade?"

Erika shook her head. "He did nothing to change the general structure. All that was required was a bit of sprucing up. Harrison paid the asking price the day it was put on the market, and that was that. It all took place no more than three days after he returned from Europe."

"As I said, miraculous."

"For the seller. Who was on the verge of bankruptcy."

"Well," Sara said, "the unfortunate man's financial skills may have been wanting, but his aesthetic sense surely was not. I love the whole Beaux-Arts thing—very tasteful."

"Without being overdone," Erika agreed. "The joining of styles was quite a coup, especially for the architect who pulled it off." The building had been a featureless five-story red brick apartment building. Twenty years ago, when the first two floors had been converted into an art gallery, the architect had applied a decorative Beaux-Arts façade in white rusticated stone to the entire length of the building, turning square windows into graceful arches with handsome male and female mascarons adorning their keystones. As his *piece de resistance*, the Roman goddess, Minerva, reclined in the keystone of the gallery's grand arched entrance.

"Shall we?" Sara asked, looping her arm through Erika's and pressing her forward. "I adore your cocktail dress, by the way. Revealing, but tasteful." She smiled. "Like the architecture. By the way, my husband sends his regrets; can't seem to shrug off his cold. Where's your husband, anyway?"

"Here, preparing. I stayed late at the office—as you know."

Sara gave her a nudge. "The truth, for a change," she said, before uttering her signature staccato laugh. "Love it," she cooed, as they dropped arms on arriving at the tall arched doors: thick glass panes framed in oak. "Massive and graceful at the same time."

Erika directed an admiring look at the etched print on the right pane: *Owen Grant Gallery.* As she reached for the pane's polished metal door pull, she spotted Harrison through the glass and her heart skipped a beat. Spotting him in the crowd at the airport had caused a similar jolt, as if his sudden appearance had been the most amazing coincidence. A miracle, she had thought, that they had ever met at all; that they had survived all the known and unknown near-fatalities that had grazed their lives, only to be thrown together at a table at the Pierre, and now, over a year later, to be reunited after what might have been a tragic plane flight—or for her, a bullet to the head shot by rogue Agent Hunter. Oh, and then to see his wondrous expression as he caught sight of her, as if her crazy revelations were matched by his, confirming them!

How hungrily they had made love that night and thereafter, she back in the master bedroom, love-making no longer a euphemism for sex, but its sole meaning, an expression of intimacy arcing from need to consummation.

"What are you smiling about?" Sara asked, as they entered the building.

"Harrison," she said, without elaborating.

* * *

Harrison had seen to it that the only name on the title page of the deed to the gallery was PAPNEA: Partnership to Aid and Promote New and Emerging Artists. Not that his generosity had anything to do with the fact that he and Erika had met at the organization's fund-raising gala at the Pierre—he was, after all, a member of PAPNEA's board—but it did add an emotional component to the transaction.

The 5,000 square foot art gallery boasted over 700 linear feet of exhibit space. The first floor was made up of two large viewing rooms with a broad archway nominally separating them and an office right off the building's entryway. The office space was multi-functional. This evening it was to serve as an hors d'oeuvres and bar station. The second floor consisted of one moderately large exhibit area and a meeting room/movie theater, where art-related discussions, lectures, and screenings would take place. Although the floor was presently not in use, an exhibit of Pratt Institute's award-winning young artists and a screening of *The Cool School*, a 2008 documentary portraying the rebellion against the Abstract Expressionist art movement, were already on PAPNEA'S September agenda.

Harrison was realigning a framed drawing hanging on the near wall when Erika and Sara stepped into the gallery's sprawling exhibit space. He turned when he heard them enter, lighting up at the sight of them. "Hi, there!" He gave the drawing's placement a final visual check and approached the women. "You two look beautiful," he said, gazing at his wife. He hugged them in turn. "Sara. Good to see you. So, do you approve?"

"I do." Waving at the wall at which he'd been tinkering, she said, "But what's all *this* about?"

240

Harrison and Erika exchanged smiles. "You mean the mysterious hinged flaps where the identifying information should be?" Erika asked, all innocence.

"Don't tease. Yes. The artist, title, media, and such."

Erika yielded to Harrison; let him have the fun.

"It looks like we're exhibiting two Titians, side by side, yes?" Harrison asked. He moved further along the wall. "And here, two Corots?"

Sara nodded.

"Lift up the flaps," he directed.

She did so. "Oh, how clever! In each pairing, one is the real thing, and one is a Hebborn forgery!"

"An interesting guessing game, don't you think?" Erika said.

"Yes, of course. How many sets do you have? And how, in heaven's name, did you get your hands on them?"

"We're very resourceful," Harrison said, smiling at Erika. "We tracked down eighteen of the nineteen forgeries Hebborn led us to. Of those, seven drawings and one oil are on loan for the duration of the exhibit. As for their authenticated mates, they're on loan from various institutions. Harvard's Fogg Museum contributed the Corot. The Met sent along Titian's *Venus and the Lute Player*." He laughed. "It's all there under the flaps."

"Excellent," Sara commented. "Hebborn would have gotten quite a kick out of this, the devil."

Harrison cocked his head. "I think *more* of a kick out of Erika's brilliant use of one of his hardcovers to nab a consortium of art criminals! How about her pretending to find Hebborn's clue to finding a couple of stolen masterpieces slipped into its binding? How wicked was *that?*" He drew Erika close to him; they gazed dreamily at each other, and then he kissed her lightly, but squarely, on the lips.

Sara rolled her eyes. "I must get away from you two before I'm tempted to run home and tell my husband to go fuck himself. If I'm not mistaken, the art of two PAPNEA contest winners are also on display? I think I recognize one of Georgia Field's Brancusi-ish sculptures in the next room." She started toward it, then looked back. "Will there be drinks, darlings?"

"The caterers are on their way," Erika said. "Give them fifteen minutes."

* * *

Amy and Matt Barlow had been Erika's neighbors in the apartment building she'd lived in before her marriage to Harrison. Stockbrokers turned caterers, the Barlows had gladly agreed to take on the opening of the Owen Grant Gallery. Five minutes before their predicted arrival, Matt Barlow wheeled into the building with an insulated food carrier hoisted onto a dolly. Harrison escorted him into the office space and then accompanied him outside to where the company's van idled at the curb. Together, the men loaded the dolly with cartons of wine, liquor bottles, and cans of soft drinks. On their final trip to fetch the ice, glasses, and the balance of party-ware, Amy, fitted with a colorful backpack, jumped out of the van. She reached back to lift a small boy from his junior car seat. Carrying him in her arms, she followed behind the men.

"We'll call when we're ready to go!" she directed to the driver of the van, as he revved the engine.

Harrison darted a glance over his shoulder at Amy and the boy.

"Don't worry, he's an angel," Amy assured him. She gave the child a noisy kiss on his cheek. "Aren't you, Sammy?"

"Who's worried?" Harrison said. "I just didn't know you had a child. Of course the little guy's welcome!" He braced one of the cartons that seemed a bit wobbly as Matt pushed the dolly.

"Sam's my nephew," Amy replied, catching up to them. "It's a story—not a long one."

While Matt was preparing the bar and buffet table in the space assigned to the catering team, Amy explained to the hosts: "My sister Kate went into labor this afternoon, two months early. I couldn't deprive my brother-in-law the joy of seeing his wife give birth, so I said I'd watch Sammy."

Erika felt Harrison's hand clamp onto hers as soon as she caught sight of the child. "How's Kate doing?" she asked, voice calm.

"Kate's doing great. We just heard it's a girl." Amy readjusted Sammy's position in her arms. "Hey, Sammy, how do you like that? A baby sister!"

Sammy, clinging to his aunt's neck, smiled cooperatively.

"I promise he won't get underfoot," Amy said. "I've brought his favorite—Legos. He'll play quietly in a cozy corner of the office."

"Legos!" Sammy exclaimed, clearly more enthusiastic about the building blocks than about his having acquired a sister.

* * *

By 6:30 the party was in full swing. The diverse assortment of guests, from curators to lawyers, were mingling like old friends, the steady flow of food and drink a catalyst to community spirit. Harrison, John, and Greg were sitting on a leather bench facing a series of mounted sculpted works by Georgia Field, one of the two young artists showcased.

"I don't understand them, but I like them," the detective commented.

"You're trying too hard," Harrison said. "Just let them speak to you. Even if you don't understand the language, the tone will convey meaning."

"Like when my Greek girlfriend broke up with me," Greg offered.

Harrison had been instrumental in choosing the artist. Her pieces were abstract distillates of organic forms, like Brancusi's classic bird and fish sculptures, only Field's works were ambivalent. The intriguing lines evoked entwining limbs or plant growths, or their amalgam. Harrison was not about to foist this interpretation on John. Instead, he gestured toward a group of women standing in the broad archway dividing the exhibit space. "The artist herself is right over there," he said. "You see? Between Charlene Miller and Andrea Stein's mother. You can speak to her directly."

John was more interested in the women's interaction. "From the looks of it, Charlene and Andrea's mother seem to be on better terms since last I was in contact. Are the Steins feeling more kindly toward their daughter's partner?"

"Apparently so," Harrison said. "They gave her their daughter's ashes. Although there must have been some pretty complicated feelings about that. As religious Jews, they don't consider cremation an acceptable option."

243

"I'm glad they worked it out," John said. "Healing together—or trying to—is always better than preserving the animus." He turned to Greg. "Are there any new developments on the felon front? Any recent arrests stemming from Candice Hunter's tell-all? Has she been allowed to leave the country?"

"In answer to your last question, yes. Two days ago Candice was escorted to the same Aeroflot gate at which the authorities intercepted her three months ago. They didn't want to release her until all the leads she provided panned out—which they did. In fact, they were most productive. Let me tell you about—ah, Harrison, here comes your wife. How did she know it was about to get interesting?"

"Felon radar, I suspect. Hi, darling. Come, sit."

Erika squeezed in between Harrison and John, causing hip-to-hip contact all around. "Are you okay?"

"We're fine," Greg said, at the far end.

"Have you taken a close look at the Williamson oils?" she asked the group. "They're brilliant! From a distance they appear to be peaceful landscapes, but as you get closer, you see that all elements of the scenes are actually composed of human forms. They emerge ghostlike into your vision, as if you imagined them. I've been speaking to the artist himself—so young to have such mastery of his medium!" She leaned forward to take them all in. "Sorry. I interrupted your conversation—aside from making you uncomfortable. Greg, you're teetering." She jammed closer to Harrison. "Let's give him room, darling."

Harrison gladly shoved over, clinging to her thigh for support. "Greg was about to give us an update—Greg?"

"I was just saying Candice Hunter—née Volkov—was allowed to leave the country two days ago."

"Was the Ministry of Culture of the Russian Federation given a heads up?" Erika asked.

"No. That was part of the agreement. The Ministry will not be alerted—that is, unless we catch the slightest hint of her coming out of retirement. She'd be facing charges in Russia and the threat of extradition back to the states. She's got dual citizenship and double trouble, and she knows it."

"It was all worth it, yes?"

"Absolutely. Let me tell you a story. About three and a half years ago, a US bank was going through a routine audit. A particular transaction caught the auditor's eye. A Willem de Kooning was being held as collateral against a sizable loan. The auditor made inquiries with the FBI and Art Loss Register. Cut to the chase: an investigation led to a drug trafficker who was using the painting to launder money. He was offered immunity and a spot in witness protection if he came clean. He did, and he informed us that he had collaborated with an authentication expert to dupe the seller into believing the de Kooning was a forgery. The purchase price was slashed, but the subsequent bank loan was based on the painting's legitimate value. The authenticator received a generous kickback, which he shared with his consortium." Greg paused. "Ringing a bell?"

"Sounds like Winston Elliot's MO," Erika said. "Did the perp give up Elliot's name?"

"No, he gave up his life. He was eliminated before the authorities could question him further." With a wry smile, Greg added, "But Candice did indeed give up the name of the authenticator when she confessed that the de Kooning hoax was the handiwork of her organization." His smile broadened. "In fact, the scammer in this case was not Elliot, but one of his stable-mates—a Russian expatriate domiciled in Cleveland. Hard to untangle it all, but we're getting there."

"At this point, what's the status of Agent Hunter?" John asked. "When the fingerprints on the lighter found in Andrea Stein's rented car turned out to be his, that should have been the nail in his coffin."

"One of many," Greg said. "His trial begins in a couple of weeks. As you know, no bail was set. He's considered a flight risk."

"What of Elliot and Randall?" Harrison asked. "What's become of them?"

"Randall was given immunity, but he had nothing much to offer. Elliot struck a plea bargain and will get a minimum sentence for a watered-down charge of fraud. He came up with a few names associated with the organization, but way lower in rank than what Candice handed us."

"The irony of it," Erika mused.

Greg sat forward. "How so?"

"The sting was created to catch Elliot in a compromising position so that he'd be persuaded to name names. Instead, by sheer luck, Agent Hunter came aboard, and the operation turned out to be way more far-reaching than expected."

"I'm curious," John said. "How did Agent Hunter and Candice Volkov hook up in the first place?"

"Good question," Greg replied. "Hunter was an FBI agent when he met Candice on an online dating site. She reeled him in. During their brief courtship, she convinced him to train for the art crime division of the FBI. She wanted someone on the inside with access to potentially useful information. She got a more aggressive recruit than she had hoped for, one who had no qualms offing problematic individuals when a good talking to would have sufficed."

Crudely put, Erika thought, thinking of Jeremy and Andrea, but keeping quiet so as not to rankle.

* * *

No sooner had the group risen from the bench than Charlene was upon them. She looked radiant—like a newlywed, Erika thought, as if she and Andrea had reunited in another dimension, more sublime.

"I haven't had a chance to thank you!" Charlene cried, embracing the Wheatleys. Releasing them, she focused on Harrison. "Andrea would have been so honored!"

Harrison's jaw dropped.

"Oh, no, I forgot. I'm so sorry. Sara told me you had sponsored the scholarship, but not to let on. She said you prefer to keeps things undercover."

"'Anonymous' sounds less dubious," Harrison said, smiling to nullify her guilt.

"I promise I told no one else." She glanced sideways at John and Greg, well within hearing.

"That's okay," Harrison said. "They can keep a secret."

It had given Harrison great pleasure to set up an in-perpetuity scholarship in Andrea Stein's name. Appropriate, he had thought, to award it annually to an individual studying Art Crime and Cultural Heritage Protection—the actual title of the post-graduate certificate granted by the Association for Research into Crimes Against Art (ARCA) located in Umbria, Italy. Harrison had in fact chosen one of their students, Hannah Rosen, as this year's recipient. Hannah, hard at work abroad, was unable to come to the opening of the gallery, but her name would surely be mentioned in the speech shortly to be delivered by the gallery's newly appointed curator.

Erika gave Charlene an extra hug. "I'm really happy to see you," she said, holding her at arm's length. "Are you doing okay?"

"It comes in sudden spasms," Charlene said. "I never know what will set it off. The other day I was peeling an orange, and I realized it was the first time I'd peeled an orange since Andrea was gone. I cried uncontrollably for half an hour, and then it was over. Just like that."

Erika understood, but would not undermine Charlene's experience with an example of her own. Instead, she squeezed Charlene's hands before letting them go. "How is it going with the Steins?"

Charlene shrugged. "If only they had shown their love for Andrea the way they now shower it on me. I sort of resent it, although I try not to. It's like being treated for dinner after you die of starvation. You know what I mean?"

"Yes."

"It is better between us, though."

"I can see that."

* * *

Shortly after, the gallery's newly hired curator stepped to the center of the exhibit space. For so young a woman, she appeared to be remarkably confident. In her right hand she held a glass of champagne, which she raised in symbolic toast before she spoke. "Hello, there," she began. "My name is Fiona Clark." Her voice was clear as a bell, requiring no artificial amplification.

As if following a written stage direction, the gathering formed a circle around Fiona. Erika and Harrison moved in accordance with the group, along with Harrison's teaching assistant, Jack Simon, to whom Erika had just been introduced.

"Is she single?" Jack whispered.

"Shh, yes," Harrison whispered back. He shot him a paternal grin. "Behave yourself." He could hardly fault Jack his animation. Three months earlier, he had asked his TA to stand in for him at the European conferences he had precipitously dropped out of. Jack had presented his in-progress masters' thesis on the influence of politics on art in the Romantic era, and it had turned out to be a big hit. He was still walking on air.

Fiona Clark got right to the point. She thanked PAPNEA for hiring her—Harrison breathed a sigh of relief; it was actually he who had plucked her out of NYU's Museum Study candidates—and then went on to congratulate the first recipient, in absentia, of the Andrea Stein Award. Again, as Harrison had firmly instructed, Fiona refrained from mentioning his name. Lastly, Fiona introduced the artists on exhibit through September—they finger-waved from the sidelines—and expressed her gratitude to NYU for sponsoring the gallery's internship program for aspiring curators.

As Fiona merged with her audience to a lively round of applause, Amy's nephew came running out of the Barlows catering center, fast as a rabbit. He was clutching something in his right hand. It looked like something that may once have been edible. Erika wasn't sure if Sammy had been heading straight for Harrison or if Harrison had stepped into his trajectory, but within seconds, he was scooping the boy off the floor, legs still pedaling.

"Hey, Sammy, how've you been?" he merrily inquired. "What have you got there? Hmm, looks like something good to eat!" He readjusted his hold on the child so that his forearm was tucked under his bottom, nice and secure.

Sammy, taken by surprise, smiled. He stuck his clenched hand in front of Harrison's face. Chicken pate was oozing from between his fingers. "Yech!"

he said, teasing a reaction out of Harrison.

Amy emerged from the refreshment station waving a wet-wipe over her head like she was about to break into the Chilean handkerchief dance. She stopped dead in her tracks as Harrison was opening his mouth to allow Sammy to jam it with a glob of pate on crushed toast point.

"Yummy," Harrison crooned dreamily, sending Sammy into gales of laughter.

Erika gazed at Harrison. *Look at him,* she marveled silently. *Just* look *at him!* She felt the tears of joy—*his* joy—well up, and ordered them not to fall from her eyes and cause drama.

Amy was back in motion, arriving at the twosome just in time to prevent Sammy from going for another smack-down with the hand that bore the remnants of chicken liver. She scrubbed Sammy's hand and drew a packet of wipes from her apron pocket, plucking one out for Harrison's use.

"Thanks," Harrison said, swiping the towelette over his mouth. Amy extended her hand, and Harrison returned the used item. "Sorry for the mess," he said.

"No, *I'm* sorry," Amy said.

Harrison shook his head vehemently. "We're fine." To Sammy, he said, "Want to take a look at a statue?" without waiting for an answer, he walked to the center of the room, where the largest of Georgia Field's tentacular creations sat on a rectangular stone plinth. Erika and Amy followed behind, mesmerized.

"Go ahead, touch it," Harrison said. "Is it scratchy or smooth?"

"Smooth," Sammy said, running his fingers along one of the intertwined circuits.

"What do you think it looks like?" Harrison asked. "I think it looks like an elephant!" He roared like one.

Sammy laughed. "It looks like monkey bars."

"Excellent!" Harrison darted a sly glance at Erika. "Like I told John earlier—let the art *speak* to you."

"Good advice," Georgia agreed, coming up from behind.

Harrison introduced Sammy to the artist. "Sammy makes things, too," he said. "With Legos."

"I'd like to see what you've made some time," Georgia said.

"Now is as good a time as any," Harrison declared. A moment later, Sammy was escorting Georgia to his personal work space.

Harrison beamed. His marriage had been restored to blissful normalcy, and he realized that he had been swept into the child's unbridled merriment as an outlet for his own contained joy. He looked to Erika to share it. Were there tears in her eyes?.

Of course! he lashed inwardly. *How else could she have reacted, watching me play the paternal buffoon!* He encircled her waist, drawing her close. *I'm not asking for anything, my love, only you,* he struggled to convey without opening his mouth.

Erika kissed his cheek in response.

"Cute kid," Jack remarked, breaking into the Wheatleys' exchange.

"Yes, he is," Erika answered, as Harrison pressed her closer.

"So, do you guys have any kids of your own?"

Harrison's intake of breath was audible. "No, we're not planning to—"

"None yet," Erika answered. She issued Harrison a smile for which no words of interpretation were needed. "But we're trying," she added anyway, just to make him smile back.

End Notes

Fiction grounded in history poses a problem. How does the reader distinguish between the two without being distracted by the question itself? Knowing the writer's mindset is a start:

I'm a stickler for historic accuracy and an incurable romantic.Without distorting history, I take off from it, filling in its gaps with events that conform to its character, and that therefore *might* have been. Then, in a kind of butterfly-effect maneuver, I fast forward to the present and drop a pair of resourceful lovers into the challenging set of circumstances that have evolved and see if the sleuthing duo can sort it out.

For this tale of murder and artful deceit, my principal sources were Eric Hebborn's memoir, *Drawn to Trouble/ Confessions of a Master Forger*, and numerous newspaper and magazine articles and independent studies, past and contemporary, on US and international agencies that deal with art theft, recovery and restitution. In researching art crimes, the Isabella Stewart Gardner Museum heist of March 21, 1990 was of particular interest.

Continued thanks to Level Best Books for bringing my art history mystery series to light. It's not often that one finds eagle-eyed focus and sunny dispositions under one roof, and in such abundance. Thanks, too, to copy editor Jeanne Thornton, whose meticulous read was of great help.Thanks, as ever, to Marcia Rosen for her continued guidance through the maze of marketing/public relations.

To my husband Bob, whose inspiration is forever entangled with mine: Thank you.

About the Author

Claudia Riess, a Vassar graduate, has worked in the editorial departments of The New Yorker and Holt, Rinehart, and Winston and has edited several art history monographs.

You can connect with me on:
- https://claudiariessbooks.com
- https://twitter.com/ClaudiaRiess
- https://www.facebook.com/ClaudiaRiessBooks

Also by Claudia Riess

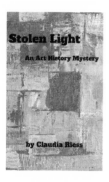

Stolen Light
An Art History Mystery (#1)

In 1958 in Cuba, the main house of sugar plantation owner, American-born WILLIAM DELANEY is vandalized by a band of Castro's rebels, who seize Delaney's art collection to raise money for weapons. Delaney is killed during the incident, and his pregnant wife, fearing for her safety and that of her unborn child, flees Cuba, never to look back.

Now, over fifty years later, Delaney's wife dies, and his daughter, Helen Gilmore, motivated by the desire to "know" the father whose life was kept shrouded in secrecy by his wife, is determined to restore what she can of his legacy. She seeks the help of a young *Art News* writer Erika Shawn and art historian, Harrison Wheatley to help solve her father's murder.

Made in the USA
Middletown, DE
05 November 2019

78027824R00156